THE LAST LIBERATOR

THE LAST LIBERATOR

a novel by
John Clive

Delacorte Press / New York

Published by
Delacorte Press
1 Dag Hammarskjold Plaza
New York, N.Y. 10017

Extracts from Hitler's Last Political and Personal Testaments and
from Goebbels's Appendix to the Fuehrer's Political Testament reprinted
from *The Last Days of Hitler* by H.R. Trevor-Roper by permission of
A.D. Peters Ltd., London.

Manufactured in the United States of America

First printing

Designed by Laura Bernay

Library of Congress Cataloging in Publication Data

Clive, John.
    The last liberator.

    1. World War, 1939–1945—Fiction. I. Title.
PZ4.C6423Las   1980   [PR6053.L53]   823'.9'14   79–19161
ISBN 0–440–05650–0

This book is dedicated to

The Movie-Makers,
who filled my head with Hollywood
and gave my imagination
an education.

Early one morning,
I heard an air raid warning,
I jumped out of bed
With a Jerry overhead.
Spitfires chasing him,
Tracer bullets tracing him,
How could you treat a poor Jerry so?
—CHILDREN'S PARODY
LONDON, CIRCA 1940.

THE LAST LIBERATOR

PROLOGUE

THE VOICE shook with emotion, and the eyes, no longer abstracted, were bright as though with fever. He paced distractedly around the small study fifty feet below ground, forgetting the pain in his leg, and gesticulating wildly as he had done at the huge rallies in the past.

The killing of Fegelein seemed to have inspired him and given him new strength, however temporarily. It did not matter that Fegelein, who had become one of his favorites after judiciously marrying Eva Braun's sister Gretl, was innocent of any plot—at least against him. In the fevered hothouse atmosphere of the Fuehrerbunker, mere absence was desertion, and desertion meant a plot to kill.

Thus Fegelein, the ex-jockey whose astute maneuvers and low cunning had taken him from the racetrack to the upper reaches of power in the Nazi hierarchy, had paid dearly for preferring his apartment in Charlottenburg to the Fuehrerbunker. He had been taken up the stairs to the Chancellery garden, which would serve as a graveyard not only for him but also for his executioner, and shot by the SS guards of the Escort.

His voice rose again as he spoke of the traitorous behavior of Himmler. Instinctively, he treated his secretary, Frau Junge, as an audience, seeking to exert his power over her as he had done over thousands.

Frau Junge's pen flew over the note-pad. She was hard put to keep up with the dictation of his last two communiqués, which were his political and personal testaments. In his mind they were a dignified and valid explanation of all that had gone before, and would serve to perpetuate Nazi philosophy in the future. But by now, even his uncertain hold on reality had given way, and much of what he dictated was repetition, recrimination. . . . He was not to blame.

Occasionally, little bursts of laughter penetrated from an adjoining room of his private suite, where Eva, Bormann, Goebbels, Frau Goebbels, and Von Below were enjoying the champagne and reminiscences long after the wedding ceremony in the conference room had been concluded.

The strange little ceremony had been presided over by one Walter Wagner, who was a Gau Inspector for Goebbels and held some kind of honorary position in the city administration, and was thus apparently empowered to perform marriages. He wore the uniform of the Nazi party but was completely unknown to anyone else in the Fuehrerbunker but Goebbels, and he disappeared as mysteriously as he had arrived.

All sense of time had vanished, with the irregular meals, the occasional periods of total darkness when the lights failed, the expectation and the tension as the Russians drew nearer. Bormann's eyes kept flicking toward the door. Frau Junge's presence in the study meant that Hitler was preparing something. Was this to be the final transfer of power? What part would he play in it? Would Hitler expect his trusted lieutenant to stay here and die with him? Bormann had no wish to die; he had no interest in Viking funerals, flamboyant gestures. He only wanted to exercise real power, which was why he had not joined Goering, Himmler, and Doenitz in the general exodus from the bunker on April 22. The only source of real power was Hitler, and Bormann had chosen to stay. He could hear the typewriter clacking faintly; the dictation was over.

Fifteen minutes later the typing stopped. Frau Junge emerged quietly from the study and stood in the doorway until she caught the eye of Heinz Linge, the Fuehrer's personal servant. She gave him a curt nod to indicate that he was wanted; then she left the suite for her own quarters.

No one except Bormann had noted this exchange, but when Linge emerged a moment later, Bormann rose to his feet and entered the study.

Hitler was sitting behind his desk, his face pale, his eyes covered again with that veil of moisture, as though he were drugged. Bormann stood stiffly before him until he flapped an arm weakly, indicating that he should sit down. The documents that Frau Junge had typed were on the desk, and he shuffled them nervously, separating them into three piles.

"There are two documents here." Hitler did not look at him but started to count the pages.

"Three copies of each one. They are my personal and political testaments." He glanced up, focusing his eyes on Bormann. "One of them involves you directly."

Bormann inclined his head. "Yes, *mein Fuehrer.*"

"These will be witnessed by you and others, and I want copies sent immediately to Field-Marshal Schoerner, and to Admiral Doenitz at his headquarters at Ploen." He paused and wiped away some of the moisture from his forehead, his hand visibly shaking. "You understand, Bormann, it is vital that these documents reach Schoerner and Doenitz." The eyes flashed momentarily as some of the old power returned. "Vital!"

Bormann had already decided. "I think Major Johannmeier is the best choice for Schoerner. He has a fine fighting record and a reputation for resourcefulness." He knew also that the choice would appeal to Hitler, since Johannmeier was his army adjutant.

Hitler nodded his approval. "Yes, yes. Johannmeier is right for this mission . . . he will do it."

Bormann was nothing if not a pragmatist. He knew that Berlin was entirely surrounded by Russian troops, and that the odds against the major's getting through their lines were high. His own escape route, though risky, was less likely to fail, and should he be caught, there were still the *Prominenten*, a group of well-connected Allied prisoners who were being held as hostages in Bavaria. There was also the fund maintained on behalf of ODESSA, the SS veterans' organization, since the thirties out of Nazi party coffers, siphoned through well-disguised corporate channels into a Swiss account which amounted to several millions by now—and to which only Bormann had access. Bormann's future was well provided for; as for Johannmeier . . . He didn't know and he didn't care, but he nodded his head reassuringly. "Yes, Major Johannmeier is a good man."

Hitler looked at him sharply.

"And Doenitz, who will you send?"

"I think both the other copies should be sent to him, even if one is intercepted, the other may get through."

He waited for Hitler's reaction.

"Yes, that is good, but who?"

Bormann paused. "My personal advisor, Standartenfuehrer Zander, and Heinz Lorenz as a representative of

Goebbels's." This last choice was cunning, implying an equal division of power between himself and Goebbels. In reality it meant nothing at all. Goebbels had already decided to kill himself, and Bormann knew it.

Hitler seemed satisfied; he nodded his head wearily. "Good, I am pleased. It has been an important day and much has been accomplished." He smiled grimly to himself. "I have even become a husband at last." He stared at the documents lying on the table for a moment. "I will leave you to read these, Bormann, and arrange to have them witnessed in my presence later. Now I must have some rest."

He rose stiffly to his feet, favoring his right leg. Bormann stood up immediately, but knew better than to offer assistance. Hitler stared down at the desk as though in a trance, then he glanced at Bormann and without speaking made his way slowly to the door.

Bormann called after him, "Good night, *mein Fuehrer*."

Hitler paused in the doorway but did not look back. The door closed softly behind him. Bormann leaned over and touched one of the documents on the desk, glanced around at the door, then sat down and began to read. It was four o'clock on the morning of April 29, 1945.

The three messengers, accompanied by a Corporal Hummerich, left the Fuehrerbunker at noon on April 29. All of them carried copies of Hitler's political testament. Johann-meier, the military adjutant, was to carry a covering letter from General Bergdorf to Field-Marshal Schoerner. The other two messengers each carried a copy of Hitler's personal testament: Zander, the SS officer, was to deliver Hitler's marriage certificate to Admiral Doenitz, and Lorenz, the civilian journalist, Goebbels's "Appendix to the Fuehrer's Political Testament."

All three messengers escaped through the Russian lines

and eventually into the British or American zones, but by then the war in Europe was over. Johannmeier returned to his family's home at Iserlohn in Westphalia and buried the documents in a bottle in the garden.

Zander went to Bavaria, changed his name to Wilhelm Paustin, and hid both documents in a trunk in the attic of a house in the village of Tegernsee.

There they would have remained but for the instinctive behavior of the journalist, Heinz Lorenz.

In the summer of 1945 Lorenz made his way to Hannover under the name of Georges Thiers; he sought employment with the British Military Government, claiming to have intimate knowledge of life in the Fuehrerbunker. Eventually he was arrested for carrying false papers and interned. In November 1945, during a routine search, the documents were found stitched into the lining of his clothes. Ultimately, this led to the discovery of the other two messengers, and all the documents were recovered—except one. Bormann had kept one last copy of Hitler's personal testament for himself.

Extracts from
Hitler's Personal Testament

ALTHOUGH during the years of struggle I believed that I could not undertake the responsibility of marriage, now, before the end of my life, I have decided to take as my wife the woman who, after many years of true friendship, came to this town, already almost besieged, of her own free will, in order to share my fate. She will go to her death with me at her own wish, as my wife. This will compensate us for what we both lost through my work in the service of my people.

My possessions, insofar as they are worth anything, belong to the Party, or if this no longer exists, to the State. If the State too is destroyed, there is no need for any further instructions on my part.

The paintings in the collections bought by me during the course of the years were never assembled for private purposes, but solely for the establishment of a picture gallery in my home town of Linz on the Danube.

It is my most heartfelt wish that this will should be duly executed.

As executor, I appoint my most faithful Party comrade, Martin Bormann. He is given full legal authority to make all decisions. He is permitted to hand over to my relatives everything which is of worth as a personal memento, or is necessary to maintain a petty-bourgeois standard of living; especially to my wife's mother and *my faithful fellow workers of both sexes who are well known to him. The chief of these are my former secretaries, Frau Winter, etc., who helped me for many years by their work.*

My wife and I choose to die in order to escape the shame of overthrow or capitulation. It is our wish that our bodies be burned immediately in the place where I have performed the greater part of my daily work during the course of my twelve years' service to my people.

Extracts from
Hitler's Political Testament

IT IS untrue that I, or anybody else in Germany, wanted war in 1939. It was wanted and provoked exclusively by those international politicians who either came of Jewish stock, or worked for Jewish interests. After all my offers of disarmament, posterity cannot place the responsibility for this war on me. . . .

After a six-year war, which in spite of all the setbacks will one day go down in history as the most glorious and heroic manifestation of a people's will to live, I cannot forsake the city which is the capital of this State. Since our forces are too small to withstand any longer the enemy's attack on this place, and since our own resistance will be gradually worn down by an army of blind automata, I wish to share the fate that millions of others have accepted and to remain in here in the city. Further, I will not fall into the hands of an enemy who requires a new spectacle, exhibited by the Jews, to divert his hysterical masses. I have therefore decided to remain in Berlin, and there to choose death voluntarily at the moment when I believe that the residence of the Fuehrer and Chancellor can no longer be held. . . .

In future may it be a point of honor with German Army officers, as it is already in our Navy, that the surrender of territory and towns is impossible, and that, above all else, commanders must set a shining example of faithful devotion to duty until death.

Before my death, I expel from the Party the former Reich Marshall, Hermann Goering, and withdraw from him all the rights conferred upon him by the Decree of June 29, 1941, and by my Reichstag speech of September 1, 1939. In his place I appoint Grand Admiral Doenitz as Reich President and Supreme Commander of the Armed Forces.

Before my death I expel from the Party and from all his offices the former Reichsfuehrer SS and Reich Minister of the Interior, Heinrich Himmler. In his stead I appoint Gauleiter Karl Hanke as Reichsfuehrer SS and Chief of the German Police, and Gauleiter Paul Giesler as Reich Minister of the Interior.

Goering and Himmler, by their secret negotiations with the enemy, without my knowledge or approval, and by their illegal attempts to seize power in the State, quite apart from their treachery to my person, have brought irreparable shame on the country and the whole people.

Finally, they [Admiral Doenitz and the new government] must above all else uphold the racial laws in all their severity, and mercilessly resist the universal poisoner of all nations, international Jewry.

Goebbels's "Appendix to the Fuehrer's Political Testament"

THE FUEHRER has ordered me, should the defense of the Reich collapse, to leave Berlin and to take part as a leading member in a government appointed by him.

For the first time in my life I must categorically refuse to obey an order of the Fuehrer. My wife and children join me in this refusal. Otherwise—quite apart from the fact that feelings of humanity and loyalty forbid us to abandon the Fuehrer in his hour of greatest need—I should appear for the rest of my life as a dishonorable traitor and common scoundrel, and should lose my own self-respect together with the respect of my fellow citizens; a respect I should need in any further attempt to shape the future of the German nation and State.

In the delirium of treachery which surrounds the Fuehrer in these most critical days of the war, there must be someone at least who will stay with him unconditionally until death, even if this conflicts with the formal and (in a material sense) entirely justifiable order which he has given in his political testament.

In doing this, I believe that I am doing the best service I can to the future of the German people. In the hard times to come, examples will be more important than men. Men will always be found to lead a nation forward into freedom, but a reconstruction of our national life *would be impossible unless developed on the basis of clear and obvious examples.*

For this reason, together with my wife, and on behalf of my children, who are too young to speak for themselves, but who would unreservedly agree with this decision if they were old enough, I express an unalterable resolution not to leave the Reich capital, even if it falls, but rather, at the side of the Fuehrer, to end a life which will have no further value to me if I cannot spend it in the service of the Fuehrer, and by his side.

BERLIN
night of
May 1, 1945

THE FRIEDRICHSTRASSE was burning; gouts of yellow
flame burst through the blackened windows of the buildings,
gutting and consuming them. What few jagged panes of glass
remained reflected the destruction of the city. Heavy fighting was taking place all around the last narrow perimeter
protecting the ruins of the Chancellery.

The noise was a curious mixture of appalling din and
strange little pools of quiet, as though everyone had stopped
for a moment and were listening. The smell was cordite and
sewer—but it seldom seeped through the terror most men
felt.

The Fuehrerbunker was deserted now except for General
Krebs, General Burgdorf, and the commander of the SS Escort, Hauptsturmfuehrer Schedle, who had been injured by a
bomb and could not walk. They had chosen to stay and no
more would be heard of them.

One by one in the flickering shadows of the street the small party of men emerging from the bunker ran the gauntlet of flame, flinging themselves to the ground whenever they heard the rattle of a machine gun or the crunch of an exploding shell. They reached the Weidendammer Bridge. At the north end was an antitank barrier facing outward, toward the advancing Russians. Several times they tried to cross the bridge but were driven back by heavy Russian fire. Some German tanks came rumbling up to the south side of the bridge and were ordered across. The leading tank managed to force a gap in the barrier and was quickly followed by several others. The group of men gathered around the leading tank in a loose formation and moved forward about three hundred yards until it reached the Ziegelstrasse.

The tank exploded, torn apart by a *Panzerfaust* antitank weapon. Kempka was temporarily blinded; Beetz and Axmann wounded; Bormann and Stumpfegger blown to the ground by the force of the explosion, but miraculously unharmed. Once again they retreated to the bridge. For a while they tried to stay together—Bormann, Naumann, Schwaegermann, Axmann, Stumpfegger, Rach, and one other—but now it was every man for himself.

Bormann and Stumpfegger started to walk east along the Invalidenstrasse toward Stettiner Station. Now they were making better time; Bormann knew it was crucial. They reached the bridge at the point where it crossed the railway line and paused, peering into the shadows whenever the flashes lit up the sky. They heard someone calling to them softly from the doorway they had just vacated. Bormann turned, recognizing a Standartenfuehrer, one of their party from the bunker. He saw the muzzle flash of the Luger, but did not hear the sound of the explosion—the bullet had already entered his chest just below the ribcage, torn through his heart, and left a gaping wound where it emerged from his back. He was dead instantly and fell silently to the ground. Stumpfegger threw up a hand to protect himself and died just as quickly and clinically. The man replaced the Luger in its holster, leaned down, and removed the last copy of Hitler's testament from Bormann's pocket. He examined it briefly, then continued to search until he found a brown envelope wrapped in oilskin. He opened the envelope and checked the document inside. It dealt with the ODESSA account and included the code number. He put it back carefully in the envelope and wrapped it once again in the oilskin. He then removed Bormann's black leather overcoat after wiping away as much of the blood as he could and put it on over his SS uniform, carefully replacing one envelope in each pocket. He walked away from the doorway, climbed through a gap in the wall, and slid down the embankment onto the railway line. It was midnight and he had four hours left to reach Lake Havel if he was to make use of Bormann's escape route.

Several times he thought he heard voices but he did not stop for an instant. Moving as swiftly as he dared, he stuck to the railway line, heading out north, then west through Charlottenburg. He came to the bridge where the railway crossed the River Spree; still no one challenged him. On his left he knew was Adolf Hitler Platz, but he did not leave the railway line until it skirted the Spandauer Chaussee. Pausing only to wait for a Russian tank to rumble by, he crossed the wide road and ran easily across the playing fields toward the Reichssportfield Stadium. As he ran, the soft pounding of his shoes in the sodden grass reminded him of another race he had run, seven years before when he was fifteen. He could still hear the cheers as he ran around the stadium representing the Hitler Youth. Now he was running in a different race—this time for his life.

He fell to the ground—he could hear voices ahead of him.

He listened; they were German. He called softly but there was no answer. He tried again. This time a high, almost girlish voice, tight with fear, replied. He talked quietly, confidently, trying to allay their fears; then slowly he raised his arms above his head, rose to his feet, and walked toward them.

They were boys, three of them, members of the Hitler Youth battalion that was holding the Pichelsdorf Bridge, still waiting hopelessly for Wenck's army to appear from the south. They took him to the battalion commander and one glance at Hitler's testament was enough to give him all the cooperation he needed. It was as he had hoped; the commander had automatically assumed that he was Bormann, because Bormann had been expected and the correct identification presented. Furthermore, Bormann was a shadowy figure to most Germans; he had assiduously avoided personal publicity and had almost never allowed himself to be photographed, except as an indistinct presence in the background of group portraits of the Nazi hierarchy.

It was now 3:30 A.M. Five minutes later he was in a rowboat heading toward Pfaueninsel, an island at the southern end of Lake Havel. On his left on the west shore was Gatow, the last airport in Berlin to fall to the Russians. He had three miles to go. He rowed steadily but did not exhaust himself. The oars had been muffled, but the rowlocks still squeaked during the occasional lulls between bursts of gunfire. He threw water over them from time to time and it seemed to work. Once or twice he heard Russian voices on the bank far off to his right and he coasted quietly until he felt it was safe to continue. By four o'clock the island began to loom up and he drew quietly into its shadow and waited.

It did not take long—the pilot knew what little chance he had would disappear with first light, and he wasted no time. He piloted the three-engined Ju-52 down through the low cloud cover, and suddenly the city was blazing beneath him. It was difficult to find landmarks, but he had already flown in three times and knew exactly where he was.

Below him was the road to Potsdam and immediately ahead Lake Havel. The pilot brought the reliable old work-horse down cautiously through a thick blanket of smoke; as he leveled off over the water he saw with relief that the flames of a burning ship at anchor on the eastern shore made the surface of the lake as bright as a mirror. He could already make out the plane's shadow on the water below. He was grateful now for the fires burning all along the shore—it made his task that much easier. The floats touched the water and he quickly taxied to a halt, turning and facing back the way he had come. The island lay ahead and to his left. Almost at once he saw the figure in the rowboat pulling swiftly toward him. The noise from his engines was already attracting the attention of the Russian infantry, and there was sporadic firing from both sides of the lake.

The pilot turned the power down to make it more difficult for them to identify his position and yelled a command to his navigator, warning him of the approaching boat. He saw the figure in the black leather overcoat hunched over the oars, thrusting them expertly into the water, and soon the boat rounded the port wing. He thought he could hear something grating against the float; then a huge explosion sent a boiling mass of flame hurtling upward. The night sky was as bright as daylight, and almost instantly bullets were clattering against the corrugated metal sides of the aircraft as the Russians found their target. He shouted to his navigator, heard his muffled response and the sound of the door banging shut. The empty rowboat began to drift away from the side of the airplane, and he waited no longer.

Full power poured into the three engines and he guided the Ju-52 down the lake, sheltered by the island, searching for as much cover as possible before dragging her reluctantly into the air over Wannsee at the south end of the lake. The water streamed from the floats; then they were into the cloud cover, banking around to the north and heading for Rechlin. It was 4:10 in the early morning of May 2, 1945.

By April 25, 1945, Berlin was completely surrounded by Russian armies, and the German perimeter within the city encircling the Chancellery was a small pocket gradually diminishing.

Nevertheless, during the last three days—April 29, April 30, and May 1—that the Fuehrerbunker beneath the Reich Chancellery was occupied by Hitler and the so-called "Reich Chancellery Group," the following managed to escape from the bunker and the majority from Berlin.

Noon, April 29, 1945

Major Willi Johannmeier (escaped)
SS Standartenfuehrer Wilhelm Zander (escaped)
Heinz Lorenz (escaped)
Corporal Hummerich (escaped)

Early Afternoon, April 29, 1945

Major Baron Freytag von Loringhoven (escaped)
Rittmeister Gerhardt Boldt (escaped)

Night of May 1, 1945
Martin Bormann's group

SS Sturmbannfuehrer Erich Kempka (escaped)
SS Standartenfuehrer Beetz (killed)

SS Hauptsturmfuehrer Guenther Schwaegermann (escaped)
Goebbels's driver, Rach (escaped)
Werner Naumann (escaped)
Reichsleiter Martin Bormann (killed)
Dr. Ludwig Stumpfegger (killed)
Reichsjugendleiter Artur Axmann* (escaped)

* Axmann later informed Allied interrogators that he had seen the bodies
of Bormann and Dr. Stumpfegger behind the Invalidenstrasse Bridge.
He did not examine the bodies, but both appeared to have been shot.

THE TESTING AND EXPERIMENTAL STATION AT RECHLIN

65 miles northwest of Berlin, morning of May 1, 1945

IT WAS bitterly cold and the rain blown by the easterly wind slanted viciously into his face, numbing his cheekbones and nose. Koessler made his way across what was left of the asphalt of the assembly area. He was grateful for the warmth of the long Luftwaffe overcoat as he pulled the high collar tight under his chin, trying to keep the rain out. He could feel the stubble on his face scraping the back of his hand.

He picked his way carefully around the bomb craters that pockmarked the landing field. Most of them were half full of mud and water, and he pitied the thinly-clad gang of old men and boys of the Volksturm who were desperately trying to fill in the holes of the only remaining runway at Rechlin.

Every day there were more to fill as the Allied bombing grew in intensity. Koessler knew it would be only a matter of time before Rechlin was overrun, and he wondered how much longer he was going to be kept in cold storage before the High Command decided to make a run for it.

Not that he cared very much; he was aware that no matter how skillful the pilot, the chance of a successful escape from Rechlin was minimal. The Russians were closing in terrifyingly fast from the east. Every day brought them closer. Time had slipped away from Hitler and Goebbels and the others, but still he had not been called upon to act. He'd had to stand by and watch as a Luftwaffe sergeant was ordered to fly Albert Speer into and out of encircled Berlin on April 23 and 24. The pilot had taken a training plane as far as Gatow, which then was still in German hands. From there he had transferred his passenger to a Fieseler-Storch and landed successfully on the East-West Axis Boulevard leading into the heart of Berlin. From there it was merely a car ride to the Chancellery and the Fuehrerbunker beneath it. He had returned the same way twenty-four hours later. This was a brilliant piece of flying and for a while the admiration Koessler felt for the sergeant had shaken off the numbness that had begun to take hold of his mind, protectively funneling all his thoughts into the simple project of getting from one day to the next.

In the early hours of April 26, Colonel General Ritter Von Greim had arrived at Rechlin with the legendary test pilot Hanna Reitsch. Once again the same pilot was assigned the mission of getting them into Berlin. This time he chose a Focke-Wulf 190. There was room for only one passenger, but since Hanna Reitsch was determined to go, and since she was small enough, she was stuffed into the tail of the aircraft through a small emergency hatch. They were accompanied this time by forty fighter planes, many of which were lost while escorting them through the Russian air cover.

At Gatow, Ritter Von Greim commandeered a training plane and flew it himself on into Berlin while the remaining fighters were sacrificed in a diversionary feint. There was heavy street fighting in the Grunewald, and ground fire tore a hole in the bottom of the plane, shattering Greim's right foot. Reitsch took over the controls, and in the last daredevil feat of her career as an aviator, landed safely on the East-West Axis Boulevard.

The boulevard would be used once more as a landing strip before Berlin was finally taken by the Russians. On April 28, with Gatow now in enemy hands, the Luftwaffe sergeant landed an Arado 96 training aircraft on the boulevard and flew Von Greim and Reitsch back to Rechlin. They had left for Doenitz's headquarters on the same day, April 29, and now two days later Rechlin seemed deserted and quiet, except for the rumble of guns getting louder and closer.

Still no one had approached Koessler to explain why he had not been used, and he had inwardly resigned himself to whatever fate awaited him here. Now the Allies were in total command of the skies without even token resistance since the loss of the fighters that had escorted Von Greim. The few remaining serviceable aircraft at Rechlin remained in the heavily fortified underground hangars. Koessler knew he was a good pilot, probably one of the best, but he didn't think that when the time came he'd get very far, and he'd seen enough men die in flames to know the fate that awaited him. He pushed these grim thoughts out of his mind and hurried on.

IN ADDITION TO THE MEMBERS OF THE "REICH CHANCEL-LERY GROUP" WHO ESCAPED FROM BERLIN ON FOOT, Albert

Speer, Ritter von Greim, AND Hanna Reitsch FLEW INTO AND OUT OF BERLIN AS DESCRIBED.

FURTHERMORE, JU-52 DID LAND AND TAKE OFF FROM THE HAVEL LAKE ON THE NIGHT AND EARLY MORNING OF MAY 2, 1945.

ZUYDER ZEE
HOLLAND
1963

SLOWLY the steel hawsers tightened as the winch took up the strain; they seemed to stretch like elastic as the drum continued to turn, but the B-17 didn't budge. The mud that had entombed it for nearly twenty years beneath the waters of the inland sea was not going to give up its catch that easily. The Dutch major watched anxiously as the hawser engaged as soon as an inch of slack appeared on the drum.

All he could see of the Flying Fortress was the tail assembly sticking up above the surface of the partially drained polder. His recovery unit, which was attached to the Royal Netherlands Air Force, had hauled a lot of broken aircraft from the mud of the polders as sections of the Zuyder Zee were gradually drained. This was the first time an almost complete B-17 had been discovered.

It moved; they heard a strange wrenching, sucking sound

as the airplane protested at being hauled from its watery grave. Bubbles of gas appeared on the surface, and the smell that assailed their nostrils was a mixture of stinking mud and something else that made one of the recovery team turn and vomit behind the winch cab.

The major had positioned the winch as close as possible to the edge of the polder, and now the bomber seemed to be moving slowly, sliding up the mudbank, grinding and sucking and blowing like a living thing as it emerged from its cocoon of mud and water.

First the flight deck poked itself above the surface, water pouring from the shattered cockpit. Then the perspex nose cone emerged, surprisingly intact. Finally all of the Fortress lay on the mudbank, damaged and stinking, but as far as the Major could see, all in one piece. He signaled to the winch operator, and as the motor ground to a halt there was an eerie silence, broken only by the sound of the water still pouring from the bomber, like muddy blood.

The major jumped down from the dyke onto the mudbank and squelched his way to the nose section. He looked closely beneath the cockpit and rubbed the mud and slime away with his gloved hand; underneath he could just make out the legend. *In Like Flynn.*

RECHLIN
morning of May 1, 1945

THE GUST of cold wind as the door opened caught the papers on Hauptmann Lange's desk, and he slammed his hand down angrily to keep them from being blown to the floor. With his hand on the papers he turned his head and stared coldly at the pilot standing in the doorway.

"Come in, Koessler," he said brusquely, "and shut the door. We don't want to die of pneumonia—at least not before the Russians get here." He smiled grimly. Koessler could see that his eyes were red-rimmed with fatigue and the lines were drawn tight around his mouth.

"I'm sorry, Herr Hauptmann. It was inconsiderate of me."

Lange did not reply, and Koessler shifted uneasily under his steady gaze.

"Koessler, I know you are one of our better pilots. I also know something of your record, but do you usually come to see your commanding officer unshaven and with dirty boots?"

Koessler was about to explain that the last of his razor blades had run out three days ago, and that it was impossible to obtain any more, but he changed his mind. "I'm sorry, Herr Hauptmann—it will not happen again." He'd have to sharpen his knife and use that.

"All right, Koessler, sit down." He indicated the chair on the other side of his desk, then sat back and gazed at the ceiling at a point somewhere over Koessler's head, assembling his thoughts. There was a silence that stretched Koessler's nerves, but he waited as calmly as he could for Lange to speak. Perhaps now, at last, they were to put him to some use—attempt an escape—but to where, he wondered, and with whom? Last night on Hamburg Radio he had heard Doenitz's proclamation—Hitler had died at the head of his troops, and Doenitz was to be his successor. He knew Doenitz was in Ploen. Since Hitler was dead, who was left in Berlin who could have escaped the Russians and reached Rechlin?

Intermittently they could hear the guns in the distance—the sound seemed to bring Lange back from his reverie. "They get closer." He paused. "I expect you have guessed why you have been kept here at Rechlin?"

"Yes, Herr Hauptmann, but I don't think it will be possible for me to get far." He had blurted that out without thinking, and he saw Lange's face harden. Now he would have to explain. "It's been left till too late. The Allies have complete control of the air." All the fear and frustration of the last week of silence burst through the barrier of discipline. "Why do we wait? Why don't they come? Forty men and fighters lost uselessly flying *into* Berlin." He rushed on: "Even if I left at night, they have excellent radar and the night fighters would be all around us immediately." He stopped.

"You do not sound hopeful, Koessler." He was dangerously calm but Koessler was not aware of it. "Perhaps you would prefer to wait here for the Russians?"

"Hope won't keep me in the air when my plane is on fire." Koessler saw the anger blaze in Lange's eyes, and he realized, belatedly, that he had gone too far.

"You will do exactly as you are ordered, Koessler." Koessler inclined his head. "Of course, Herr Hauptmann. I will try to go wherever you send me."

As quickly as it had come, the anger disappeared, and Lange suddenly looked very old and tired. He rubbed his face with his hands and stared at the floor. "I'm sorry, Koessler. I understand your frustration and the dangers you face, but believe me,"—he looked up—"I wish someone would offer me a chance like this."

The guns rumbled again and Lange stood up, clearing his throat as though he were trying to clear away the pervading sense of gloom. "Now then, what do you know of KG 200?" The question surprised Koessler; it would not be the only surprise he would get that morning.

"Very little, Herr Hauptmann." He paused. "I have heard it mentioned only once, and then it was just a rumor about one of their operations."

Lange nodded his head wearily. "Yes, of course. Security is very tight." He glanced at Koessler curiously. "I believe it is referred to as the 'Ghost Geschwader' by the other units?"

"Yes, Herr Hauptmann, I've heard it called that."

Lange seemed satisfied. "Good, that's good." He turned to the inner door. "Well, let us see how true these rumors are, Oberleutnant." He led Koessler through the administration block to a concrete bunker. Inside was an elevator just big enough for the two of them. Lange pressed the button and they began to descend slowly. "I understand you were with Lufthansa for a time before the war?"

Koessler deliberately avoided looking at him, wondering what was behind the question. "Yes, but not for long. I qualified as a pilot in late '38, after. . . ."

Lange interrupted him. "However, you were with them

long enough to fly one of the two Boeing 247's that Lufthansa had acquired."

It was a statement more than a question. Koessler realized that Lange knew a lot more about him than he had anticipated. He remembered the 247 well. It had been one of the first twin-engined American commercial planes to use the low wing under the fuselage—in fact the ten passengers it carried had to step over the wing spar that ran through the cabin. Nevertheless, it had been a speedy, comfortable plane to fly, and once the new controllable-pitch propellers and geared engines had been installed, it had performed well. Now the American Army Air Force had renamed it the C-73 and was using it for transport and training operations.

"Yes, that's true, Herr Hauptmann." He decided to elaborate. "I've always been interested in aircraft of all kinds. Whenever I had a stop-over, I'd take the opportunity to have a look at whatever was on the ground."

Lange glanced at the steel door of the elevator. "Not always on the ground, Koessler."

He tried not to show his surprise—he didn't think anyone had found out about that episode. The descent ended abruptly, and the doors slid open without a sound. They stared down a long gray concrete corridor, in which Lange's voice echoed hollowly as they walked.

"Yes, we know you once persuaded an American pilot to let you fly a DC-3—unofficially, of course."

Koessler did not comment—it seemed better to say nothing.

"As a matter of fact we very nearly brought you into KG 200 much earlier. We had many ex-Lufthansa personnel in our group. Unfortunately, casualties have been high. It was thought that your record as a fighter pilot was so good that it was better you remain where you were—at least until we needed you."

They were approaching a huge steel bulkhead door which

spanned the corridor. Lange began turning the flywheel in the middle of the door. It reminded Koessler of the water-tight hatches he had seen in U-boats, and it appeared to be very heavy; he helped Lange push it open. As they did so the noise from the huge underground hangar flooded in. Koessler stepped through and Lange followed, then stood beside him, ordering two mechanics nearby to reclose the door.

Koessler found it difficult to believe what he was seeing. There were several German aircraft in the hangar, but all the activity was centered on a four-engined bomber in the far corner. About twenty mechanics were working on it frantically, and Koessler instantly recognized the twin tailfins and the long, slender wings set high up on the trim fuselage.

It was a USAAF B-24 Liberator, slightly the worse for wear but being rapidly put back into shape by the feverish activity of the ground crew.

"Well," said Lange, and this time his eyes were smiling, "perhaps you will have a slightly better chance than you anticipated, Koessler."

Koessler gazed at the Liberator. His eyes narrowed, the adrenaline started to flow, and he could feel his palms getting sweaty as he realized the implications. His mind was racing ahead, working out the details, evaluating the chances —how far? what destination? how much fuel? He suddenly felt alive again, and it came as a shock to realize just how far the despair had sunk in—moments before he had secretly welcomed the thought of a quick death. Better that than some Siberian prison camp, dying slowly, painfully. Now he had a chance to live.

He said quietly, "Herr Hauptmann."

Lange turned and looked at him curiously, aware of the intensity in the young man's voice.

"I swear I will get this machine wherever you want it to go."

Their eyes met in a moment of understanding.

"I believe you, Koessler—I believe you." Lange nodded his head and slapped him on the shoulder. "Come, let us have a look at your famous American Liberator." He laughed. "Perhaps it's going to liberate a few its designers didn't have in mind, Oberleutnant?"

Koessler actually found himself laughing—he couldn't remember the last time he had.

They walked over to the B-24 and stood beneath the port wing.

"We were lucky with this one; as you can see she suffered only superficial damage, mostly to the undercarriage." Lange pointed to the hydraulic retraction system. "We are able to carry out most repairs by cannibalizing parts from other crashed Allied aircraft that are otherwise unusable."

Koessler could contain his curiosity no longer. "We have been flying these planes, their own aircraft, on missions against them?" He seemed shocked.

"Yes, Koessler—you do not approve?"

He did not reply. Lange continued. "Your attitude does not surprise me, but what we are doing is not without precedent." He paused momentarily. "During the Napoleonic Wars the British Navy often sailed their men-of-war into French ports under the French tricolor. Once inside the defenses they would hoist the Union Jack and fire away."

Koessler continued to examine the Liberator. He could not accept what Lange had said as a justification—it was too pat, as though he'd said it a thousand times before. Perhaps as a pilot he had seen the agony of death too many times. He knew the rage, the sense of betrayal, he would feel if he were attacked by a German fighter with an American pilot.

Lange had been waiting for him to answer; his voice hardened a little. "Let me show you something." He walked toward the nose section of the fuselage. "Here in the bombardier's compartment we discovered why the American bombers were able to hit their targets so accurately from more than four miles up. We recovered intact the Norden bombsight. It is very ingenious, Koessler. It has a gyro-stabilized automatic pilot which takes over on the final run and compensates for any errors the pilot might have made. We have examined it very carefully. There are over two thousand components in it and it detects any deviation from course—whether the nose is up or down. Crosswinds do not affect its accuracy. It is a beautiful piece of equipment, Oberleutnant, and it has reduced many of our cities to smoldering rubble. Unfortunately, I fear we have discovered its secrets too late."

There was nothing Koessler could say, nothing he wanted to say. He did not want to think about the devastation of Dresden and Hamburg. He was empty and numb. All he wanted was to be back in that pilot seat again, doing what he did best. This American plane would test him, but he would fly it—he would fly it till the wings fell off. Lange had been watching him, and now expected an answer.

"Well, Koessler?"

Koessler turned and faced him, his mind made up. "She will do, Herr Hauptmann, you can be sure . . . when?"

"Tonight, Oberleutnant. The operation will begin tonight."

Lange was standing in front of a large-scale map of Europe, and Koessler was concentrating hard on everything he said, trying to commit it all to memory.

"This will be your route." Lange traced a ruler slowly westward across the face of the map from Rechlin. "As you can see, much of it is now in Allied hands. However, the latest information that I have indicates that the Wehrmacht is still holding Hamburg, Kiel, and Flensburg, and there is bitter fighting in the vicinity of Oldenburg. Since you will be flying in what is ostensibly an enemy aircraft, you would do well to avoid our antiaircraft emplacements, particularly those protecting the ports of Wilhelmshaven and Bremerhaven. Ironically, the sooner you are over Montgomery's Twenty-first Army Group the safer you should be. Unfortunately, for security reasons we cannot inform the Luftwaffe of your presence, but"—he made a slight inclination of his head—"as you have already pointed out, there is little activity in that area. The same cannot be said of the Allies; both General Bradley's and Montgomery's army groups are advancing into Germany, and I am afraid there is not much that we can do to stop them." He glanced at Koessler. "Which is why this operation of yours must succeed."

The ruler continued its progress through Holland, across the North Sea, the Midlands of England, Wales, then the Irish Sea, and came to rest on the west coast of Ireland.

"And this, Koessler, is where you will land, close to Liscammor Bay in County Clare. We have friends there who will look after you and your passenger, and see you safely to the U-boat that will pick you up the following day. Your code-name will be 'Wolf Wing,' and in here, since you will have to navigate as well, are all your coordinates and instructions." He handed Koessler a brown leather wallet. "No doubt there are questions you would like to ask?"

Koessler had it all in his head; he doubted if he needed the contents of the wallet. "There is one thing, Herr Hauptmann."

"That is?"

"Surely American aircraft are no more authorized to fly over Ireland than we are?"

Hauptmann Lange seemed relieved. "Since they do not have any air force to speak of, Oberleutnant, and since you will be flying at night, I do not think that will cause you many problems." He paused and looked at Koessler, weighing his words carefully. "There is perhaps another question you would like to ask?"

"Herr Hauptmann?"

Lange gazed silently at him for a moment, then smiled. "My dear Koessler, I cannot believe that you are entirely without curiosity. Your passenger's identity, does that not intrigue you?" He continued before Koessler could reply. "I realize that ignorance of these matters can sometimes be a useful asset, but under the circumstances I think it would be wiser if you knew." Koessler inclined his head in assent. "Your passenger, Oberleutnant, will be Reichsleiter Bormann, head of the Party Chancery. It seems he, at least, did not die when the Fuehrer was killed."

Koessler acknowledged this piece of information, though in truth the news that his passenger was to be perhaps the most powerful man in the Party now that Hitler was dead meant little to him. Martin Bormann was just a name; he did not even know what he looked like. Bormann was giving him his only chance to escape, but for Koessler all that mattered was the chance to fly, with at least a hope of succeeding —he could not expect any more.

HOLLAND
August 1963

THE RAIN that had been threatening ever since he had crossed the German border began splattering onto his wind shield as he drove out of Amersfoort. It did not concern him too much. There was very little traffic at one o'clock in the morning, and he had thoroughly planned his route at least a dozen times.

The windshield wipers slapped back and forth on the flat windows of the Land-Rover. He had deliberately avoided using a German car. And the view from the high position of the driver's seat of the Rover, particularly on this dark night, reminded him of the view from the interior of a cockpit.

The road to Harderwijk stretched out before him, and occasionally a pair of headlights would materialize out of the darkness ahead and pass him in a cloud of spray. Not many Dutchmen on the road. He smiled to himself. Most of them went to bed early in this respectable corner of Holland.

The rain began to ease up as he neared Ermelo, and he slowed down to look for the road that led to the inland sea. He passed a few scattered houses, then saw the bandstand set back from the road on the green. He turned left off the main road as soon as he had passed it.

On his right was the village dancehall, a converted windmill, darkened now and deserted; he wondered how many promises were made and broken there on a Saturday night. Past a few shops, then the railroad crossing—the barriers were up. No train would pass until it was light, when the commuters to Amsterdam began to stir themselves. The Land-Rover bumped heavily over the rails at the crossing, and he lowered the window to check his bearings. The rain had stopped, and mixed with the damp scent of the grass he could smell the sea.

The narrow lane twisted past several farmhouses. He drove slowly; the last thing he needed now was to end up in a ditch. When he saw the sports field on the right, he knew he was near his destination. Now there were reeds growing on either side of the lane, and the lane itself finally petered out on a muddy flat that gleamed wetly in the headlights. He stopped the Land-Rover and backed up a few yards, so that the tall reeds would provide some cover in the unlikely event that anyone might come down to this deserted beach in the dead of night.

He switched off the headlights, then the engine, and waited for his eyes to adjust to the dark. Occasionally, he could hear funny little plopping sounds as bubbles of marsh gas seeped up through the mud. As he waited a wisp of fog crept up the lane from the sea—not enough to cause any problems, but he hoped it would not get any thicker.

He glanced at the luminous dial of his watch—he had six hours before dawn. By then he should have removed all trace of evidence that might connect him to the sunken aircraft. It had kept his secret well for nearly twenty years and would perhaps have continued to do so if the industrious Dutch with their inflexible will to wrest the land from the sea hadn't started to work on this part of the Ijsselmeer. Even before the war a great Barrier Dam had been built across this shallow arm of the North Sea called Zuyder Zee. The freshwater inland sea thus created inside the dam was now known as the Ijsselmeer. Soon the water would be drained away to reveal a graveyard of broken aircraft—one at least he was determined they would not find.

Carefully, he eased the inflatable rubber dinghy from the back of the Land-Rover—a tear in that now would be disastrous. Mentally ticking off each item one by one, he got all of the equipment together: oxygen tanks, black frogman's suit, two powerful underwater lamps, red marker light, metal spear and line, and finally a small battery-operated radio impulse transmitter. After inflating the dinghy he eased himself into the frogman's suit, checked again to be sure that he had everything in the dinghy, picked up the mooring line, and started to pull it slowly across the mud flats.

It was much more difficult than he had anticipated. The heavy rain had softened the mud; it was more porous and clinging than the last time he had reconnoitered this area. The combination of the heavily laden dinghy and the rubber suit made him sweat, and several times he had to pause and rest.

Once he thought he was finished when he sank up to his thighs in mud and was unable to pull himself free. Worse, he could feel himself sinking further into the morass. He knew that if he struggled, he was finished—the Zuyder Zee would get the victim it had failed to claim once before. Fortunately, he hadn't let go of the line. He pulled the dinghy slowly toward him until it was within reach. Then he pushed one side up, so that the equipment slid over and gave him some weight to balance against. Hooking his arms over the dinghy, he gradually eased himself out of the thick, stinking mud, pulling himself into the dinghy, where he lay flat, exhausted.

Not a good start, he thought grimly to himself, but now he could see the ragged white fringe of the shoreline not too far ahead. Using the paddle as a lever, he was able to push the dinghy onto a firmer surface. He glanced at his watch; it had taken him nearly an hour to reach the shore. Checking his position with the night glasses, he set the red marker light down at his feet; he had no wish to return the way he had come. He picked up the radio impulse transmitter and switched it on, then turned and scanned the Zuyder Zee with his night glasses until he found what he was looking for—a dim white light, blinking once every ten seconds, that he had anchored in position on his previous visit.

He washed some of the mud from his legs, put on his flippers, and strapped on the oxygen tanks, meticulously checking his equipment once again. Satisfied that all was in order, he started paddling the dinghy toward the light. The water was calm and flat with no breeze to ruffle the surface— at least conditions were in his favor now.

He tied the dinghy to the positioning light, then pushed the underwater lamp over the side, grabbed the metal spear, and slid backwards into the cold, muddy water. It was black below the surface and even the powerful lamp seemed to penetrate only a few yards ahead. Fortunately it was not deep—no more than forty feet—and he quickly reached the bottom, so quickly he had to thrust out one leg and push himself off before he could glide forward again. Immediately, he was surrounded by eddying swirls of sediment, and the light from the lamp was almost extinguished. He swam out of the cloud of mud and steadied himself, hovering about three feet from the bottom. He'd never find anything if he stirred that up again. Treading water, he slowly pushed the metal spear into the seabed until it felt secure, then unwound about three feet of the attached line. Using the spear as an anchor, he began to swim in a widening circle, gradually playing out the line, looking for anything that might conceivably be wreckage from the bomber.

He knew that it could easily have broken up by now, silted over, and sunk into the mud. It came as a shock when something glinted dully in the gloom in front of him, reflecting the light from his lamp. He cautiously swam closer and found himself gazing directly down at the flight deck of the sunken bomber.

RECHLIN
early morning, May 2, 1945

THE RUNWAY stretched ahead of him in total darkness, illuminated only by the occasional flashes of the Russian guns off to his left. Koessler sniffed the light breeze, using all his senses and experience to evaluate what the take-off and flying conditions would be like. It had stopped raining now, but the cloud ceiling was still low—so far so good.

Everything had been prepared. The Liberator had been brought to the surface by the giant hydraulic lift and was waiting in the blacked-out hangar behind him. He had watched over everything, carefully supervising as the ground crew filled the fuel tanks—aviation gas was as precious as gold dust—warming up the Pratt-Whitney engines, and familiarizing himself with the cockpit and instrument panel. He had seen the heavy wooden crates being loaded into the bomber, and he didn't need two guesses to know what kind of cargo he would be carrying. Nothing that wasn't very compact, extremely valuable, and easily convertible into cash—and perhaps a few of the more valuable paintings looted from the art collections of Europe. However, the plane was well under its maximum load, and he had made sure that the cargo was stowed away correctly. He didn't want it causing problems if he had to take drastic evasive action.

Now all he was waiting for was his passenger, Reichsleiter Bormann, and Koessler wasn't curious. His overlords, the High Command, meant nothing to him anymore. In fact, he was aware that he felt little about anything anymore. Everything was pared down, concentrated on one thing, this flight. He was lucky to have this chance, and he didn't intend to let any scruples or emotions get in his way.

Koessler took a deep breath of the damp air. My God, he could actually smell the acrid smoke of the Russian guns. As he started to walk back toward the hangar he heard, faintly at first, the intermittent drone of a German aircraft engine; he stopped and listened. It was unmistakable—three engines, a Ju-52. Suddenly, the runway lights flicked on as the old transport rumbled in on her final approach. As it came over the end of the runway, Koessler leaned forward, staring intently. There were seaplane floats fitted just above the landing wheels. He smiled to himself—they'd turned old "Auntie" into an amphibian. She dropped down to the runway, bounced once heavily, and before she had come to a stop, the landing lights flicked off again.

Lange came running out of the hangar and called to the ground crew to fetch landing steps, but before they could respond, the door was flung open and a man in an SS uniform and a black leather overcoat jumped down onto the runway. Koessler saw him produce an envelope from his pocket and show it briefly to Lange, who saluted and indicated the darkened hangar. They walked into the gloomy interior, and

THE LAST LIBERATOR : 45

Koessler pulled on his flying gloves and followed them inside. Lange was standing at the bottom of the short set of metal steps leading up to the rear hatch of the bomber. He saw Koessler and hurried over, looking anxiously back over his shoulder.

"Your passenger is now on board, Oberleutnant. Are you ready to proceed?"

Koessler nodded. "Yes, Herr Hauptmann, there is nothing else. Can we have the rest of the lights off in the hangar at once? The quicker my eyes adjust, the better."

"Of course." Lange called out the instructions. Almost at once the hangar was plunged into complete darkness. Gradually the huge door started to slide open, and the flashes from the east lit up the bomber, their glow reflected on the canopy and casting strange shadows high on the hangar walls.

Lange and his young pilot began to walk toward the Liberator. Lange gripped his arm.

"Koessler, you are not supposed to know what your final destination is, but I have decided to tell you."

Koessler interrupted him. "South America?"

Lange smiled. Koessler could see his teeth gleaming in the dark. "Ah, Koessler, I'm glad they picked you. You give me some hope for the future, but if you reach Ireland safely, I suggest you regard everyone as a potential danger. . . . Everyone," he repeated.

Koessler stared at him, trying to read the expression in his eyes.

"Your passenger—the Reichsleiter. He has been entrusted with vital documents. Hitler's testament, no less. That must survive, but as for its bearer . . . I have my doubts. Be careful, Koessler."

Koessler felt some of the numbness leaving him. He gripped the older man's hand. "Come with us. Perhaps I can get you out of this."

Lange shook his head. "I would like to, but I cannot. All my family are here, and if I survive the Ivanses' next assault, perhaps in time I will be allowed to go back to them." He squeezed Koessler's hand. "But I thank you for the thought, Oberleutnant. . . . Now you must go." He stepped back. *"Auf Wiedersehen,"* then loudly, *"Heil Hitler!"* Koessler smiled, returned the salute, and just as loudly—*"Heil Hitler!"* Then he turned and climbed the steps into the Liberator, slamming the hatch behind him.

He made his way through the carefully stacked crates, past the blacked-out side gunner's window, and along the catwalk between the bomb bays, now also stacked with booty. He deliberately avoided looking at the shadowy figure sitting in the radio operator's compartment, hauled himself into the cockpit, and began checking his instruments for the last time. He was still wearing the Luftwaffe overcoat, although Lange had suggested an American uniform. Koessler had refused, since no one would be able to see who was flying the Liberator at night, and he certainly did not want to be shot as a spy should they be forced down. He had also taken the precaution of bringing a few personal letters that might prove useful should he be captured and interrogated. It had been a hard decision for Koessler, since it directly contravened everything he had been trained to do—but then, so too did flying an American bomber.

He picked up the leather map-case his mother had bought him on the day of his promotion and slipped the letters in behind the map. She had been proud of him, and had had his name, rank, and number embossed in gold on the black leather. It had proved very useful; he could slide a folded map into the sleeve, which had a transparent celluloid panel on one side so he could check his position, and a strap so that he could belt it to his thigh. He was glad that he had pleased her. He ran his fingers over the embossed leather, remembering the day that she had given it to him, how she had traced out the gold letters with her finger—*Oberleutnant der Luftwaffe*. Truly something they could both be proud of . . . and what would she call him now? A coward? A deserter?

He thrust these thoughts from his mind abruptly, strapped the map-case to his thigh, and began concentrating on the task at hand. He pressed the starters, and one by one the four engines roared into life. Everything was ready; he could see Lange standing by the port wingtip. Lange raised his arm slowly, and Koessler thought he was going to give the Hitler salute, but he seemed to change his mind and waved his hand just once. Koessler raised a gloved hand in reply and eased the throttles forward, gently releasing the brakes. The Liberator rolled slowly through the hangar door and out onto the asphalt, which the Volksturm had been repairing all day.

He strained forward in his seat, looking for the two red lights that marked the end of the runway. As he caught sight of them, he felt the bomber lurch as it passed over a freshly filled-in crater, and he heard his passenger swear as he pulled himself back into his seat.

Koessler smiled to himself and started to ease the Liberator forward over the bumpy ground until it lined up between the two red lights and was in position at the end of the runway. Swiftly he ran his eyes over the instrument panel, then switched on the radio.

"Now."

Immediately, the two rows of lights along the runway blazed into life ahead of him, glittering in the cold like the twin strands of a diamond bracelet. At once he pushed the throttles forward; the engines roared in crescendo, and he could feel the airframe trembling as they strained to push the Liberator forward. Koessler released the brakes, and he was thrust back into his seat as the Liberator hurtled down the runway.

His eyes flicked between the airspeed indicator and the runway below. Easing the throttles up to full power, he kept the Liberator steady until the moment was right; then he pulled back gently on the wheel, and the bomber was airborne.

The runway lights blinked out at once, and the take-off had gone so smoothly that Koessler doubted if the Russian gunners had even seen them.

He caught a glimpse of the barrage flickering and glowing away to his left; then they were into the clouds. He banked the Liberator gently toward the west.

HOLLAND
April 1945

KLAUS SCHURER was thirty-two and he had been in the Wehrmacht since 1931, during the depths of the Depression. Then, the Wehrmacht had seemed to be his only guarantee of three squares a day and regular work.

He'd had no cause for regret during the early thirties, when so many were starving, and later, when Hitler came to power and things generally began to look up, new equipment—tanks—had come in, the Panzer divisions had been formed, and truthfully he had found it all very exciting.

Now he was a sergeant in charge of an antiaircraft unit stationed on a V-2 site near The Hague, and he still had no regrets—why should he? He'd seen action in Poland, followed right behind the forward columns through Belgium and France, and finally ended up here the year before, after the V-1 sites down the coast had been abandoned and the first V-2 rockets were being launched from Holland.

That summer the Allies had landed in Normandy, and all through the autumn of '44 and the bitter winter that followed he had been aware of their progress—creeping nearer every day until the winter had stopped them south of the Maas. There they had been entrenched for nearly three months, waiting for the spring.

It did not take an expert to know that once the weather eased up (and it had been one of the coldest winters Schurer could remember), they would move out. Some of the younger men had been loudly critical—though not in his presence. They thought they should have been withdrawn farther, closer to Germany, so they could help defend the cities that were taking such a hammering from the bombers. Some of the stories that had trickled out of Dresden were too horrible to believe, though, God knows, they had been busy enough themselves, what with the increasing interest the fighter bombers had shown in their operations.

In March, the British Second Army under General Dempsey, the Canadian II Corps reinforced by the I Corps, veterans of the Italian campaign, and the Polish 1st Armored Division, struck.

LOWER SAXONY
May 1, 1945

THE FIGHTING in northern Germany was bitter and confused. Patton's spectacular progress further south had met with little effective resistance, but here the watery terrain, crisscrossed by canals and streams, favored the defenders, and as each successive defensive line was breached small, stubborn pockets of Germans remained in place to harass the Allies from the rear. During most of their advance the Allied troops and vehicles had to stick closely to the roads; otherwise they found themselves completely bogged down in the muddy fields, and this created bottlenecks that were held by small parties of Germans who fought with incredible ferocity.

Klaus Schurer's party had fought their way back from The Hague, trying to avoid the advancing Polish armored division; Schurer had no wish to fall into their hands. They had been driven from Meppen on April 8 when the Canadian tanks had crossed the River Ems. Now he did not know where they were, but since they were retreating eastward and had not yet reached the Weser, he estimated they were somewhere south of Oldenburg. They had spent the whole of that cold, wet first day of May boobytrapping a road junction with a few of their precious antiaircraft shells and the last of the bombs that they had scavenged from an abandoned Luftwaffe supply dump. A 20-mm. Flakvierling antiaircraft gun was still hitched to the SD halftrack personnel carrier that Schurer had hidden in the woods. He had insisted they bring the gun with them. His men could not understand the reason for this; they felt that it merely slowed them down, and he hadn't taken the trouble to explain—they would find out soon enough if they ran into any tanks. He had seen antiaircraft guns used effectively against armor in Poland, but they were too young to remember that.

All day the Allied aircraft had skimmed by, insultingly close, safe in the knowledge that they had control of the skies and arrogant in their assumption that there was nothing to fear from the ground. They had been tempting targets for an experienced flak crew, but Schurer knew better than to try anything during daylight, when they would give away their position and invite swift retribution from the American fighters.

Tonight, however, he intended to surprise some of those cocky bomber crews and use the flak gun for the last time . . . on the targets for which it was intended.

OVER GERMANY
4:51 A.M., May 2, 1945

AS KOESSLER settled back for the long flight to Ireland he heard a sigh of relief from behind him.

"You did well," his passenger said. "We're safely away now." It was more of a question than a statement.

Koessler did not turn his head. "Yes, we were lucky. Everything has gone exactly as planned."

He had not intended this remark to be ironic, but his passenger chuckled.

"Not *exactly*, Oberleutnant. If everything had gone exactly as planned, I would not be requiring your services at the moment."

Koessler did not reply. He did not want to be distracted with reflections on national policy. His greatest danger would come now, over Germany. If they were to survive, it would require every shred of concentration and experience he could muster.

He had spent most of his active service flying nightfighters, and he knew how effective and deadly they had become since the introduction of the SN-2 radar apparatus. Earlier RAF Bomber Command had introduced the devious tactic of dropping clouds of aluminum foil from the "Pathfinder" advance squadrons that guided the bombers to their target. This left "Himmelbett," the ground radar network, baffled and completely helpless, and, more important, this gave the British a clear run over Hamburg in the summer of '43—fifty thousand civilian casualties in a single week. Fortunately the brains at Reich Air Defense had come up with one highly successful counterstroke, and the pilots and crews with another. First, the existing radar stations were fitted out with the new "Korfu" and "Naxburg" scanners; these could track British bombers by homing in on their own navigational radar beams. Now, Himmelbett could give warning of a mass bomber attack as soon as the bombers left the ground, and then lead the nightfighters straight to their quarry. Fighters equipped with the new SN-2 radar started coming off the line that autumn; the SN-2 beam could track the enemy bombers in the air, and it had a long enough wavelength so that the fighters couldn't be thrown off the scent by dumping aluminum foil.

And second, a far more troublesome point as far as Koessler was concerned, the aptly named "Crazy Music" technique of mounting the wing cannons at an oblique angle allowed a pilot to approach a bomber from below and behind—the blind side, even if they were using radar—then rake him from tail to nose without firing tracers and giving himself away. Koessler had made four kills that way in a single night when they had first tried out the new tactics.

At least he wouldn't be needing any radar to find that godforsaken Irish bay. But an unprotected plane would still have trouble sneaking past Himmelbett. All it would take would be a single nightfighter with a full tank of gas to spot him . . . and he wouldn't even have time to ask his distinguished passenger to crawl into the ball turret and start shooting.

His passenger stirred again. "How long before we reach Ireland?" Koessler, irritated by the interruption, tore off his headset. "About four to five hours, depending on headwinds —and now, if you will excuse me, I will have to concentrate on getting us there safely."

The Reichsleiter did not reply, but Koessler could sense the barely repressed anger, feel the eyes boring into the back of his head. Whatever possibilities of escape there might have been for him with his passenger, they'd just disappeared. Not that he'd minded after what Lange had said; he wanted to have his future in his own hands.

He readjusted the headset and checked his radio frequency again. He was tuned in to find out if any of the Himmelbett controllers were still on the air, and he hoped to pick up any report on him that they might pass along to the German nightfighters. Naturally, they knew nothing of this operation; the risks of a leak at this stage were too high. The allies would give almost anything—or pay almost anything—if they could intercept Koessler's passenger and his cargo.

As usual, the British were trying to jam the frequency, and in addition to their electronic wails and groans, one of the British transmitters was somewhat originally giving a nonstop reading from Goethe. However, with the new high-powered transmitters, the German operators could still make themselves heard when they had to, and this was what Koessler was listening for. When the word did come, it nearly blew his head off—the B-24's radio was much more powerful than the ones he was used to. He quickly turned down the gain, half-deafened by the noise. He listened carefully—it hadn't taken them long. They were on to him, and for once he wished they hadn't been so damned efficient. Air Defense HQ had picked him up, and they were already relaying his coordinates to a nightfighter over Hannover.

Koessler checked his position on the map. He was slightly to the north of Celle, and he estimated the closing position would be somewhere near Nienburg. Koessler waited; soon the nightfighter would make radar contact. He felt nothing except a certain sense of relief. This was what he was good at; his mind was clear, his senses alert, and his concentration total.

There, they'd found him. The nightfighter's radio operator was talking to the Himmelbett controller now. "We have him on Emil Emil"—that meant the radar had picked him up, and there wouldn't be any more chatter over the radio until they had a visual sighting. That gave him a few minutes to anticipate his colleague's next move as the fighter moved into striking position.

Koessler held the Liberator steady, gently testing his controls. He hoped the B-24 was as sturdy as Lange had made out—he'd soon find out. The silence stretched agonizingly, and Koessler prayed that he had guessed right; otherwise the first warning he would get would be the shuddering blast as the cannon fire tore through the side of his plane. Then he heard the pilot again: "We've spotted him." He let out a long sigh of relief. He knew the drill now and mentally ticked off the maneuvers one by one—move in . . . drop down . . . open up.

Koessler pushed the stick hard, forward and to the right. The Liberator immediately sank into a dive, plunging into the thick cloud cover that extended over the whole of northern Germany. This was what he was counting on. He heard the nightfighter pleading with Himmelbett for new coordinates, then a burst of incomprehensible static. Koessler watched his altimeter; he was down to ten thousand feet, and he could feel the huge aircraft beginning to shudder as its speed increased. Nine, eight; they were still in thick clouds. The Liberator was well over its maximum safe airspeed, and Koessler gently eased the stick back. He could feel the blood draining out of his face as gravity flattened him against the seat and seemed about to tear the wings off the B-24; but Lange had been right. The frame protested and whined and shuddered, but held, and gradually Koessler brought her up into a shallow dive, leveling off at about three thousand feet. As quickly as he dared, he brought her down until they were skimming over the treetops. No radar would find him here, at least.

He switched off the radio—Himmelbett was coming through quite clearly again, angrily berating the nightfighter pilot. Only then did he remember his passenger. He risked a quick look over his shoulder and saw the shadowy outline and the faint glint of his belt buckle.

"Are you all right?" he called anxiously.

His passenger grunted. "You are testing my patience, Oberleutnant. I hope you had a good reason for tossing this plane about like a fighter."

Koessler looked at his instruments with some relief and checked his position once again.

"Yes, Herr Reichsleiter, I think so. We've lost the nightfighter and soon we will be over the North Sea."

They had crossed the Weser and were about forty miles from the Dutch border, south of Oldenburg.

LOWER SAXONY
May 2,1945

THE GUN was ready, the black barrel pointing straight up at the sky—waiting. His men were tired; they'd worked hard all day preparing the boobytrap, but they had responded just as he had hoped. They wanted this last chance to get at those bloody arrogant bombers so badly that they could almost claw them out of the sky with their bare hands. Schurer knew the effect it had on their morale to watch Allied planes flying effortlessly overhead without being able to have a crack at them. They were an experienced antiaircraft crew with a good record, and it was an affront to their professional pride. Well, soon he was going to put that right. It didn't matter if they didn't hit anything, just so long as they got the chance. And one thing he was sure of—somebody was in for a nasty surprise.

They were still waiting. Schurer couldn't understand it. Nobody had flown in or out. It was incredible; every night since they had fled from The Hague it had been almost impossible to sleep because of the noise the bombers made. Now they had disappeared as if they had never existed at all. The sergeant rubbed the sleep from his eyes and looked at the luminous dial of his watch. It was after midnight, and still the skies were empty. It was almost as if the Allies had guessed where they were and decided to fly around them.

This was no good. They were accomplishing nothing— just losing sleep—and tomorrow their lives might depend on how alert they were. He decided to turn half of them in for the first shift until three. There was some grumbling at this; most of them wanted to stay up and keep watch. Schurer stayed awake, and at around five thirty, just before dawn, his vigil was rewarded. He listened intently; his men fell silent, straining to hear. There—it was unmistakable, the roar of a four-engined bomber approaching from the east.

Immediately their mood changed. They slipped silently into their positions around the gun, frozen like predators crouched to spring. Schurer was absolutely still, his eyes raised, listening, praying, willing the bomber to come their way. The noise of the engines grew louder, and the sergeant raised his arm, ready to give the signal.

They all saw the faint outline of the Liberator at the same time, dark against the sky. Immediately, Schurer dropped his arm and shouted the command. The tracers started arcing into the night sky and quickly lined up on the target. It seemed they couldn't miss. The flak was bursting all around the bomber, yet unbelieveably it seemed to be undamaged. Then, as the sound of the engines started to fade, the sergeant saw what he was looking for. The outer port engine was on fire, and his men began to cheer as the crippled bomber disappeared from sight. He wanted to join them, leap about and slap them all on the back, laugh and cry, but he couldn't. He knew how important discipline was going to be if his men were to have a chance of surviving this war. He couldn't see any further than that and he didn't want to. So he resisted the impulse, but permitted himself a quiet smile of triumph.

The tracers started pumping toward him like a stream of red lights just as he was beginning to think they were over Allied territory and safe from German ground attack. The flak bursts were tossing the Liberator from side to side, and he thanked God he'd decided to give himself a little more altitude before they struck the Dutch coastline.

He had no time to think; instinctively he tried to make it as difficult as possible for them, pulling back hard on the stick and banking to the left. Then he nearly lost control as an enormous explosion below the port wing wrenched the stick from his hand, and the outer port engine burst into flames. The big plane started to slip down to starboard, but Koessler grabbed the stick and straightened her out, then switched off the burning engine and activated the dousing control. He checked his instruments—the oil pressure on the inner port engine was dropping rapidly, and he knew they were finished. He tried rapidly to calculate how much longer the inner port engine would last before it seized up, and he began to scan the terrain ahead for a place to set the Liberator down.

Now his passenger was clutching his shoulder and yelling in his ear above the roar of the slipstream. It was only then that he realized the Plexiglas on the other side of the flight-deck screen was shattered, and the gale was screaming in through the broken nose-canopy. He couldn't make out what he was saying, nor could he see him properly, just a shadowy impression under the high-peaked cap of eyes and nostrils dilated with fear. The grip on his shoulder was painful, and he pushed his hand away. The flying suit was torn, and he felt the wetness on his hand and knew he was bleeding. He couldn't tell how badly he was hurt. His shoulder was numb, but he could still move his arm.

The face wouldn't go away, and the hands kept tearing at him. Koessler half turned in his seat, put the heel of his palm under the other's chin, and pushed hard. He went down, sprawling on the cabin floor behind him. They were down to three thousand feet, and Koessler could see sheets and ribbons of water glittering in the moonlight where canals crossed the half-flooded lowlands. He didn't want to end up in that. There would be banks and dykes, and if the big bomber slid into one of them, nobody would get out alive.

His passenger had reappeared. Incredibly, he was pointing a pistol at him. Koessler almost laughed—at that moment, with one engine still blazing and another about to seize up, the pistol seemed about as lethal as a peashooter. His passenger was mouthing something and pointing upward. Koessler assumed he was being ordered to gain altitude— and he would have given a lot to be able to oblige—but it simply wasn't possible. The bomber was doomed, and now it was just a matter of minutes. The gauge for the inner port engine began to oscillate violently, and he knew he could delay no longer. As he leaned forward to switch off, the engine seized up, the propeller cracked, and a fragment flew off, slicing through the fuselage like a blade through putty. Before Koessler could react, it had slashed the high peaked cap from his passenger's head, cut a red bloody weal across his forehead, and opened up the front of his scalp. He remained upright for a. moment, spattering Koessler with his blood, then fell backward and disappeared from sight.

Koessler felt the port wing dipping into a stall, and it took all of his strength and skill to hold on to the controls and prevent the big ship from spilling out of the sky in an uncontrollable dive. But there was still nothing he could do about the altitude. Slowly, the Liberator was being dragged down to the sodden fields, and Koessler knew he didn't have much time left, and no time to think, no time to calculate. Every part of him was fighting to keep the Liberator airborne and under control until he could find a place to set her down.

He was not sure of his position, but from occasional glimpses of the moon appearing from behind the nest of clouds he could tell he was still heading west. He felt no pain from the wound in his shoulder, and the gale coming in from the broken canopy hammered in his ears, drowning out the sounds of the big ship in her death throes.

He didn't know how long he had managed to keep her in the air; he just had a blurred impression of fighting to hang on to the controls as they sought to rip themselves from his grasp, and the wind lashing at his face.

The moon emerged once more from behind the clouds, and there, shimmering in front of him, was the Zuyder Zee, smooth and unruffled and shining like glass. That was it— that was what he had been hoping for; he was being given another chance. He switched off the starboard engines and trimmed up the port wing, so that the Liberator was no longer wallowing along with one wing pointing at the sky. He pushed the stick forward, keeping her nose down to maintain airspeed; and all he could hear was the rattle of the plane and the wind blowing through the splintered Plexiglas.

The edge of the sea came sliding up toward him, and he lifted her gently over the dyke, flattening out his approach so that the Liberator would hit the surface of the water with as little force as possible. Just before the impact he lifted the nose slightly, then set her down. She hit the water once, glanced off, hit again. Koessler was jerked forward in his harness, the pain from his injured shoulder knifing through his body as he flung up his arms in front of his face. Then she was down, the nose section sheared off just in front of the cockpit, and the water was streaming in through the nose-canopy. The Liberator slid to a stop; the fuselage split and filled with water almost at once.

Koessler struggled painfully with his harness as the water crept up swiftly to his knees, to his chest. Then he was free, and he clambered out through the broken panel and up on top of the plane.

The cockpit was already flooded, and water was bubbling up through the canopy before he realized that his map-case was no longer strapped to his knee. It must have been torn off when he had been struggling with the harness—there was no way he could get it now. He was not afraid; his mind was working so fast that everything seemed to be standing still. He tried desperately to release the liferaft cradle, but the hatch was jammed. He tried again and it moved slightly, then stuck fast. He knew he had to try and get a rough fix on his position. He turned to face the rear of the plane, and through the tailfins he could see the faint outline of dry ground rising from the water. Off to his left, where the shore curved around on the other side of the inland sea, was a shape like a tall building. At first Koessler thought it was a church, then he recognized the vanes of a windmill. The metal skin of the Liberator was already awash when Koessler started swimming back toward the spot where the bomber had skimmed over the dyke just moments before.

ZUYDER ZEE
August 1963

THE OUTLINE of the Liberator was clearly visible; it was lying in about forty feet of water, and it appeared to be intact—apart from the missing nose section and the tail assembly, which must have been wrenched off by the impact of the crash. The wings appeared to be resting on the soft seabed, apparently undamaged, and as Koessler swam down to the bomber he saw that the greater part of the fuselage, everything below wing-level, was totally immersed in the mud, almost up to the cockpit. He could see the broken nose-canopy through which he had escaped; it also seemed to be the best way to get back in.

Koessler swam slowly down to the flight deck and shone the lamp inside. It was impossible to see anything—the water was too muddy. He would have to get into the cockpit; perhaps in a confined space the lamp would reveal more. He eased himself toward the hole in the nose section—it looked big enough to accommodate him even with the oxygen cylinder on his back. Slowly, feet first, he pushed himself through, careful not to let the cylinder snag on the jagged edges of the panel. At once he realized that the external appearance of the Liberator was deceptive. The flight deck was almost half full of mud, and his first tentative movements had already disturbed the sediment. He swung the underwater lamp around—the mud had covered everything. It was clear that he was only going to get one try at finding the mapcase that he had come so far to recover. The only link between him and this bomber, but it could destroy everything that he had worked so hard to achieve since the end of the war.

Koessler positioned himself as best he could over the spot where the pilot's seat ought to be. He could just see the top of the control panel, and he tried to make a rough estimate of where the map-case might have fallen. He wedged the lamp into the broken section so that the beam was pointing down at the mud, and he gripped the top of the control panel with his left hand. Slowly, he thrust his right hand down into the mud. It was very loosely packed, and he had no trouble pressing his hand down toward the floor of the flight deck. Almost at once the light from the lamp grew faint as a thick cloud of sediment surrounded him. Koessler felt his hand touch the steel floor, and he scrabbled around with his fingers, searching for anything that could possibly be the map-case.

There was nothing, just the sickening, slimy mud. He shifted his position slightly, reached further back. The mud was all around him now, and the lamp was just a dim flicker of light at the mouth of a black cavern. His hand brushed against something, and he held it absolutely still, then slowly stretched out his fingers. It felt soft through the gloves, and he gripped it in one hand and pulled it toward him; as it pulled free of the mud he let go of the control panel and felt it with his other hand. He was holding the leather sleeve of his passenger's overcoat. Koessler dropped it in disgust and pulled himself back toward the broken canopy. He had to get out. He felt a sudden claustrophobic sense of alarm, and the dank steel cage of the flight deck seemed to be closing in on him. His sudden motion must have dislodged the lamp, because suddenly he was in darkness, and the water seemed as black and thick as ink. His head struck the roof, and he fell back stunned, instinctively throwing up one hand to try to feel the bruise through his rubber headpiece.

He tried to move again and found that one leg was immersed up to the thigh in thick, gluey mud. He felt completely disoriented, and he began to thrash around in a blind panic, trying to escape from the tomblike flight deck. Twice he crashed blindly into the cabin wall and almost lost his mouthpiece before he stopped and just let himself float, desperately choking down the fear and claustrophobia. He knew that if he was going to get out he would have to work his way back calmly and methodically to the broken nose-canopy. He reached out with one hand until he found the side of the cabin wall, then slowly worked his way along until he came to the hatchway that led back into the rear of the fuselage. He had been going the wrong way. He felt the panic rising again as he paddled through the black, filthy water, but he resisted the urge to strike out and swim straight for the nose section. Once again, he clawed his way along the side of the cabin, one hand in front of the other. He stopped; his hand touched empty space.

He reached out farther and found the edge of the broken nose-canopy. He felt all around it with both hands. There was a gray, opaque space in front of him, and he pulled himself through it slowly, deliberately fighting back the temptation to hurry in case he snagged his gear and trapped himself forever in the sunken wreck. He was clear. He pushed himself away from the hull of the Liberator, swimming upward as strongly as he could. The water began to get clearer, and suddenly he broke through the surface; he could see the stars glittering high overhead. He tore off his facemask, spat out his mouthpiece, and breathed in the cold night air. It tasted good. Koessler was utterly exhausted and very glad to see his marker light, not fifty yards away. He swam toward it, and it took all of his remaining strength to haul himself into the dinghy. He collapsed on the bottom and lay there a long time before he started to paddle back to the shore and the waiting Land-Rover.

CHATHAM ENGLAND
August 1963

HE FELT really pissed off—in addition to everything else, he'd just finished what was probably his clumsiest docking since he was fifteen years old. Then he might have had some excuse, now he had none. Wally had left without saying a word; he didn't have to. The look he'd given him had said it all.

Manderson knelt down on the quay and examined the side of his boat. The paintwork was badly scratched where she'd scraped against the granite facing of the quay and there were a few nasty splinters, which he carefully removed. A stupid blunder, but it wasn't serious. *Lucky Lady* had at least lived up to her name. He patted the wooden hull.

"Sorry, old girl, it won't happen again."

He couldn't afford to let it happen again. He'd thrown everything he had into this venture, and he'd hocked himself up to the eyebrows just to get it started, but things were not going well. Maybe Chatham was not the right place, maybe he'd have to move farther down the coast, closer to the big shipping—Portsmouth, somewhere like that. Fareham would be a good berth if he could get it.

He pulled on his leather jacket. He felt cold and hungry, and he remembered he'd had nothing to eat all day. In spite of the weather forecast he and a slightly hungover Wally had sailed *Lucky Lady* out through the Medway and into the Thames Estuary. As they rounded Sheerness the bad weather had really hit them, but he needed the job, and in spite of the heavy seas and Wally Bannen's sickly smile they had reached Margate in reasonable time.

The job had gone; the client was very sorry, but he'd given it to another diving rig. He added somewhat superciliously that he didn't think anyone would have sailed from Chatham on a day like this.

Tom Manderson had resisted the urge to grab this safe little man by the lapels and explain just how badly he'd needed that job. Instead he had swallowed it, turned, and walked out, biting off the words he wanted to say and feeling contemptuous of himself for playing safe.

He trudged up the hill and around the headland to the hotel where he rented a room. He got it cheap because he was a permanent guest, not just seasonal—besides, he hated cooking for himself, and sometimes the company was interesting. The foyer was warm, and he was glad to get out of the cold wind. Maggie, the receptionist, had her head buried in a paperback thriller. She went through them as though they were going out of fashion, and at the moment she was devouring Chandler.

She hadn't noticed him come in, so he slid quietly up beside her and whispered sibilantly in her ear.

"Okay, sweetheart . . . gimme the keys."

She lowered the book slightly so that she could see across the top and surveyed him coldly for a moment.

"You know, Tom, one of these days you'll do that once too often, and I'll kick you right where it hurts."

He raised his hands in mock alarm.

"Maggie, what a terrible thing to say to a regular client!"

The innuendo was unmistakable, and Maggie was annoyed. She swore in most unladylike fashion and threw the book at him. Tom clutched it to his stomach and pretended to be hurt.

"Ahhh. I'm ruined for life. Now are you satisfied?"

Maggie smiled. "If I've ruined you, I'm never going to be satisfied."

Tom laughed. She was good for him, and he liked her more than any other woman he'd known who'd mattered to him. It was an ingredient that he hadn't noticed in any other relationship. He regarded her steadily, and she returned his gaze a little defiantly, although her tummy turned over. It always did when he looked at her like that.

Finally he asked, "Are you busy?"

Her mouth set firmly; she was angry again, although she didn't know why. "Yes, I am," she said pointedly. He didn't look like he believed her, and Maggie fumed.

"I do have a job to do, you know."

He raised his hands defensively. "Sorry." He gave her a questioning look. "I'll go and get a drink then." She didn't reply, and then she sensed a change in his mood as he dropped the banter. "Sorry, Maggie, it's been a lousy day." He turned and started toward the bar.

You bastard, she thought, then called out softly, "I finish at seven."

He looked around, grinned, and raised one finger in acknowledgment. "Right, I'll make that two drinks." He disappeared into the bar.

He threw the letter angrily onto the floor. "Shit! That's just what I needed. What the hell am I going to do now?"

Maggie stared at him as he paced the bedroom floor. She was worried—she'd never seen him in this mood before. He was angry, but beneath that she sensed that he was badly shaken. She'd known for some time that the diving rig was not doing as well as he'd hoped, but he'd never let on to her just how bad things were.

"What did they say?"

"Oh, the usual thing. They've turned down the bloody tender"—he slammed his fist down on the table—"and I know it was the lowest. I'd cut it right down to the bone, barely enough to cover the expenses."

She wanted to put her arms around him, but she knew that he wouldn't let himself be consoled. She tried to be practical. "Then why, Tom? There must be a reason."

"Oh, there's a reason all right." She wanted him to calm down; his anger frightened her. "It's because they've never heard of me. I'm a new boy, not someone they're prepared to give a chance to, even though my record is good."

Maggie tried again. "You can't give up now, Tom, not after you've put in so much. Just keep plugging away. Something'll turn up."

"Something'll turn up," he repeated scornfully. "Jesus, woman, you haven't heard a word I've said, have you?" He held up his finger an inch from her nose. She could see that his hand was shaking, and she stood very still.

"Listen, I've been submitting tenders and estimates for anything that was going within a thirty-mile radius for six months now." He turned and went to the desk, picking up a handful of letters. "This is all I ever get back—no sir, no sir . . . no way, sir, go away, we only deal with the people we know. Jesus Christ! How does anyone ever get started in this country?"

Maggie was close to tears. She knew he was taking his anger and frustration out on her, but that wasn't it. She loved him and wanted to help, but she couldn't. She sat down on the side of the bed and looked at the floor so that he wouldn't see how much he had hurt her.

"I'm sorry, Tom."

He stood by the desk, looking at her, all the anger draining away from him, knowing what a bastard he'd been. He put the letters back on the desk and crossed the room, kneeling in front of her. He took her face in his hands and saw the tears. He tried ineffectually to brush them away with his hand.

"Jesus, Maggie." He was biting his lip and close to tears himself. "I'm sorry."

He kissed her gently at first, but then with an intensity, a need, that Maggie had never felt before. He pushed her back onto the bed, and started undressing her slowly and deliberately. His desire communicated itself fiercely to her, and she wanted him inside her, to feel his love, his passion, his hard muscular body close to hers. She twisted this way and that, helping him undress her, and she tore at his clothes until they were both naked, and she could feel him inside her. His loving was passionate but tender. He wanted her to know that this was different. There was a yearning inside him—an ache, a need to make this woman his own. For too long he had held back from a commitment to anyone; perhaps it was selfish, but he wanted most of all to succeed on his own terms, owing nothing to anyone. Now that he wanted to speak the words, he found that he couldn't, and Maggie, sensing this, didn't force it. She understood, without being told, what was happening to him, and she knew that sooner or later, if he felt the way she did, it would happen. A wise girl was Maggie.

IN THE EASTERN MEDITERRANEAN
December 1945

THE SMELL from the stinking, packed humanity on board
the tramp steamer could be detected three miles downwind,
but so far they had been lucky. None of the British patrol
boats blockading the harbors of Haifa and Tel Aviv had
found them yet, and unusually bad weather had grounded
the observation planes searching for illegal immigrant ships,
but most of those on board felt it was only a matter of time.
No one intended making it easy for the British to prevent
them from reaching their goal. Waterhoses, rotten fruit,
even spoiled tins of tomatoes were in readiness to receive the
boarding parties, though many found it impossible to believe that the British, of all people, would send them back.

For most of them it had taken six years or more to come
this far. They were the lucky ones—the survivors of Hitler's
deathcamps. For them the sickness and the overcrowding on
this vessel meant little or nothing. The stink of human ex-

crement could be tolerated—and the vessel's primitive sanitary arrangements made it inevitable. The first outbreak of dysentery had claimed the weakest of the survivors, and now even the strongest were beginning to show the pale-blue skin and sunken eyes of the cholera victim. But the buoyant hope of a new life, a home in the state of Israel, still sustained them—without this they would have let themselves die long ago.

For Franz, the squalor was horrific, but it was the fear of disease that frightened him—of dying before he could accomplish what mattered to him most. When the stench became so overpowering he couldn't help vomiting, he began to search the ship for a place where he might survive, safe from contact with anyone else.

Every inch seemed to be occupied. It was almost impossible to move from one part of the vessel to another. They spilled out onto the decks and into the lifeboats—even the roof of the bridge was crowded. Three days out from Genoa the bad weather had started to hit them hard, and several had been swept overboard, but others quickly took their places, ready to risk anything for the comparatively fresh air on deck.

Franz had one advantage. He was small for a fourteen-year-old and very strong. The regime of the boarding school at Heilbronn and his training in the Hitler Youth had hardened him physically and mentally, and he had never seen the inside of a concentration camp. There was still one place on the steamer that no one had attempted to occupy. High above the deck on the forward mast that formed part of the derrick which was used to load and unload cargo was a crow's-nest, a long disused relic of the days before radio and well-charted shipping lanes. Franz waited until it was dark and filled his rucksack with enough food and water for several days. He swung along the steel halyard that raised and lowered the cargo boom, then slid carefully down the boom until he reached the mast. Now came the most difficult part. The ladder that had once led up to the crosstree had long since been removed, and Franz had to wrap his arms and legs around the mast and, using his rubber sneakers to brace himself, shin up the mast a foot at a time. Luckily the sea was fairly calm, but the swells were still strong enough to make the mast sway from side to side in a slow arc, and more than once he was nearly flung down to the steel decks below.

The crow's-nest was full of bird droppings, but once he had cleared it out, he was mercifully free from most of the foul odors from below. He was to spend five days and nights in the crow's-nest, and he had plenty of time to retrace the steps of his journey thus far.

He couldn't remember when the idea of this journey had first come to him. Slowly, it had grown stronger, brighter, giving him some sort of hope in the misery and unhappiness of his years at the boarding school. Memories hurt, but now that he was alone, with only the sea, the sky, and the birds for company, they started to come back, crowding into his mind whenever he relaxed or closed his eyes. He remembered the boarding school, the headmaster, Schlenke, and most clearly of all . . . the unspeakable Lutz Beyer.

From the moment of his arrival he had been the focus of Beyer's interest. It almost seemed as if he knew that Franz was Jewish. Some atavistic sixth sense, probing, smelling out the racial overtones, had told him that Franz was not quite the same. And yet he seemed drawn toward the blue-eyed, fair-haired younger boy, alternately bullying and taunting him, then seeking out his company. Franz had learned to hate very quickly here, particularly the Hitler Youth. He was immediately enlisted; Beyer had seen to that. There was no alternative; you were either with them or against.

He had not excelled in their games, on the playing field or

off, unlike some. He remembered the frantic rush after school to change into uniform for the evening rollcall—all of them standing at attention in the quadrangle like toy soldiers. Their names would be imprinted on his memory forever. Beginning with the eldest—Lischke, Beyer, Gerling, Vogel, right down the line until they got to him among the juniors.

What had happened to them? he wondered. He knew the older ones had fought in the war. Beyer had been decorated, and Franz had cheered at assembly as loud and as long as the others, hating them all, particularly Lutz Beyer, who had taunted him for his reluctance to join in the Jew-baiting— something Lutz was especially good at.

He remembered how Beyer had led a small group of their Hitler Youth brigade into town one night. All of them were older than Franz, but Beyer had insisted that he accompany them. The road had semed endless, and the heavy stone jug Beyer forced him to carry made his arm ache. He soon had difficulty keeping pace with the others. It was a still, damp night and as the moon crept up, its shape and luminosity fluctuated weirdly through the heavy mist that had settled on the fields. Once it had risen, it shone full and bright, cheering the boys with its light and glinting off the brightly polished buckles of their uniforms.

After a couple of miles Beyer called a halt, took the heavy jug from Franz's aching arms, and opened it, wiping the mouth with his hand. He started to raise the jug to his lips, then changed his mind and proffered it to Franz.

"Since you have had to carry it so far, perhaps you should be the first to taste it."

Nervously, Franz took the jug, knowing that all eyes were watching him. He raised it to his lips and took a swallow; the bitter lager soured his tongue and he choked and spat it out, coughing uncontrollably.

Beyer laughed and pounded him heavily on the back. This broke the tension, and the others were happy to join in. As Franz caught his breath he looked up and saw that Beyer was staring at him, waiting for him to stop coughing. The others took their cue from him and gradually the laughter died away. Now all Franz could hear was the croaking of a frog in the pond behind the grove.

Beyer had taken the jug from him to keep it from spilling and now he offered it to him again. "You must drink some. You are the youngest and must set an example for us all."

Franz was frightened. He had never disobeyed Beyer before, but he knew he could not swallow any of that foul liquid; he was sure it would make him vomit. He shook his head, not daring to look up. Beyer was furious.

"Drink it!"

Still Franz did not respond, hardly daring to move. Abruptly Beyer took a pace forward, grabbed a handful of his hair, and jerked his head back. Franz struggled; the pain made his eyes water as Beyer kept holding tightly by the hair. Franz flailed about, trying to break his grip, but too frightened of Beyer to strike him. Beyer ordered one of the other boys to grip his arms, and another to hold his nose. When Franz opened his mouth to breathe, Beyer poured the beer down his throat, pumping him on the back to make sure he swallowed it.

When he was satisfied that Franz had had enough, he brushed the others aside and stepped back, letting Franz fall to his knees, choking and sobbing. Beyer looked down at him contemptuously and wiped the mouth of the jug with his hand.

"Anyone would think it was poison."

He raised the jug, took a long drink, and handed it to the nearest boy.

"Taste it."

He lifted it slowly, wondering what was inside but not daring to defy him. He took a swallow and coughed slightly at the unexpected bitterness. Then he smiled, recognizing the taste.

"It's beer!"

Then he took another swig and passed the jug down the line. After they'd all had some, Beyer retrieved the jug and sealed his dominance over them by finishing it off. Then he handed the empty jug to Franz, who was still on his knees, sniffling.

"Here, you carry this. Perhaps it's all you're good for, carrying empties."

Franz's humiliation was complete, and the last mile into town was like a nightmare. The singing became more raucous, the marching less orderly, and Franz trailed miserably behind, clutching the jug and wanting to be sick. The trees swirled above him, and the alcohol affected his balance, but the fear of Beyer and his own shame forced him to keep it down.

The trees began to thin out; now tall, solid family houses were scattered along the roadside. Beyer motioned them to be silent and moved over to the side of the road, the others following. Soon there was pavement underfoot, and widely spaced street lamps cast pools of light onto the shrubbery bordering the gardens. The houses here sat well back from the road, and sometimes Franz could see inside the bright, warm rooms of those who lived in this wealthy section. But this was not the place Beyer was after, and he led them on, into the commercial part of the town. Occasionally a car went by, but there were not many people about after ten in this provincial German town.

Beyer stopped outside a shop and pointed at the sign— Benjamin Dreifuss, Jeweler & Watch Repairer. It occurred to Franz that he must be quite rich to own a jeweler's shop.

Then he saw Beyer take a can of paint that one of the boys had been carrying, and he realized the purpose of their journey.

Slowly and with great concentration Beyer began to write a single word in huge capitals across the walls and window, JUDE, JUDE, repeated many times over. Then he gave the brush to another boy, who followed suit. One of them added *Jewish pig* and turned to Beyer for approval. He gazed at this embellishment silently for a moment, and they all waited for his reaction. He put his hands together slowly and began applauding. One of the boys cheered and clapped his hands together, imitating Beyer. Immediately they all did the same, the slow, rhythmic applause echoing down the street in small bursts of sound.

A light went on in a window above the shop. Then the window was flung open, and a man of about thirty stuck his head out. The applause stopped suddenly. Franz could see the man's face—he gazed incredulously at the dripping letters splashed across the front of his shop. Franz heard a woman's voice from inside, questioning. Then the woman joined the man at the window, and Beyer broke the silence, chanting softly at first *"Jude, Jude."* The others picked it up, and the chant grew louder. Franz could see that the woman was screaming at them, but her voice was drowned by the chanting. The man was trying to pull her back inside, but she broke away from him, and suddenly the door of the shop was thrown open, and she stood there in her nightdress, clutching a riding crop.

The chanting stopped, and there was an uneasy silence. No one moved. Beyer threw back his head and laughed, pointing between the woman's legs, where the black pubic hair showed through her nightdress. He shouted an obscenity, and the boys laughed nervously. The woman's eyes, dark, glittering with hatred, fell upon Beyer, and she advanced on him. He stood his ground, but for the first time he appeared a little unsure of himself.

She stopped in front of him, then spat right in his face. The spittle trickled down the side of his nose, and he cried out, trying to wipe it away before it reached his mouth. The woman struck him with the riding crop. A red-speckled weal seemed to glow on his cheek, and he lifted one arm to protect himself. She began to hit him again and again, ripping his shirt open. He threw up both arms in front of his face, and using the handle of the crop like a truncheon, she jabbed it sharply into his unprotected groin. He screamed with pain and fell to the ground, hugging his knees up to his chest, trying to ease the agony between his legs. Frightened, the others turned and ran. Franz stood dumbly, unable to move. Beyer cried out, throwing up his arms and turning his head toward Franz. There was a look of terror in his eyes.

"Stop her, please! For God's sake, Franz! Stop her!" The anguish in Beyer's voice jerked Franz out of his nightmare. He stepped forward, raised both arms, and brought the stone jug down on the back of the woman's head. She fell limply across Beyer; he thrust her dead weight away violently and rose unsteadily to his feet. She was pitched over on her back, her eyes gazing sightlessly up at the moon, her head resting in a dark pool of blood. Beyer grabbed his arm, and Franz found himself running back past the tall family houses; they slowly grew farther and farther apart. The street lights disappeared, then the pavement, and he was still running.

He hadn't stopped, and he ran as far away as he could. When the war ended, he joined the thousands of homeless refugees flooding the roads out of the bombed cities. Franz walked the fifty miles to the small town where his family lived and found the little shop shattered and empty. He did not linger. He was an intelligent boy, and he had had a long time to think about his next move. Eventually he made contact with the Youth Aliyah Organization, which helped him to escape from Europe. Most of the journey was along well-traveled routes, across the Alps and down to Genoa, where he finally boarded the steamer in December 1945. The weather had gotten worse as they approached the Palestinian coast, and sometimes Franz had to wedge himself firmly into the crow's-nest to keep from being flung out into the sea. Although no one knew it at the time, the weather had been their salvation. The tramp steamer was one of only five ships that successfully negotiated the blockade, out of sixty-three that attempted it between 1945 and 1948. Franz and the other survivors were put ashore at night, south of Haifa, and he set foot on the shores of his new country in late December.

It was to be a long time before Franz Herrimann would return to Europe and again make use of his Aryan appearance, thus turning full circle. . . .

EASTBOURNE
September 1963

THE SUN was warm on his back, and Manderson felt a
comfortable drowsiness settling over him. Already the worries and frustrations that had assailed him ever since he
bought the diving rig seemed far away, and slightly unreal.
He stretched out, cradled his head on his arms, and breathed
in the smell of freshly cut grass. He closed his eyes; the familiar sounds of children playing down by the seashore
mingled with the brushing of the waves over Eastbourne's
pebbled beach.

He liked Eastbourne. He'd come down here two or three
summers on the trot after finishing his National Service in
the Marines at Poole—working the deck chairs, doling out
the tickets, and making a little bit on the side whenever he
got the chance. Eastbourne was a surprisingly attractive
place for an unattached male in the summer. He remembered "Rannie's" girls. High-income, high-spirited, and just

a little debbie, escaping from their finishing-off domestic-science courses in the grand building beside an even grander Grand Hotel. They were fresh and ready for anything, and Manderson fitted the bill. He intrigued them because he didn't fit in, and they knew little or nothing of his background. The chairs did a roaring trade when he was working, so that when he occasionally pocketed the ticket money, he felt he was getting no more than he deserved. The local council increased its profit—so did he, and when Rannie's girls departed, the French invasion began. Here to learn the language, they boarded with local families and spent their spare time, as did everyone else, on the beach. He smiled when he remembered how their arrival every summer caused great consternation among the local adolescents. Winter romances broke up and the locals swapped affections with the Continental talent. Yes, he'd spent a lot of time consoling broken hearts on Eastbourne's stony beach.

Thus it was not surprising that when he decided he'd had enough of his problems for the moment, he'd slipped down here without saying a word to anyone. He'd go back in a few days. Meanwhile, he needed a break—a breathing space—and this was just the place for it.

He was lying on the grassy knoll below the martello tower, known locally as the Wish Tower because it commanded a fine view of the Channel from Wish Point. He didn't know how long he'd been dozing when he was awakened by the sound of a woman's voice, and he gradually realized that she was talking to him. He rolled over on his back and looked up, shielding his eyes from the sun. It was bright and behind her, and he could only perceive her outline. She realized that he hadn't heard her.

"Hello, Tom."

"Maggie!"

"I thought I'd find you here."

She pointed to the deck chair on which he had thrown his jacket and shirt. "Mind if I sit down?"

Manderson hastily grabbed the clothes from the seat. "No, of course not."

She sat down wearily, closed her eyes, and let the late September sun warm her face. "Sorry if I've spoiled it for you."

Manderson looked at her curiously. Once again she had surprised him. "No, you've not spoiled anything. But how did you know where I was?"

She opened her eyes and looked at him. "Oh, that wasn't difficult. You don't live with a bloke for three months without knowing something about him."

"But I didn't—"

"Yes, you did. You often went on about this place"—she looked at him out of the corner of her eye—"how marvelous it was—all those French girls." Maggie smiled. "Well, I wasn't gonna let them get their hands on you, was I?"

Manderson laughed and knelt in front of her, between her legs. "You're incredible. Do you know that, Maggie? Incredible." He leaned forward to kiss her, but she put her hand on his chest and pushed him back.

"First make yourself useful. You can take my shoes off for a start. I've been walking around this town for hours looking for you, and my feet are killing me."

He grinned. "All right, Maggie, anything you say. . . . It's the least I can do." He carefully removed her shoes, then he pulled up some of Eastbourne's hallowed grass and rubbed her aching feet with it. Maggie looked down at him gently, rubbing her feet, and she felt like crying with happiness and relief. Instead, she ruffled his hair.

"You want to know something?"

"What?"

"It was almost worth the journey just for this."

This time he did kiss her. She rolled off the deck chair and fell into his arms, much to the annoyance of the elderly gent in a panama hat who was sitting in the next chair. "No decorum these days," he muttered to the equally old lady beside him. "No decorum at all."

She watched Maggie and Tom's passionate reunion with a vague smile. "Oh, I don't know, Albert. I think they're rather nice."

He was exhausted, rivulets of sweat ran down his neck and chest, soaking his T-shirt. The small discotheque below Finch's coffee bar was packed, and he was having a tough time trying to keep up with Maggie, who was dancing with an abandon, an invention, that literally took his breath away. She was like a bird released from a cage. She twisted and turned and wiggled her bottom, and his eyes were glued to her bra-less blouse. He wiped the sweat from his forehead with the back of his hand and yelled at her, trying to make himself heard above the sounds of The Searchers and "Sweets for my Sweet" at full volume.

"How about a drink?"

It only seemed to spur her on to further efforts.

"Come on—you can't be tired yet. I'm the one who's been traveling all day."

She grabbed his hand and started to jive, bobbing and turning, then sliding down between his legs and rolling across his back, taking most of the initiative herself and making Manderson look a better dancer than he was. The music stopped; there was a burst of applause, and he realized they had the floor to themselves. He looked around at the sea of faces in the tiny room, most of the men grinning and staring enviously at Maggie, who was eager to continue as soon as the music started up again.

He shook his head, releasing a fine spray of perspiration, grabbed her hand, and hauled her off the floor and up the staircase. They collapsed onto two seats at an alcove table, and he pulled at the neck of his T-shirt to cool himself off.

"What was that all about? I've never seen anybody move like that before."

"That's because you don't have to spend nearly every day of every week sitting behind a desk in the foyer of a crummy hotel. This is different. Makes me feel alive."

Manderson could see that. She was excited, her eyes dilated, taking in everything.

"I'm glad you've enjoyed yourself."

"Oh, I have—I really have, Tom. Thanks for bringing me here."

She took his hand in both of hers and kissed it. She did it without thinking, excitement and pleasure mingled, totally instinctively. Manderson looked at her steadily; at this moment he wanted her more than anything else in the world. His hand tightened on hers.

"Shall we go?"

Maggie nodded brightly.

"Your place or mine?" he asked.

She smiled. "All I've got is a beach."

Manderson paused momentarily. "Mine, I think."

His place was cozy. A small flat over a wool shop next to the Lamb Inn, just a kitchen, hall, and bedroom with bay windows and a huge double bed.

"You like it?" he asked, sipping his tea and nodding toward the bed.

Maggie pulled the covers back, then snuggled into his arms. "Yes, I think that's what sold me on the place."

He set the cup of tea down on the sideboard and slid his hands up inside her blouse; her bare breasts under the fabric always came as a pleasant surprise. He turned her around and cupped her breasts in his hands, burying his face in her damp hair. Maggie reached behind her and felt for the zipper on his jeans, pulling it down slowly and reaching her right hand inside, feeling for his penis, now engorged with blood and pressing hard against her buttocks. She slid round and faced him, her mouth searching hungrily for his as she pushed his jeans and shorts to the floor. Her hands caressed him tenderly, feeling his balls now tight against his body. His hand was between her legs.

Slowly, he pushed her back onto the bed, sliding the tight briefs down her legs. Then he was inside her, thrusting hard and rhythmically. Maggie was full, her body responding totally to his. He grabbed the brass rails above her head, arching his back and pushing himself into her with all his strength. Maggie felt that she was about to split in two; then he was coming, and she could feel the quickening pulsations as he ejaculated into her. It triggered her own response. She was flooding, holding his taut, lean buttocks and pulling him as deeply into her as she could. Then, as suddenly as their lovemaking had begun, it was over, and they lay exhausted beside each other. Manderson gazed up at the ceiling and started to chuckle. Disconcerted, Maggie raised herself up on one elbow and peered down at him.

"What's so funny?"

"I was just thinking."

"Thinking what?"

"They're right, you know."

"Who's right?" she demanded exasperatedly.

"They are. Someone once told me to get into the hotel business. I never thought it would be this nice."

Maggie tried to look offended, then collapsed into his arms, giggling like a schoolgirl.

LONDON
November 1963

MANDERSON was intrigued. He'd been running over the phone call in his head all the way up from Chatham, trying to work out what the possibilities were, but he was still no wiser. The man had been polite, a little vague, and had coughed a lot, but the message had come through loud and clear. If he was interested in an unusual diving job that demanded absolute secrecy, then there was money to be made. Manderson hadn't needed to think twice about it, and the nearer he came to his destination in London, the more curious he got.

The cab turned left off Victoria Street and then right into a narrow road just wide enough to accommodate the taxi. The driver peered out, checked the numbers, and pulled back the sliding window.

"Forty-six, did you say, guvnor?"

"Yes, that's right."

"Gets a bit difficult sometimes," the driver said. "Not all of them are numbered in streets like this. You have to work it out from them that are." The cab crawled along a bit farther until the driver pulled up.

"There we are, on the right—forty-six."

Manderson paid the driver and looked up at the somewhat decrepit Victorian building in front of him. Inside it was better; the place had obviously been converted into a block of offices and recently redecorated. Fortunately, they hadn't tried to alter the character of the place and give it a modern gloss, but had concentrated on restoring the former glories of the brass and woodwork. The office he was looking for—J. H. Pennyman Ltd.—was on the third floor. There was an old-fashioned self-service elevator in the corner, which carried him slowly upward, and from what Manderson could see through the grill, most of the offices seemed to be occupied by chartered surveyors and solicitors.

Manderson slid back the doors, stepped out, and then made sure they were closed properly behind him. He hated it when someone had left them open and he had to trudge up the stairs.

The office was on the right at the end of the passageway; it had a plain wooden door marked simply *J. H. Pennyman* and, below that, *Enter*. He knocked once, opened the door, and found himself alone in a small anteroom with several filing cabinets, a desk, a buzzer, and a sign—*Please Ring*. He pressed the buzzer and waited. Through the inner door he heard a low buzz of conversation, punctuated by long silences and a great deal of coughing. At last came the sound of a telephone receiver being replaced on its cradle, and a voice called out to him.

"Come in, please. Come in."

Manderson opened the door. It was a large room, high-ceilinged and airy; the sunlight slanted down through the two big bay windows, falling in two bright pools on the faded carpet. The room was furnished with a few pieces of ancient but good-quality furniture, and behind an enormous desk a gray-haired old man sat in a leather chair. He stood up with some difficulty and thrust out his bony hand.

"Hello, young man," he wheezed. "You must be Manderson."

His watery eyes peered over his glasses and seemed to be regarding him with some amusement—there was a definite twinkle. Manderson gripped his hand and was surprised to find himself saying, "That's right, sir, Tom Manderson." He felt as if he were back at school, talking to headmaster.

The eyes twinkled again, and he rubbed the side of his nose.

"Right, well, sit yourself down, Manderson, and make yourself comfortable." He sat back in his own chair, pursed his lips, and then started rummaging through a stack of papers on his desk. "Let's see, now. I've got it here somewhere." He seemed to be talking to himself, and Manderson couldn't resist a smile. It would be hard to imagine anyone less likely to be engaged in something nefarious.

The old man stopped rummaging for a moment. "Would you like a cup of tea?" he enquired. "I've got some nice hot sweet stuff here in a flask." He took the flask out of a drawer and waggled it in front of him. Manderson declined. "Hope you don't mind if I do. Helps me think. Besides, I don't go out to lunch these days. The restaurants are all too crowded round here."

He poured some tea into a mug, then started to put the flask back in the drawer. He paused, pushing his glasses up on his nose.

"Ah, here we are." He reached into the drawer and pulled out a large brown envelope. "Knew I'd seen it somewhere." He set the flask absentmindedly on the floor and closed the drawer.

"I expect you're wondering what this is all about." It was

more of a comment than a question. He opened the envelope and scanned the letter inside.

"It all sounds very exciting, I must admit. Don't get many commissions like this." He tapped the letter with his glasses and chuckled; the chuckle became a wheezing cough, and the old boy started getting very red in the face. Manderson was concerned. He stood up, wondering whether he should try patting him on the back, but the old man looked so frail that it was likely to do more harm than good.

"Are you all right, sir?"

The old man nodded vigorously. "Yes," he spluttered, and picked up the mug, swallowing some of the tea. "Quite all right, thanks." He seemed recovered and his color had already returned to normal.

"It's just that I'm trying to give up smoking, you see, and every time I do that, I develop this silly cough. Thought it was supposed to be the other way round. Never had one when I smoked a pipe!"

Manderson thought it best to say nothing.

"Now, where was I?" He stared vaguely at the desk as though he were looking for something.

"The letter?" Manderson prompted.

"What?"

"The letter, sir"—he pointed—"in your hand."

"Ah, yes, of course," he adjusted his glasses again.

"Now, let's see what this says. 'Dear Mister Pennyman' "
—he glanced up—"that's me, by the way, forgot to introduce myself—very rude of me."

"What does the letter say, sir?" Manderson interrupted gently, trying to keep the edge out of his voice.

Pennyman looked at him gravely. "Sorry, Manderson— down to business, quite right." He started to read through the letter in a completely inaudible drone, and Manderson waited as patiently as he could. Finally, Pennyman put the letter down.

"What it boils down to is this. I've been asked by a Dutch businessman, who wishes to remain anonymous, to approach you and see if you might be interested in a diving job that could recover some wartime booty. You would get five thousand pounds, half now, half when completed, and five percent of whatever the operation might realize. At this stage, there is apparently no way of knowing just what that might amount to. Naturally, this would have to be done in complete secrecy, otherwise various governments might have a claim on the items recovered. Before I tell you anything else, I must ask you if you are interested." His rheumy eyes regarded Manderson expectantly. "What do you say, young man?"

Manderson cleared his throat. It was much more than he had expected, and there was no doubt in his mind, but, instinctively, he started to haggle.

"If I get ten percent of whatever I recover, and the job is feasible . . . yes, I am."

The old man smiled. "Good, good, well done. I'm glad you said that. I am authorized to go as high as ten percent." He seemed genuinely pleased. "Now then, I have here all your instructions and maps, in detail, but briefly the situation as I understand it is this." He glanced down at the papers. "There is a sunken Second World War aircraft in a part of the Zuyder Zee that is shortly to be drained. Inside that aircraft are some packing cases and the skeleton of a dead man that your principal thinks is German." He paused, his eyes gleaming with excitement. "Marvelous, isn't it? Now, he believes that these packing cases contain war booty that the German was trying to escape with when the war ended, and he makes it very clear that you must recover intact everything down there—map-cases, documents—if they have survived. It's quite possible, incidentally; he points out that when the previous polder was drained—

that's a section of the Zuyder Zee, by the way—they found all
sorts of things—scarves, bottles of scent, and so on—"

"How did he find the plane?" Manderson interjected.

For the first time Pennyman looked uncomfortable.

"Yes, I was afraid you might ask that question." He waved
his hand at the papers in front of him. "That seems to be a
rather gray area." Manderson was not surprised. "There is
no direct reference to that here," Pennyman continued, "except to say that he found the wreck by accident and that he
has examined it"—he peered at his papers again, "wearing a
frogman's suit?" He glanced inquiringly at Manderson.

"That's right," Manderson explained. "It's made of rubber."

The old man shook his head in disbelief. "Good heavens, a
rubber suit . . . what'll they think of next?" Manderson
didn't bother to explain that they had been used since the
Second World War; this would only have delayed matters,
and he was eager to find out the full extent of this operation.

Pennyman continued, still plainly amused by the concept
of a rubber suit. "The aeroplane lies in about forty feet of
water; it is heavily silted up and will certainly need clearing
out." Pennyman put down his glasses. "However, all the details, maps, references, and so on are here. It seems to my
untutored eye to be quite comprehensive."

Manderson tried to conceal his excitement. He'd guessed
that it might be a recovery job of some sort, possibly an old
wreck, something like that, but this was more interesting and
perhaps more lucrative.

"Let me see the maps, Mr. Pennyman."

"Not yet, young man, not yet. First, there is a little matter
to be settled." He took another document from the manila
envelope.

"This is a contract. Bascially, what it says is that you agree
to recover from the wrecked aeroplane whatever you find

down there and hand it over to his agent—which is me—and he will attempt to realize the full value of the, er, proceeds of your undertaking. In return you will get ten percent, as we agreed"—he filled in the figure on the contract—"you also get twenty-five hundred pounds now, and a further twenty-five hundred when the job is completed."

He paused and peered at Manderson over his glasses. "There is one other thing that you may find inhibiting. . . ."

"Yes?"

The old man seemed embarrassed. "Well, er, one of the conditions is that you must complete this job entirely by yourself."

Manderson's eyes widened in surprise. "What?"

"Yes." He hunted for his place in the contract. "That is what it says here, I'm afraid, and indeed he also mentions it in his correspondence."

"But that's impossible," Manderson protested. "Maybe he doesn't understand diving procedure, but there must always be someone on top in case anything goes wrong."

"I thought you might take that point of view, but, in fact," Pennyman said, "he says he understands this might be a problem, but that he has gone into it, and he believes it is possible. In any case that is the stipulation, Manderson, and you must decide whether or not you want to go ahead on that basis. If you agree, then you sign here. Then you can see the maps." He handed the contract over. "You'd better read that."

Manderson read quickly through the contract. He knew that he had no choice. Besides, if what the old man had said was true, then it might just be possible. He signed.

"Now, sir, if you don't mind, the maps."

Pennyman sighed with relief, took the contract from him, blotted the signature, and reached into the envelope once more. "Here we are. There are also detailed instructions on where you can stay in Harderwijk, the tides, and so forth."

Manderson looked through the maps and diagrams. They had been drawn with meticulous accuracy. No detail had been omitted—the phases of the moon, the projected weather forecasts for that time of year. Manderson glanced up; the old man was quietly watching him.

"These are good, Mr. Pennyman, very good. You mentioned something about money?"

"Of course"—he rubbed the bridge of his nose again—"if you are satisfied that you can proceed at once?"

Manderson was beginning to realize that the old man's appearance was deceptive. He was certainly no fool. He used vagueness and an apparently woolly mind as a front and made it work for him.

"Yes, I can leave for Holland just as soon as I get back and tidy up a few things."

"Ah, that reminds me," Pennyman began. "You will, of course, tell no one about this, and finally, I should feel a lot happier if your preparations didn't make it appear that you were going very far."

Manderson smiled. "Of course. Anything else?" he added, with just a hint of malice, which Pennyman ignored.

"No." He rubbed his hands gleefully. "I'm glad that's settled." He took a drink from the mug and produced a set of keys from his waistcoat pocket, then reached down to another drawer and pulled out a steel cashbox. Manderson watched impatiently as the old man tried each key in turn.

"Sorry, I always have trouble with keys. I can never get them to open anything."

Eventually he succeeded in finding the key and removed two bundles of ten-pound notes from the cashbox, passing one over to Manderson.

"You'll find that is correct. I've checked myself." He put the other sheaf of notes back in the box and locked it, after apologetically going through the key business again. Manderson was sitting quite still, looking at the money. It meant so much, and yet looked like so little. He felt exultant and angry at once, unable to pin down his reactions. He smiled. *Mixed feelings* would just about sum it up. The old man was looking at him quizzically. Manderson realized he'd been asked a question.

"Sorry?"

"I said, aren't you going to count it?"

"No, I don't think so, Mr. Pennyman. You've got everything else right, so I expect it's all there." He put the money in the envelope with the maps and instructions and stood up.

"Is there anything else?"

The old man pushed himself out of his chair and walked around the desk.

"Just one thing. I'd like to wish you luck, young man." He gripped his hand and shook it firmly. "Chance of a lifetime, you know. Don't mess it up."

"I won't." Manderson turned and walked to the door. He paused, remembering something.

"What made you think of me, Mr. Pennyman?"

The old man shook his head. "I didn't. My client seemed to know all about you, and I'm bound to say I think he's made a good choice."

Manderson warmed to him. "Thank you, Mr. Pennyman."

MUNICH
November 1963

HELMUT LANGE was enjoying the show, and so was the American he was entertaining. He hadn't been to the cabaret theater in the Schwabing for a long time, although he had always had a soft spot for it. The stage in the corner was still not much bigger than a postage stamp, and he marveled at how skillfully the actors created the illusion that the tiny stage was whatever they wanted it to be.

Lange had first come to the "Lachen- und Scheissegesellschaft" years ago when he was a young officer. He'd loved the cosmopolitan atmosphere of the place—the audiences of students from the university, politicians, businessmen, and a fair smattering of the stars of the day. He'd once seen Peter Lorre there before he had gone off to America.

Later, when Hitler came to power, the outspokenness of some of the satire had incurred the Fuehrer's displeasure, and the audiences wisely faded away, as did the actors, although a few of them paid a heavier price for their nerve.

Now the place was crowded and even more popular than before the war. Tonight things were a bit different, which was why Lange had brought his American visitor along. The resident German company was playing in a London nightclub, and tonight's attraction in Munich was an English revue with the provocative title *England Versus Germany— Love All.*

The four actors, three men and a tall, willowy blonde, were doing well. The performance, which was in English and easily understood by most of the audience, took the form of a series of quick sketches and songs, plus a send-up of the Bond cult. Lange had particularly liked the opening song:

> *If it hadn't happened from '39*
> *To Hiroshima in '45*
> *No German officer could cross the Rhine,*
> *And dear old Adolf would still be alive. . . .*

The bitterness of the lyrics took the audience totally by surprise, but then the actors stood to attention and sang, *"Deutschland, Deutschland ueber Alles"*—their right arms rose slowly in the salute— "means that we love you!"—The salute had relaxed into a hilariously silly wave. Shock gave way to delighted laughter from the audience. Finally, as the applause subsided the little Englishman on the right exclaimed in mock alarm, "My God, the room's full of Germans!" He ran offstage and reappeared a moment later, brandishing a tommygun. Another actor restrained him, saying, "No, no, it's all right! It's all over," then turned to the audience with his arms raised in surrender. *"Kamerad! Kamerad!"* Blackout, finish. Lange was amused; the English actors were less serious, more irreverent than their German counterparts, and it made a refreshing change.

After the show Lange and his guest retired to the bar and talked some business; the American was interested in distributing Lange's line of stationery in the States. Most of the main points were settled over schnapps, and all that remained were details. Lange was well pleased with the progress they had made by the time he drove the American back to his hotel, and they made arrangements for their final meeting the next day.

He drove his Mercedes slowly back home through the suburbs of Munich. His visit to the cabaret had revived many half-forgotten memories, some of them happy ones, particularly of the times that he had been there with his wife. He missed his wife; it was incredible that they could have gone through so much together. Those awful black days just after the war, locked away in a Russian POW camp and not knowing if she was alive or dead, or if he would live long enough to find out.

Eventually, over a year later, they released him and he made his way back through the shattered ruins of Germany to Munich. He'd found her working in a shoe store, and not even the shock of how weary and old she looked would ever take away the joy of that moment. He had held her silently in his arms, the tears running down his unshaven face. Neither of them spoke; they were content just to hold each other again. No one in the shop took any notice—it was a scene that had been repeated a thousand times. Then, a few weeks later, she caught a harmless cold, then influenza, then fatal pneumonia, and for a long time he had wanted to die himself.

He was driving automatically, and he only noticed the car overtaking him when it suddenly accelerated and pulled up across the road in front of him. Lange braked abruptly and was forced to run his wheels up on the sidewalk to avoid a collision. As he brought the Mercedes to a shuddering halt, two men leapt from the other car; they were wearing black woolen helmets that completely covered their faces. One of them yanked his door open before he'd even taken his foot off the brake pedal and pulled him roughly from the car. The other covered him with what appeared to be a submachine gun, and he was unceremoniously bundled into the back of the other car, which accelerated sharply away, the tires squealing on the road surface. Someone threw a blanket over his head and tied his hands behind his back. All this had taken place in an eerie silence that was unbroken throughout the journey that followed.

He tried once to speak to his captors through the blanket and received a sharp painful jab in the ribs for his trouble; after that he kept quiet, though his nerves were stretched to the breaking point. After what must have been about an hour the car stopped and skidded slightly on what sounded like gravel. They took him out of the car and led him up some steps. He heard a door slam behind him, and he was inside a building, walking along a corridor perhaps, then down some steps. The air was colder and it felt damp. Then he was shoved through a door, and he heard the bolt being shot behind him.

He stood quite still for a moment, listening, wondering if there was anyone else in the room with him. Not a sound. He bent over and managed to shake the blanket off his head, but he still could not see anything. He was in total darkness. He edged his way slowly along the walls, exploring. He felt his leg brush against something, which turned out to be a low cot, made of canvas and wood. He managed to lie face down on the cot and half cover himself with the rough woolen blanket.

As one hour crawled slowly into the next, the cramp in his arms became almost intolerable. He tried flexing his muscles to loosen the bonds, then jumping up and down to keep the circulation going, but nothing really worked. He recalled the technique. It was a preliminary exercise the Gestapo had perfected in cases where they were particularly eager to get a piece of information. Later would come the cruder forms of torture.

He couldn't see his watch, but after what must have been about four hours, a light suddenly went on. He was almost blinded by its brilliance. The door was unbolted, and the two men in the black woolen masks came in. One pulled a chair from the corner and sat facing him while the other lounged against the wall. Neither of them spoke. Lange could stand the pain in his arms no longer.

"Please, would you untie my hands. I have cramps in my arms." The man in the chair stood up, took a knife from the other's belt, and quickly sliced through the cords on his wrists. Lange tried to rub his arms but couldn't move his fingers, so he simply shook them loosely by his sides. The man on the chair spoke. Lange noticed for the first time that he was cradling a pistol in his lap.

"You are Helmut Lange."

He nodded.

"Formerly Hauptmann Lange?"

"That's right."

"You were commanding officer at Rechlin when the war ended?"

Lange knew there was no point in denying it, and perhaps if he appeared to cooperate with them, it might improve his chances.

"Yes."

"I want you to think back to the time after the Russians began to cross the Oder on April 16."

"I remember."

"Good." He paused. "Now then, between April 30 and May 2 how many planes left Rechlin?"

Lange was cautious. He thought he knew what they were after.

"A few."

"A few?"

"That's right."

His captor whipped the barrel of the pistol across his face, laying his cheek open to the bone. Lange fell back on the bed, clutching his face, the warm blood pouring through his fingers. The man in the chair threw him a handkerchief.

"Cover it with that, and in future do not insult my intelligence. Do you understand?"

Lange nodded; the pain was unbearable, and he could feel his eye closing.

"Now then, how many?"

"There was one," he mumbled. It hurt when he talked.

"Good." He sounded pleased. "Yes, we know there was only one. You see, it's much better when you speak the truth, Lange." His voice hardened. "Who was on board?"

Lange was beaten. They already knew too much for him to preserve his secret. Besides, who was there to protect? He certainly felt no allegiance to the Nazis, and he didn't want to die. That surprised him—his will to live. It was still as strong as ever. But he could not tell them the name of the passenger. Of one thing he was certain, he would not leave this room alive if he spoke the name of Bormann. It was obvious that their intelligence had been thorough, and they would know that, apart from his involvement in this escape, his military record was unblemished. If he could disguise his knowledge, he might have a chance.

He flexed his fingers; the blood was returning to them now, and they throbbed painfully. The man with the pistol had been watching him carefully; it was clear that he had come to a decision.

"There was a pilot and one passenger." The man leaning

against the wall slowly stood upright, and his interrogator could not keep the edge of excitement out of his voice.

"Who were they?"

"The pilot was Oberleutnant Koessler—"

His interrogator leaned forward in the chair, interrupting him. "And the passenger, Lange—who was he?"

"I am not sure."

His captor was on his feet, the pistol raised.

"Don't lie." His voice was tight with anger. Lange held up one hand in front of him, the other still cupped over the handkerchief that was pressed against his cheek.

"I swear to you—that is the truth. No one was allowed to know. Not the pilot, not even myself." He rushed on quickly, fearing the lash of the pistol. "It was dark when he arrived; the plane had to take off at night, otherwise it would not have had a chance. The hangar lights were turned off, and he never let me see his face."

His interrogator lowered the pistol. "All right. Describe what you *did* see of him."

Lange knew he had no alternative but to cooperate fully. He thought back over the years, trying to remember everything about that night, choosing his words carefully.

"He was an SS man, average height. He wore a leather overcoat, and he was carrying a letter in an envelope that he showed to me."

"What did the letter say?"

"I don't know. He only showed me the envelope."

The pistol jerked upward threateningly. Lange raised an arm to shield his face.

"He said it was the Fuehrer's last testament—it had his insignia on it. This was what I had been told to expect."

The pistol dropped.

"You say he wore a leather coat?"

"Yes. Black, I think."

"Was he also wearing a wide belt with a heavy, square steel buckle?" His voice was quieter now, and Lange understood the question was important. He nodded. Yes, he did remember the belt. He had caught a glimpse of it during a flash of Russian gunfire.

The two men exchanged glances, and Lange thought he saw his interrogator give an almost imperceptible nod. He could feel the tension relax and a sense of elation replace it. He turned back to Lange.

"The pilot's name was Koessler, you say?"

"Yes, Oberleutnant Koessler."

"He was in your unit?"

The question surprised Lange, and he hesitated. "He was with nightfighters."

"You had nightfighters under your command?"

"No, he . . . he'd been transferred to us a few days before."

"What was his destination?"

"He was flying to Ireland, somewhere near the west coast. A U-boat was going to pick them up the following night."

"And it didn't pick them up?"

Lange shook his head. "No, they never arrived, and the U-boat couldn't wait. It seemed obvious that they'd been shot down."

His interrogator said nothing for a long time, and Lange knew what he was thinking. He waited.

"How did the pilot intend to get to Ireland? The Allies had complete control of the air. Besides, he would have to fly directly across England." His interrogator leaned forward in the chair, staring hard at him. "There is something you are not telling me, or else you are lying." He raised the pistol and pointed it directly at Lange's face. "Well?"

Lange swallowed hard; his throat was dry.

"It was an American plane, a B-24." He paused. "We made a joke about its being called a Liberator."

His interrogator stood up and started to pace the small

room. "The plane, the Liberator, did it have German markings?"

"No, we wanted them to think it was one of theirs."

"Koessler—what became of him? Do you know?"

"No, I never heard from him again." That was the second time Lange had dared to lie. He waited for the reaction, hardly daring to breathe.

His interrogator seemed satisfied. He turned and signaled for the other man to leave the room. He'd said nothing during the whole of the questioning, and he left just as quietly. He reminded Lange of a predatory cat denied a meal.

His interrogator stared at him quietly for a long time. Lange waited fearfully, knowing his fate was being decided.

"Listen carefully. You have created a position for yourself here in Munich, a good one. We have no desire to kill you. You were never involved in war crimes, otherwise you would not be leaving this building tonight. That much is certain." He stopped for a moment to let this sink in. "But I caution you not to repeat anything of this to anyone, not even your daughter." Lange looked up, surprised. "Yes, we know all about you. We know how your wife died, and if you don't want your daughter to join her—do as I say." He leaned down and held the gun under his chin. "Understood?"

Lange looked straight into the cold blue eyes and said hoarsely, "I understand."

His captor stood up abruptly and walked to the door. He paused for a moment in the doorway.

"You will be able to leave this room in half an hour, not a moment sooner. I hope that this is good-bye, Lange. It would be a pity if I had to look you up again." He shut the door quietly behind him. Lange checked his watch and sat down on the bed, not moving until half an hour had elapsed. Then he quietly walked to the door and climbed slowly up the stairs and out of the front door into the cold gray light of the early morning sky.

CHATHAM
November 1963

MANDERSON was proud of *Lucky Lady*. He'd searched a long time for the right boat before he found her, deserted and slowly rotting at her moorings in Newhaven, but Tom knew instantly that she was the one he had been looking for. She was a high-prowed motor fishing vessel built by the government during the war to supplement the fishing fleets.

She was about forty-five feet long with a fifteen-foot beam; Tom knew that her round bottom would make her a bit of a gut-roller, but the heavy keel would give him the stability he needed for his diving operations. The Gardner engine had a relatively slow top speed of nine knots; this might prove to be an inconvenience, but not a critical one.

In the event, the owners were happy to get rid of her for £3,000, which had left Manderson with the remaining £2,000 of his savings for the conversion. That was when Wally arrived on the scene. Tom had managed to sail the old tub to Chatham, which he hoped would prove a promising base for his rig. Wally had turned up one day while Manderson was ripping out the old fittings from the hold, which he intended to convert into a cabin area. He'd asked if Tom needed a hand, and he obviously knew his way around boats. On instinct Tom hired him. Wally was unkempt, of indeterminate age. He could have been anything between forty and sixty, with a permanent growth of gray stubble that never got any longer, or entirely disappeared.

Wally proved to be something of a double-edged sword. He'd probably forgotten more than Tom would ever know about boats, and he could turn his hand to anything from a blocked fuel line to whipping up something edible on a pitching galley in a force-eight gale. However, he was never entirely sober, and he tended to gabble on endlessly, mostly to himself. Tom quickly learned that the best way to deal with him was to keep liquor or loose cash out of his reach and only reply to direct questions—both were easier said than done. After a while it more or less worked out; at least, it was the basis for a working relationship.

Lucky Lady was his first boat. It was something he'd been working for all his life. When he was a kid he'd been fascinated by stories of sunken wrecks and mysterious disasters at sea. It had begun during the war when he had been evacuated to a small fishing village up on the east coast. His imagination had been fired by stories of a sunken Spanish Galleon, one of the fleeing remnants of the Armada, that had been wrecked nearby after Drake's great victory in the Calais roads. Some of the fishermen had claimed to have recovered coins from the wreck, and Tom was determined that one day he'd find it.

The truth was that Manderson had never completely grown out of his childhood ambition. He'd worked hard learning all there was to know about small boats and diving.

During his National Service stint in the Marines at Poole he'd picked up a lot of technical knowledge and some practical diving experience. So it came as a bitter blow to his pride, and ambition, when it began to seem as if every door were closed to him, and the debts kept mounting. The money from Pennyman had come only just in time. He paid off the absolutely essential bills and used what little remained to hire a low-pressure, high-volume air compressor for use with a suction airlift. He would need that to clear the mud from the interior of the sunken plane. He had a diesel pump and some old fireman's hose he could use as a water jet should the sediment need breaking up.

Getting rid of Wally was more difficult. He'd been suspicious and nosy, and was greatly intrigued by Manderson's journey to London. Tom didn't like having to lose the old man. He was beginning to feel a certain reluctant sense of responsibility for him. But it would only be temporary, until after this Dutch job, and so he'd made up a story about a London bank that had lent him enough to pay off his debts, and a charter for a fishing trip on the south coast that wouldn't require Wally's help. It was plausible, but Manderson had a feeling that Wally did not entirely believe it.

Maggie certainly didn't. She remembered his sudden escape to Eastbourne a few weeks earlier, and she wondered if this was going to be a repeat performance. Although Maggie had said nothing, Manderson knew he had hurt her unnecessarily, and for that he was sorry. At least this time she had been forewarned, and curiously, Manderson felt he owed her some sort of explanation—curious because he had never felt that he owed a woman anything before. He told her the truth, or as much of it as he dared; he didn't want her to know the risks that would be involved in this operation. She was delighted that he had gotten a commission at last, and Manderson visibly relaxed as he prepared for the job that he did best.

Confidence returned and their involvement deepened in the brief time between his return from London and his sailing date. For Maggie, they were perhaps the happiest moments that she had had with Manderson.

He was under no illusions about this job. Without Wally he knew he was taking risks that he would never consider normally. No diver likes to go down without someone on top—too many things can go wrong. A line can get tangled, the weather can turn suddenly, but in this instance he was prepared to risk it.

The risks were acceptable; the wreck was only under forty feet of water, and the Zuyder Zee was sheltered from the North Sea. In any case he had little choice if *Lucky Lady* was going to continue to be his rig.

He expected the run up the Thames Estuary and across the North Sea would take him the best part of a day and a night. He had two options open to him when he reached the Netherlands. He could make his entrance into the Zuyder Zee either through the North Sea Canal, which ran from Ijmuiden on the coast, through Amsterdam, to the inland sea. Or he could approach it from the north, through the Great Barrier Dam at Den Oever. He decided on the northern route. He had been on the North Sea Canal before, but he had never been through the lock system at Den Oever, and since he had no way of knowing how fast he might be trying to leave Holland, he thought it best that he find out all there was to know about his only possible escape routes.

Two days after returning from London he was ready, and as *Lucky Lady* slipped her moorings and eased slowly out toward the estuary, Maggie stood on the seawall and waved as he moved off. Manderson glanced back at her from time to time as the seawall gradually receded into the distance.

Once more, before he rounded the point, she waved, then she was gone, and Manderson felt a sense of loss. He shook his head ruefully and busied himself about the vessel. There would be no time for that kind of sentiment on this trip. He was alone, and there was much to do. *Lucky Lady* slipped past the muddy flats of the Isle of Sheppey on the early morning tide, rounded Sheerness, and headed up the Black Deep in the Thames Estuary toward the North Sea. It was flat and calm, and the late-autumn mist, which would clear as soon as the sun poked up over the horizon, effectively concealed the small motor cruiser that followed closely in *Lucky Lady*'s wake. Wally Bannen was curious.

LONDON
November 1963

KOESSLER was asleep when the phone rang. He felt his wife move and half cry out in protest. He uncurled her arm from around his waist and fumbled for the light switch, nearly knocking the bedside lamp over. *Why are the damn things always falling over?* he thought irritably. He switched it on, then picked up the phone, blinking in the bright light. Greta pulled the covers up over her head.

"Hello." his voice was clogged with sleep. He heard the phone pipping as the coins dropped into the box at the other end. There seemed to be a lot of them.

"Hello. Is that you, Koessler?" The voice at the other end sounded strained.

"Yes." His voice came out hoarse and scratchy. "I'm sorry. I've got a bit of a frog in my throat."

"That's all right, I understand. You must have been asleep. I'm sorry I had to wake you, but I couldn't call until it got dark." There was a pause, and the line fell silent for a moment.

Koessler called out, "Hello, are you still there?"

"Yes, yes, of course. This is Lange. How are you, Koessler?"

He hadn't recognized the voice. It must have been at least five years since he had last seen his old commanding officer.

"Lange, my dear fellow! How nice to hear from you after all this time! But why are you calling in the middle of the night?"

"I'm sorry, Koessler, but I had to. I couldn't call from my home or office in case they had the line bugged."

Koessler felt a sudden chill of apprehension.

"What is it, Lange?" His voice had lost all of its warmth. He could hear Lange's labored breathing.

"They picked me up last night, here in Munich, and I had to tell them." Koessler heard the break in his voice, and realized that Lange was close to the edge.

"That's all right, Lange, I understand." He tried to sound authoritative and reassuring. "Just tell me what happened."

The pips started to go again. Lange called out, "Hold on, I have more coins."

Koessler heard them going into the box, then Lange came back on the line. "Hello, Koessler?"

"Yes, I'm still here. Go on."

"They took me from my car last night—"

"Who were they, Lange?" Koessler broke in.

"I don't know, but they want your passenger." The line was silent for a moment. "You know who I mean, Koessler?"

Koessler was sweating. He could smell his fear. "Yes, I know who you mean." He paused for a moment. "Were they a terrorist group—Israelis?"

Lange's words came out in a rush. "Yes, yes, they were, Koessler. There were two of them. They wanted to know everything, and they seemed to know so much already. I had to tell them about the plane and its destination, and your name, but they don't know what happened. I told them that the bomber never reached Ireland, and that we thought you'd been shot down. I said I had never seen you again."

Koessler wiped the sweat from his upper lip. "So they know my name, but not that I am still alive?" He glanced at his wife, wondering if she had heard him, but she was breathing deeply, still sleeping.

"Yes, that's right. You must get your Luftwaffe file removed from records; otherwise they may find you. But your name is a common one, and there is no reason for them to connect *you* with all that. In fact, your present position makes it less likely."

Koessler knew he was right. "Thank you, Lange. I will not forget this. Now go home and try to put this out of your mind. Do not contact me again unless they come back. All right?"

"Yes, of course." His voice was thick with emotion. "Koessler?"

"Yes?"

"May I wish you good luck once again?"

"Thank you, Lange. You are a good friend."

He heard him whisper *"Wiederhoeren,"* then the line clicked and went dead.

Koessler sat motionless on the bed for a moment, then dialed a number in Bonn. A sleepy voice answered, but quickly snapped to attention when he identified himself. He gave him the instructions, then lay back on the bed, switching the light off.

His Luftwaffe file was standard, except that it contained no photograph of him, nor did it mention his brief attachment to KG 200. He had never tried to hide the fact that he had been a pilot during the war, indeed it would have been impossible, and his good record had served him well in many ways, not least when British Intelligence had run a check on him before his appointment as Ambassador of the Federal Republic to the Court of St. James.

Greta put her arm around him again, snuggling against his shoulder. "Who was that, darling?" she mumbled, still more asleep than awake.

"Nothing," he replied, "nothing important."

The lie froze him in the warm bed, and he felt a cold trickle of sweat slide down under his arm. He turned away from his wife, knowing she might sense his fear even in her sleep. He was wide awake now, the adrenaline rushing into his bloodstream, putting every nerve on edge. He put his hand over his eyes. Oh, God, what was he going to do? Would he lose everything that he had worked so hard for since the war? It wasn't his fault that he'd been forced to fly Bormann out of Germany.

Even as the self-pitying thought flashed across his mind, he rejected it. It had been a lifeline for him as well, and whatever the circumstances at the time, he knew there could be no excuses. He had naturally said nothing about the Liberator when the Canadians had picked him up near Harderwijk. Flying an American bomber full of plundered gold and God knows what, and a top Nazi with Hitler's testament in his pocket, could not have been explained away. He would have been interned for years—perhaps shot. At the time he had no way of knowing, so he had said nothing, merely given his name, rank, and number, and the information that he had crashed in the Ijsselmeer.

Since the end of the war Bormann had become the subject of increasing speculation, putting more and more pressure on him to conceal the evidence of his role in Bormann's disappearance. It would be impossible for him to remain here in London if his connection with the Liberator was ever discovered. Oh, they'd probably make use of his record in the Luftwaffe, and the hoary excuse that he had merely been carrying out orders, but politically he would be finished, even if he escaped prosecution, and Koessler had his hopes set much higher. He was already being touted back home, among those who made it their business to spot promising new men, and they had started to put out feelers about a seat in the Bundestag. All that would go—he'd probably be lucky to finish up on the board of some pushy little industrial combine.

Methodically he reevaluated his position. Because the Dutch had decided to drain that particular section of the Zuyder Zee, he would have to recover the map-case and the letters from the cockpit of the bomber before they were found. He had failed once himself. The memory of that muddy tomb inside the Liberator, and his panic when at first he had been unable to escape, caused him to shrink with fear even now. He could never go back again, but perhaps Manderson would have better luck. Koessler knew that by involving Manderson and Pennyman, he was putting himself at risk, but there was no alternative. To find that map-case was crucial, and the task required, as he well knew, the skill of a professional diver.

It had taken a lot of hard and careful work to find a man with Manderson's qualities. Not bent—that might have made him inquisitive and ready for blackmail—but in tight enough circumstances to accept a job that involved some risk, and for a price that would get him out of his troubles and that was high enough to make him turn a blind eye to the rest.

Now the Israelis were after his passenger and the testament. They had already traced Lange, and the year before executed Eichmann after abducting him from South America. Could they find him? It was possible, and he did not underestimate their ability to get their hands on vital information, but he had already made his first move to check them. Koessler toyed briefly with the idea of informing the Israelis where his passenger was, and rejected it. First, he had to put himself in the clear.

He rolled over onto his back, tormented by the suspicion that he had forgotten something. He heard Greta stirring in her sleep, and he lay still, hoping she would not wake up.

Her hand slid up over his chest, and she could feel the sweat. "Werner?" No answer. "Werner, I know you are awake."

He grunted, and pretended that she had awakened him. "Mmmmm, what is it, darling?"

She sat up in bed and looked down at him, concerned. "Tell me what's wrong, Werner. Was it that phone call?"

"No, no." He turned his head away. "Well, yes, it woke me up, and I can't get back to sleep again. It's probably that dinner we had. My stomach is too full."

Greta smiled and slid back down under the covers again, rubbing his stomach in a slow circular motion. "Poor darling, I did warn you. You should have had the fish."

Koessler slipped his arm underneath her shoulders and held her tightly for a moment. "Yes, I know, but the meat was nice. Besides, I had to satisfy your demands later. All that leaping about on a full tum." He chuckled. "Can't be good for the digestion."

He felt her relax, and her hand rested lightly between his legs as she slipped back into sleep again.

A car went by outside, and the headlights traced a pattern across the ceiling. When he was a boy, he'd often stayed awake for hours watching the shadows creep across the bedroom, and he knew that he wasn't going to get much sleep that night.

MUNICH
November 1963

FRANZ was surprised to see that his fingers were trembling when he opened the file on Koessler. His contact at records had done well to trace the file so quickly, and a copy had been sent by fast car from Bonn at once.

The details of Werner Koessler's background were typical of many Luftwaffe pilots. However, it quickly became clear that he had been an outstanding flyer, and his qualities had been noted by more than one superior officer. He thumbed through the various reports to the last page, which gave details of his operations as a nightfighter pilot up to the beginning of 1945.

It ended with a single cryptic sentence: "Captured on May 2, 1945, by Canadian troops at Harderwijk after being reported missing in action, later transferred to a POW camp in England."

He hurriedly checked back through the report for next of

kin. It simply said "deceased," and Hauptmann Lange was conspicuous by his absence, which only confirmed the story he had given Franz the night before. It seemed like another dead end. No mention of which POW camp in England, and finding a pin named Koessler in that particular haystack was going to take forever. There could be dozens of Werner Koesslers to check through.

Franz threw down the file in disgust and started pacing his small hotel room. He stared out of the window at the traffic in the wet streets and wondered why German motorists always seemed to be driving as though there were no tomorrow—perhaps it was the sudden taste of freedom after the discipline of working so hard all day at their jobs. Strangely, he felt no animosity toward them, in many ways he admired them. Objectively, he could separate the Germany of today from the country he had grown up in, but he could not forget the horror of that boarding school. How he'd had to join in the Jew-baiting, the lessons on "race science," the struggle of the Aryans against the alien Jew, the bullying—and finally the headmaster's quietly taking him back to his house one evening to tell him that his parents would not be coming to see him, nor could he go home to see them.

He remembered the empty classrooms during the holidays. Sometimes he'd climb the echoing stairs to the highest floor in the building, just to look out through the window as far as he could in the direction of home.

He was often tempted to run away during one of these awful periods, but then he'd see his father's face and hear his warning. Later, there was no need; he knew they had been sent to a concentration camp.

Franz continued to gaze sightlessly out of the hotel window. Something was troubling him about this case, an emotion he had never felt before. That thought gave him the answer. For some reason he *did* feel emotionally involved this time. He'd always known that it was an obsession, this quest to track down the Nazi warlords who had escaped trial at Nuremburg. And although the deep hatred he felt had persisted, it had been divested of passion. Made more effective by a clinical approach. Cold and sharp like a surgeon's knife.

But this case was getting to him; he felt excited, involved, and yet, curiously, there was something else too. A sense of personal responsibility. Perhaps it had something to do with the place. Being back in Germany for the first time since 1945—he felt close to his childhood; he'd avoided thinking about that for years.

The red neon sign across the street was flicking on and off, giving his blond hair a slightly garish tint. It was ironic that a Jew should look as Germanic as he did, but he knew it was the only reason he had survived the war. That, and Alfred Schlenke, the headmaster, who had forged his entry papers into the school, fed him, paid his fees when his parents were taken away, and protected him from the Nazis until the war ended.

He had wanted Franz to stay with him, but there was only one place he'd wanted to go. Now he was trading on his Aryan looks again, and no one would suspect his connection with Israel and the Mossad. Certainly the Luftwaffe veteran who had told him about the landing of the Ju-52 at Rechlin would never know that his convivial and generous beerhouse acquaintance was a Jew.

That apparently accidental meeting had taken days to arrange, and longer to research. It was routine, one of dozens that he would make of one kind or another, but this time he'd struck gold.

Franz knew that a Ju-52 had successfully landed and taken off from Lake Havel in Berlin, in the early morning of May

2, 1945, but reliable information had always indicated that the plane had flown back empty to Admiral Doenitz's HQ at Ploen in Schleswig-Holstein. Now he knew better. Tracing Lange, the former commanding officer at Rechlin, had not been difficult, and he had quickly confirmed his suspicions that a top Nazi had been on board, but who? Could it possibly have been Bormann? Perhaps; he did not know. The description of the man's clothing tallied with photographs of Bormann at the time. Not that it mattered; whoever it was that had escaped from the Fuehrerbunker, Franz wanted.

He turned quickly away from the window, picked up the file again, and stared at that last sentence. "Captured on May 2, 1945, by Canadian troops at Harderwijk after being reported missing in action, later transferred to a POW camp in England." Plainly, that was as far as he had got in the Liberator, and if he had survived, then perhaps his passenger had also. Harderwijk! There was something about that name that was striking a chord, but he couldn't place it.

He put on his overcoat and went down to the foyer. The bookstall there was closed, so he left the hotel and walked through the busy streets. The office workers had given way to a fresh crowd of theatergoers and pleasure seekers, and he was glad to be out of his small, overheated room.

He found what he was looking for in a narrow back street near the Schwabing, and asked if he could look at a map of the Netherlands. Then he remembered. He had been reading a magazine article about the draining of the Zuyder Zee; the article had mentioned Harderwijk more than once.

The attractive salesclerk gave him the map, lingering over it as long as she dared, but he didn't even notice her. He spread the map out on the counter and found Harderwijk immediately. A small town on the innermost point of the inland sea.

He could hardly contain his excitement. He folded the

map and thrust it into his pocket. The girl looked at him with interest.

"Did you find what you wanted?"

He saw her for the first time, and smiled. "Yes, yes, I think I have."

Franz was a normal enough four-year-old boy growing up in a small town not far from Stuttgart. He found his younger sister a bit of a nuisance, always wanting to go where he went and always dragging along miles behind him, but then he was beginning to figure out that most girls were a nuisance anyway. His father, Otto Herrimann, had a shop where he mended clothes, and on a good day Franz helped out with the customers. He was always too busy to spend much time with him, but his mother, Becki, would sometimes take him and his sister into Stuttgart, where the high point of the trip was a visit to the pastry shop.

The pastry shop was very special, the window like an Alladin's cave full of cakes made into houses and castles with their towers spiraling upward, gleaming icily in the sun, and every time they went it was different. Sometimes there would be a whole train with puffs of white cotton-wool coming out of the smokestack. Franz remembered those trips best of all.

He also remembered the night that had changed everything. He had been asleep when they had thrown the bricks through the glass front of the shop downstairs. He leapt out of his bed and ran to the window; there were lots of people in the street, some of whom he'd recognized. They all looked different now, their eyes glittering in the torchlight, looking up at him, the mouths all open at the same time, shouting *"Jude, Jude, Jude."* Then his father had pulled him away from the window, and they sat down on the bed, his mother trying to keep his sister from crying, and his father clutching him tighter than he had ever remembered before.

One night, about a week later, they had crept silently out of the house carrying a few blankets, got into the old car his father had been so proud of, and drove to the boarding school. The journey was a long one, but Franz was too excited to sleep. It was like a fabulous adventure, driving through the night. Occasionally the headlights of other cars would come blazing toward them like the eyes of the tiger in his storybook.

When they finally arrived it was still dark, and surprisingly, the headmaster was waiting. He showed them into his house, which adjoined the school. Franz's sister, as usual, had woken in a bad temper, and his mother was trying to console her. Franz wandered around the house, his eyes getting wider as he discovered there were books practically everywhere. Books had always fascinated him, and he ran back to the living room to tell his father. He knew at once something was wrong, and his half-formed sentence trailed off as both men turned and looked at him gravely. His father took him aside, sat down, and simply stared without speaking for a very long time.

Franz wanted to tell him about the books, but something in his father's eyes silenced him and he waited. His father started to talk, slowly and carefully, telling him that from now on he would be staying here at the school and that he was going to have a new name—Hagen, Franz Hagen. He started to listen with growing excitement when his father told him that in future no one must know that he was a Jew. Franz knew that his fair hair and blue eyes would make the secret easy to keep. Sometimes he had been ragged by his friends for looking so German, but he had managed to hold his own. He remembered what his father had said, he told them he *was* a German, but also a Jew. . . . they had never understood. His father had always been determined that he would go to boarding school, and the headmaster, Alfred

Schlenke, was an old friend; they had served together in the Great War. He had often visited their house, bringing books for him to read, telling him about the games he would play at school and the famous people who had been there when they were boys. Franz was not due to go for another year, and the headmaster had not been to see them for a long time, but his father said it had all been arranged.

Instinctively, Franz felt the intensity of his father's feelings. He wanted to fling himself into his arms, but again something stopped him, and he just stood there and nodded his agreement.

It was his mother who broke the long silence. She told him that they would, of course, be coming to see him from time to time, and that he was not to worry, just be a good boy and do as his father had told him.

Franz could see that she was on the verge of crying, so he tried to cheer her up. "I'll be home around Christmas, Momma." He didn't want her to cry in front of the headmaster. Then his sister, who had been strangely quiet, started to make a fuss, and it was time for them to go.

They all went out to the car, his father busying himself clearing the windows, which had gotten fogged up. His mother kissed him, and he thought she was going to cry again. His sister refused to say good-bye, so he shook hands with his father. Then they all got back into the old car, and he kept waving to them until it disappeared down the road behind the trees. Quite suddenly he felt his throat tighten, and he knew he was crying. He felt the headmaster put his arm around his shoulders—that was the beginning.

MUNICH
November 1963

LANGE came out of the telephone booth, glanced quickly around the deserted station, and made his way back to the car. He'd left it in a side street, and there were few people about at that time of night; those who were had muffled themselves up against the first chill blast of winter.

He could not see anyone taking any untoward interest in him. He drove carefully, keeping a watchful eye on the rearview mirror; the events of the night before had shaken him up more than he had admitted to himself. He had tried to give the impression to his colleagues at the office that nothing unusual had happened, and he explained the plaster on his cheek, covering the stitches, with a story of an ordinary traffic accident. Nevertheless, the strain was beginning to tell, and all he really wanted was to sleep.

But sleep wouldn't come. He laid awake in his bed, thinking of Koessler and his passenger and the terrorists who had shattered the calm of his well-ordered life. Time and again he ran over the details, but it didn't get any clearer, and eventually he fell into a troubled sleep.

In his nightmare he was standing in a muddy field at night, trying desperately to light some flares in time for the stricken Liberator to make a landing, but the mud was clinging to his boots, and he found it almost impossible to move.

Then he saw it, like a big black shadow angling down from the sky with all its engines burning. It came skimming down toward him without making a sound. He couldn't move. It came closer, and he knew that it would crush him, but he was transfixed, eyes wide with terror, as the huge black shadow with the flames pouring from it descended on him. Then he saw the face behind the windscreen. It wasn't Koessler—it was the passenger, and he screamed as he felt the plane falling on him, crushing the life from his body, suffocating him.

Then he was awake, his arms flailing wildly, trying to remove the pillow from his face, but the burly figure in the raincoat held it down firmly until the thrashing stopped. Then quickly he removed it, lowered his head to Lange's face, and listened. Good, he was unconscious but still breathing. He slapped his face lightly, on both cheeks. He saw the eyelids flicker, and he bent down to whisper in Lange's ear. "Come on, now, wake up."

Lange groaned.

"No screams this time, please. Otherwise I shall have to put the pillow back over your face."

Lange's eyes were still closed. He slapped him once, harder, and they suddenly opened wide, staring fearfully up at him.

"That's better, Lange. I think you must have been having a bad dream. I tried to wake you, but you screamed, so I had to shut you up with this." He held the pillow up so that Lange could see it.

Lange was sweating. He knew he was awake now. He could feel the weight of the man sitting on the bed beside him. Faintly, in the light that came through the curtains, he could see his squat outline.

The man pulled himself over on the bed, using all of his weight to pin Lange down. Lange could sense a feeling of physical power, like a coiled spring waiting to be released. He could not make out the color of his hair, but it curled long over his collar.

He cleared his throat, trying to speak. "Who are you?" he said hoarsely.

"Now, now, Lange, don't upset me, please. You don't remember who I am?"

Lange remained silent, sweating, an awful fear beginning to creep through him. The man sighed and ran his hand over Lange's face, pushing back his hair. He started back in the bed, trying to draw away from him. The heavy hand pushed down hard on his chest, pressing the breath from his body.

"You must not try to move, Lange," the voice said quietly, almost soothingly. "I just want you to relax and talk to me. After all, we are comrades, you and I. True, it was a long time ago." Lange could feel the eyes boring into him.

"Do you remember when, Lange?" he asked softly.

And suddenly, Lange did know. He sucked in his breath sharply, remembering the night at Rechlin and the SS officer in the black leather overcoat.

"Yes, yes, I know who you are."

"Good."

Although the face was in shadow, Lange sensed that he was smiling. He paused, brushing the hair back from Lange's face again as though he were a little boy. Lange could feel the roughness of his palm as it passed across his forehead.

"Now then, Lange, I want you to tell me something more. Who was the pilot of that Liberator? The one who did so well to get me out of Rechlin."

Lange was more frightened than he had ever been in his life. He could feel it in his throat, choking him.

"He was Koessler, Herr Reichsleiter—Werner Koessler."

The man nodded his head approvingly.

"Ah, yes, Koessler." He sighed; then his voice sharpened. "Where is he now?"

Lange did not hesitate, not for a moment. Everything he knew or had heard about Koessler, the visit from the Israeli agents—it all came tumbling out, the words tripped over each other in his haste to tell it all. The secret he had kept all those years was sprung from him; he had responded instinctively to authority, as he had always done. When he had finished, and he lay back panting on the bed, almost sobbing with relief, his visitor spoke to him softly.

"You did well, Lange. You have nothing to reproach yourself for. You have kept this from our enemies for a long time. It is natural that you should be distressed. Now I must go and find our friend Koessler. You have served your country well, Lange, and I salute you."

Lange was gasping with relief; then he saw him pick up the pillow. The fear surged up through his body and he screamed. "No!" The pillow came down on his face with incredible force, pushing him back into the bed, his arms pinned beneath the blankets and the weight of his killer crushing his chest.

Finally Lange stopped thrashing, but the passenger kept the pillow firmly in place until he was sure. Then he took it away, checked that he was dead, and replaced the pillow under his head, tidied up the bed, and tucked him in—then left.

THAMES ESTUARY
November 1963

THE WEATHER conditions were good. A slight offshore breeze made the sea a little choppy, but the sun shone brightly and the sky was clear for November.

Manderson checked his position on the map once again and glanced out through the cabin porthole. He was making progress. He'd already rounded the Isle of Sheppey, and he could see Whitstable and Herne Bay off his starboard bow. He intended to hug the southern shore of the Thames Estuary as far as Margate, cross the North Sea overnight, and with luck raise the Dutch coast sometime the following day.

The blue motor cruiser was still tagging along behind him. It hadn't gone into Herne Bay—not that that was significant, since there were still a number of places it could be making for. Nevertheless, he was curious. It had been with him all the way from Chatham, and that was worth a look.

He picked up his binoculars and focused them on the

boat, which was about two miles astern. He could see the lettering on her bow as she rose on the swell, *Blue Waters.* She belonged to a hire firm in Chatham, used mainly by fishing parties, but there was no party on her now. He could just make out one person at the wheel, and unless there were more below, which was unlikely on a fine day like this, he was alone.

Manderson lowered the binoculars and switched over to a higher magnification. The man at the helm was holding something dark and shiny in front of his face—a telescope? Manderson steadied the binoculars, and a quick flash of sunlight glinted on the upraised bottle as Wally Bannen poured some more of the delicious juice down his throat.

Manderson put down the binoculars and laughed out loud. Well, well, well, fancy that! Old Wally Bannen going to all that trouble and expense, just to see what he was up to. He might have guessed; he knew that Wally's curiosity was insatiable, but where had he got the money to hire the boat? Everything he gave him always went straight down the old rummy's throat. Maybe he'd just nicked it—he wouldn't put that past him. Not that he cared much about the hire firm's property rights, but if Wally *had* stolen the boat, Manderson didn't want to spend the next two days assisting the coast guard in their inquiries. He was going to have to lose Wally, but there was plenty of time for that. Wally wouldn't be expecting him to continue into the North Sea, and once it was dark, it would not be difficult to shake him off.

By late afternoon he had cleared the estuary and was well out to sea. Wally was still holding his own, but the wind had freshened a good deal and the barometer was falling quickly. Manderson was beginning to feel concerned about Wally, but he was determined to get through the locks at Den Oever and into the Zuyder Zee before nightfall of the next day.

By five thirty there was a force-eight wind blowing and Manderson knew that he was in for a dark and dangerous night. The waves were breaking right over the high prow of *Lucky Lady*, and the wipers were struggling to keep the forward windows clear. He glanced back anxiously, and through the clouds of spray he could just make out the shape of Wally's boat as it topped the crest of a particularly vicious wave.

Manderson was worried about Wally. He was a fine seaman with years of experience behind him, but he was getting old now, and the years and the alcohol had sapped his strength. Manderson knew that strength as much as skill would be necessary to survive this night in the North Sea.

Both *Lucky Lady* and *Blue Waters* were now facing into the gale that was howling down from the Arctic Ocean, and Manderson was trying to maneuver his boat as close as he could, but Wally was still a good five hundred yards astern when Manderson first saw the mountainous wave building up in front of him. He slammed his engine up to full revs and braced himself against the wheel and binnacle. It was huge, a giant gray mass bearing down on *Lucky Lady* like an express train. Momentarily, it towered above him; then *Lucky Lady* was rising like a lift in a skyscraper. Manderson felt as if his feet had been screwed to the deck, and his stomach dragged into his boots. Then he saw the crest of the wave closing over his head, and *Lucky Lady* screamed and shrieked as the weight of the water pressed her bows down and the screws threshed thin air. The port window shattered, and the cabin door flew open, flapping and banging in the gale. The sea poured in, but somehow he managed to hold on to the wheel as the receding water tried to suck him out of the cabin. Then it cleared, and they were out again, battered but still afloat.

He looked back. Thank God he had the compressor securely lashed down. The tarpaulin had torn loose and was flapping in the gale, but the compressor hadn't budged an inch. Astern was the retreating gray mass of the wave, but he could see no sign of Wally's boat. Then *Blue Waters* emerged, side onto the storm and listing heavily to starboard. Manderson waited until *Lucky Lady* dipped into a trough, then flicked the wheel. She turned like a dancer and showed her stern to the gale. As they rose on the next wave he adjusted his position, trying to bring *Lucky Lady* as close as he dared to the sinking motor cruiser.

Visibility was very bad now, and although he was close it was difficult to see her. He kept his eyes glued on the cabin, looking for some sign of life. He knew that once he lost sight of her, he'd never find her again in this storm.

He maneuvered *Lucky Lady*, using the screws for steerage until he could get in for a closer look. As he cleared the bow of *Blue Waters* he saw Wally clinging to the lee side of the cabin; he was still clutching a bottle in his free hand, which he waved cheerfully when he saw Manderson coming alongside.

He grinned and yelled something that was torn away by the wind. Manderson waited for the moment, then he lashed the wheel into position, grabbed a line, and rushed out of the wheelhouse. The wind clutched at him, trying to knock him over. He had time for only one cast, and he flung it high over the cabin as the motor cruiser was slipping sideways beneath the waves.

Wally let go of his hold on the cabin and grabbed the rope easily, as though he were standing on the quay at Chatham and not the heaving deck of a motor cruiser in a North Sea gale.

Wally went over the side, and sank in the dark water before Manderson could haul him sputtering over the side and into the wheelhouse. He unlashed the wheel and brought

her about, face into the storm again. Only then did he turn
and look at Wally.

"Well, you old bastard, what do you think you were up
to?"

Wally was slumped against the bulkhead, his head on his
chest, still clutching his bottle. He lifted his head and waved
a reproving finger.

"You're not gonna go away on some job without me, Tom
—you might find yourself in all sorts of trouble."

Then he started to cackle and took a swig from the bottle.
He choked and nearly gagged, then held the bottle up and
examined it.

"Goddamn, the bloody thing's full of water!"

MUNICH
November 1963

FRANZ HAGEN set out early from Munich. He was using
the name that he detested most, but it seemed appropriate.
The weather was good, and the autobahn rolled out endlessly in front of him, bringing him closer to the country he
was familiar with. He knew he could bypass Stuttgart, but as
the road signs flicked by he felt himself being drawn toward
it.

Stuttgart had changed; the bombed-out heart of the city
had been replaced by wide, straight boulevards filled with
prosperous modern shops and prosperous modern shoppers.
There was a fine new library and an interesting-looking theater complex; the English choreographer John Cranko was
said to be a great success with the German company.

Franz parked the car and wandered aimlessly through the
streets, looking for some place he recognized. Illogically, he
resented what had happened to Stuttgart. This was not the

city his mother had brought him to on those exciting special days. He felt alone and alien. He realized it had been a mistake to come here.

As he turned to make his way back to the car, he saw it. The street hadn't altered at all. It still twisted and turned, and Franz walked along slowly, the years falling away from him as he took in the familiar shops and smells.

Then there was the stronger, warmer smell of fresh bread and cake, and he was standing in front of the pastry shop looking through the window of his childhood. There stood the castle, the icing glinting as brightly as ever; it was as if nothing had happened. He stared at his reflection in the window and half expected to see his mother standing beside him, to hear his sister crying for one of the cakes, but there was no one.

Again he felt the bitterness and pain welling up inside him. The girl behind the counter had been watching him curiously, and she suddenly felt frightened as the pitiless blue eyes focused on her. She felt the hatred as strongly as if he had struck her. She was terrified, fascinated, and she could not avert her gaze . . . then he turned and was gone.

He drove through the small town that had destroyed his father, looking neither to the right nor the left. The road to Heilbronn and the boarding school lay on the other side of town, and he wondered if Alfred Schlenke was still alive. The eyes of his tiger came back to haunt him now, but he knew he had to make this journey, see everything as it was and remember how it had been.

He would never forget until he was sure they had all been accounted for. He pulled up in front of the headmaster's old house, where he'd spent so many empty school holidays. He switched off the engine and sat looking out over the playing fields toward the huge, ugly building that for nearly ten

years had been his home. It was strange; he did not remember the school as being ugly, only some of the inmates. Franz
began to sweat; he sat quite still and tried to relax, but it was
impossible. He knew what was happening, but he had to face
it somehow, this time—now. This was the place where it had
begun all those years ago. The memories that tormented him
were a part of this place. This school had saved his life, pre-
served him from one concentration camp perhaps, yet con-
demned him to another. One of his own making, and he was
the only inmate—a place where he died every day and every
sleepless night, every time the memories came creeping back.

And so he tried to shut them out, concentrate his mind on
those he hated most, on those he could be avenged on. And
now? Now that he was here, could he face it? He didn't
know. Suddenly the car was unbearably hot. He threw open
the door, crossed the packed reddish soil of the running
track, and started to walk across the empty playing fields.
He heard a faint burst of laughter from one of the classrooms, and he wondered if anyone would come out to use
the soccer field. He walked on slowly until he came to the
goalposts on the far side of the field, then stood beneath the
crossbar.

He remembered how he had tried to head out a particularly fierce shot from an opposing forward. It would have
been a certain goal if he hadn't attempted it—the goalkeeper
was beaten, sprawled in the mud ten yards away. The raw
leather of the heavy old-fashioned soccer ball was sodden
with mud and water. Franz had leaped toward the ball,
closed his eyes—half hoping he wouldn't make contact. In so
doing he made the elementary mistake of not making sure
he met the ball cleanly with his forehead. Instead it smacked
heavily onto the top of his head, knocking him out. He regained consciousness a minute or two later to find himself
lying in the muddy goal area, surrounded by a ring of anx-

ious faces. They yanked him to his feet, brushed the mud from his face, and for a few brief moments he had almost felt that he belonged.

Franz wandered on across the running track and up the hill, through the trees, away from the school. The trees grew thicker, the undergrowth more tangled, but now Franz knew where he was going. He increased his pace, ignoring the bushes that clutched at his legs, the thin branches whipping across his face.

He stopped when he reached the clearing. It was exactly as he remembered it—no more than thirty feet across and in the center a small grassy hollow, almost like an overgrown bomb crater. Beyer had taken him to this glade, claiming it was the secret place where his final initiation into the Hitler Youth would take place. Franz did not know if this was true or not, but it didn't matter—whatever Beyer said, he would do. Since the nightmare in the town when he had crashed the stone jug onto the head of the jeweler's wife—he did not even think of her as a Jew—he had fallen more and more under Beyer's influence. The police had made a few routine inquiries at the school, but nothing had happened, and now it seemed as if the older boy had taken him under his wing. He had become Beyer's fair-haired, blue-eyed boy.

As they entered the clearing Beyer turned to him and flung out one arm.

"There, you see? Didn't I tell you it was here? You would never have found this place if I hadn't led you to it."

Franz nodded his head solemnly. The sun was directly overhead, and the trees formed a green roof over the clearing; the sunlight fell only in the grassy hollow. Beyer ran up to the bank and slid down, disappearing from sight. Suddenly everything in the glade was silent. Franz waited for Beyer to appear, but no sound came from the hollow.

He called out apprehensively, "Beyer!" And again, louder: "Beyer! Are you there?"

Then he remembered what Beyer had said about the initiation.

"Beyer, you're just pretending, trying to frighten me."

He walked slowly toward the hollow. The grass was long, almost up to his knees, and he followed the swath Beyer had trampled through it. He felt sure Beyer was just testing his fieldcraft. When he reached the edge of the hollow, there was no one there. The grass in the hollow was short—no trail to follow. He sensed that someone was standing behind him, and a hot unreasoning fear welled up in his throat. He tried to turn, but he was pushed violently from behind. He fell forward, rolling over down the bank until he reached the bottom. Beyer was standing on the lip of the hollow, grinning down at him.

Franz closed his eyes with relief, and just lay there on his back in the warm sunshine that shone down through the gap in the green roof.

He felt Beyer's hand on his forehead, and he opened his eyes, surprised. Beyer was kneeling beside him; his face was flushed. He seemed concerned.

"Are you all right? I didn't mean to hurt you." Franz sprang to his feet, brushing himself off.

"Yes, I'm fine. You just surprised me, that's all."

Beyer stood up; he seemed embarrassed somehow.

"Good. I'm sorry if I frightened you." Beyer pointed to a tiny notch in the rim of the hollow, almost hidden by the undergrowth. "But you see how perfect his place would be if you were under attack. I was able to crawl through that, circle around, and take you from behind. If you had been the enemy, I would have killed you with this." He touched the scout knife at his belt.

Franz laughed uneasily. "I'm glad I am not your enemy."

Beyer stared at him intently.

"I noticed that you were following the track I made through the grass. That was correct, but in a hunting situation you would never have come right up to the bank with no cover. You should have waited, kept still—then you might have heard me moving around behind you. You should only have approached the bank when you were satisfied that there was nothing moving—and you should have got down on your knees and elbows." He demonstrated this, then took the knife from his belt.

"If you are being followed and you want to set up an ambush, then when you come to a suitable spot, don't stop. Go straight past it for maybe twenty feet or so. Then double back along the track you've made." He led Franz back toward the edge of the clearing along the trampled trail they had made through the long grass.

"Remember, if your pursuer had seen the trail ending suddenly, he would have gotten suspicious, and you would lose the vital element of surprise. But now, since you've backtracked to your ambush position, you have an excellent chance of eliminating him. By using your fieldcraft, you've tipped the odds in your favor."

The young boy was deeply impressed.

"How do you know about this, Beyer?"

"Because I have acted upon the principles laid down by the Fuehrer in our movement. I have read all I could about fieldcraft. Some of the things I have learned from reading about the Red Indians in America. Their chiefs, Geronimo, Sitting Bull, were the best hunters in the world. They were men of great courage, and to become a warrior you had to demonstrate your bravery to the rest of the tribe. This is what you must do, Franz."

Beyer began to hack at a clump of saplings with his knife until he had three or four pliable branches of roughly the same length, which he tied together at one end with a piece of string from his pocket. He led Franz back toward the hollow, then stripped to the waist and handed Franz the rough switch that he had made.

"I will not ask you to submit to anything I am not prepared to undergo myself. You will use the switch twelve times on my back."

Franz protested. "I do not wish to hurt you, Beyer."

The older boy grabbed his arm, squeezing it tightly.

"Listen, I intend to make you my second-in-command. You were the only one who didn't run away the night that Jewish bitch struck me with the riding crop. You dealt with her exactly as I would have done."

Franz bit hard on his lower lip, holding back the tears. Beyer saw the stricken look that crossed his face, and he put his hands on his shoulders.

"You did the right thing, Franz. You have nothing to be ashamed of. You must forget what happened, think of it only as a useful step in your training." He smacked the switch against his leg, testing it. "Now you must take this and use it on me. I will show you how brave a true Nazi can be."

Beyer handed Franz the switch and sank to his knees, his back toward him, his head bowed. Franz stared at Beyer's strong, well-muscled back, hating and fearing him with an intensity that made him tremble. He tested the switch on his leg once or twice as Beyer had done, then raised his arm slowly. He stood there frozen, his arm locked above Beyer's back. He could not bring himself to do it.

Beyer turned and looked up at him. "Hit me," he said, his teeth clenched in anticipation of the blow.

Franz shook his head. "I can't," he sobbed.

Beyer's eyes were cold, glittering. "Hit me," he repeated. "The way you hit the Jew."

Beyer had been searching for a way of goading Franz into action, but he could not have expected the savagery of his response. The younger boy lashed out with all the hatred and fear that had tormented him since his arrival at the school behind every stroke. The weals quickly reddened as the switch bit deep into his flesh. Beyer shut his eyes, biting down on his finger to keep from crying out. Concentrating every thought on counting the strokes of the switch. Eight, nine, ten, eleven, twelve. He gasped with relief and started to straighten up, but the switch struck him again. Beyer shrieked and spun around, his teeth bared in pain and anger.

Franz had totally lost control of himself; his eyes were glazed, his mouth slack and dribbling. He tried to hit Beyer again; the birch was flecked with blood. Beyer brushed it aside, sprang to his feet, and smashed his clenched fist into the side of Franz's face as hard as he could.

Franz's head snapped back, and he slumped to the ground, unconscious. Beyer threw himself on top of him, snarling, clutching at his neck with both hands, throttling the life from him. Franz lay still, unresisting, and the fury that had made Beyer spring upon him evaporated.

Beyer stopped; the stillness of Franz's body frightened him. He began to think he might have killed him. He took the water bottle from his belt and poured it on his handkerchief, wiping Franz's face, then shaking him by the shoulders, trying desperately to bring him to. Franz's eyelids fluttered and parted. Beyer bent his head over him.

"Thank God," he said softly. He stroked Franz's hair. "I thought I had killed you." He lay down next to Franz, his face streaked with tears.

"I thought you were dead. I couldn't bear it, Franz, if you died. I . . . I would have killed myself." All Beyer's arrogance had left him. Stripped of his self-control, his discipline, he was a pathetic, empty adolescent, vainly seeking some human contact.

He leaned down and kissed Franz, then picked him up and clutched him to himself, unaware of what he was doing, or why he was doing it. He kissed him again, burying his face in his shoulder.

Franz felt as if he were suffocating in his bed. He struggled to throw back the covers from his face, to breath the clean air, but he could not move—his arms were pinned to his sides. Two pinpricks of light were drilling into his head, dilating, growing more intense. He tried to open his eyes, but he could not. He thrashed around desperately, and suddenly he could breathe again.

He gulped in great breaths of the clean air, and as his eyes opened the sunlight blazed down through the circular gap in the trees, directly into his face.

There was another face, wild-eyed, tears streaming down the cheeks. His mouth open, pressing against his. He heard Beyer whisper, "I love you, Franz. I love you. Please forgive me."

Franz was terrified; he fought to free himself; Beyer seemed to possess the strength of a madman. He clawed at Beyer's back, his nails shredding the torn skin, digging into the raw flesh. Beyer screamed in agony and slammed Franz to the ground with incredible ferocity. He tore at Franz's clothing, cursing, until he had stripped him naked and pushed him down on the grassy bank. Franz was barely conscious, and only dimly aware of the pain between his buttocks as Beyer spreadeagled him face down on the ground and spent himself inside him.

The pain would only come later, but it was not physical pain that would vanish with time. Rather it was a pain that would grow, overpowering other emotions with rage—obsessing him, possessing him. Now, twenty-five years later, as he stood by the edge of the hollow, the memory was so sharp, so bitter, he could taste it. He raised his arms to the sky and bellowed like an animal. The cry echoed through the trees, flushing startled birds from the upper branches. Franz slumped to his knees, his face buried in his hands.

He knelt there, waiting, but no tears would come. Not for himself, not for his childhood, not for anyone. There was no contact, not even with the earth. He stood up as the sun passed its zenith, leaving the hollow in deep shadow. He returned slowly, by the way he had come, until he found himself standing in front of the headmaster's house. He wanted to get back into his car and drive away, but he knew he could not. Alfred Schlenke was as much a part of this as Beyer, perhaps more. He walked up the short path that led to the front door and knocked twice.

AMSTERDAM
November 1963

THE HOUSE was modern but not lacking in elegance. Set on three acres of the most expensive real estate on the outskirts of Amsterdam, it could be nothing less. It had a solidity that seemed to belong to a much earlier time. Perhaps it was the superb way the architect had blended the weathered, half-timbered upper stories into the massive stonework below. At any rate all the parts made up a complete and satisfying whole. It was a big house which had been furnished warmly and comfortably—none of the rooms echoed hollowly the way large houses sometimes do.

To the young woman who was standing by the upstairs window gazing disconsolately out at the wet, empty grounds, it seemed more like a prison. Oh, she could go anytime she wanted, she knew that. The point was, where? And what for? She had all she wanted here—clothes, jewelry, a car—and Schumacher, "Mackie" as she called him, was not unattractive. A man of medium height, in his early forties, he had kept himself in good shape. His face was rugged, craggy, his eyes startlingly blue. But it was the scar that had somehow drawn her to him. She remembered how it had fascinated her the first time she saw him in that Paris bar, two years before. Peter van Oost, a Dutch politician she had met through her work as an interpreter, had introduced him to her. The scar ran from left to right across the top of his forehead, and disappeared beneath his hairline. At once he had sensed her eyes on it.

"I'm sorry about this"—he touched it lightly with his forefinger. "The result of a car accident, I'm afraid. I hope it does not distress you."

His blue eyes had seemed to mock her, and she had found it difficult to hide her confusion.

He was very different from the younger men she had dated in Paris—old-fashioned, almost courtly—and she was flattered by his attentions and impressed by his obvious wealth. There was something else—a magnetism, a kind of power—that was difficult to define, but she felt it unmistakably every time he looked at her. The blue eyes, half veiled, drew her and yet simultaneously sent cold shudders down her spine.

Her life had changed quickly; within a week he had made a proposal. Not marriage, simply "making a home together," as he had quaintly called it. She never had the slightest intention of turning him down. Lydia Bowen was a poor girl from Texas; she had had to fight for a decent education and a good job. It was not surprising that she found wealth attractive. Now, Schumacher's wealth, at least, was still a consolation—just attractive enough to stifle any thoughts of walking away from it.

She heard the front door slam, and watched the elderly housekeeper move as quickly as she could around to the side of the car that was parked in the drive. She clambered stiffly inside, and after a long interlude of fiddling with her handbag, she found her keys and drove off. Schumacher, she knew, was in Amsterdam, and now she was alone.

Lydia made her way down the wide sweeping oak staircase into the main part of the house. On at least four occasions since she had lived here Schumacher had held all-night meetings in his study, from which she had been politely but firmly excluded. Usually he tried to find some pretext to get her out of the house—a trip to Paris to visit a girlfriend, or maybe an evening in Amsterdam. Schumacher was obviously unused to dealing with women; his methods lacked subtlety, and Lydia was far too intelligent to be deceived, and far too curious to be put off. On one of these evenings she feigned sickness and retired to her room. Much later, after the mysterious visitors had arrived, she made her way out the back and around to the study windows. Earlier she had carefully arranged the curtains in the study to leave a narrow space next to the window-frame.

From her observation post she was able to see that most of the guests were middle-aged and appeared to be respectable. Some she recognized as colleagues and business acquaintances of Schumacher's. One old gentleman she thought was a judge; his picture had been in the newspaper when he retired.

After some drinks and convivial conversation, Schumacher walked over to the bookshelves, held one of the books by the binding and pulled it toward him like a small lever. A section of the bookcase swung open, revealing a door inside, and Lydia, still pressed against the windowpane, suppressed a giggle. All we need now, she thought, is Basil Rathbone and the faithful Watson. Still, if you thought about it, where else would you hide a door? At least it wasn't behind the fireplace. Schumacher's guests trooped through the door and did not emerge for hours. Lydia had tired of waiting for them and gone back to her room; she heard them leave at about three in the morning. Now she intended to find out what was behind that bookcase.

Feeling a little like Bette Davis in an old Warner Brothers' movie, she pushed open the doors to the study, making sure they were shut behind her—nor did she forget to press her back against the panels and lean enticingly on the door knobs. Really, she thought, Herbert Marshall ought to be at that big desk across the room, looking at her quizzically, but with affection.

She shook her head, annoyed with herself—that's enough of the role-playing. But she couldn't help it, it was impossible to avoid the feeling that this was all some kind of game. She went over to the bookcase. She knew which shelf the book was on, and more or less where it was on the shelf. The fourth one did the trick. "Bingo," she murmured to herself. The heavy steel door behind the bookcase opened easily on weighted rockers.

It was dark behind the door, and she felt around for the light switches. She was on the landing of a staircase that led downward. "Uh-huh," she said to herself, "Dracula's den, I presume." Actually, talking to herself was quite comforting—the fact was, she was scared. She almost leapt out of her skin as the bookcase thudded quietly back into place behind her. This reminded her to close the steel door, after making sure that she could open it again. Lydia had always despised those movie heroines who continued to make such ridiculous mistakes, giving the hero plenty of opportunity to do the rescue bit.

Happily, the stairs did not creak, nor were they shrouded with cobwebs. There was a small hallway at the bottom, two single doors, and a pair of double doors facing the stairs.

Lydia pushed the double doors open, then stopped in amazement. The lights must have come on when she flicked

the switch at the head of the stairs. The gallery was beautifully lit. Six partitions, about forty feet long, were hung with
paintings and prints. The temperature was warm but not
bone-dry, without a trace of damp. Plainly Schumacher did
not intend to risk the deterioration of any of these evidently
priceless works of art.

Lydia walked slowly down each row in turn, pausing before those that appealed to her most. She was dumbfounded,
delighted—but why had Schumacher not let her see them?
He knew that she had studied art history in college; in fact,
she remembered him commenting favorably on her knowledge of the subject. She stopped in front of a painting she
had never seen before, peering at the title—*Portrait of a
Man in a Black Cap*, she read, by Hans Memling. The name
rang a bell—Flemish, fifteenth century or thereabouts. A
beautiful still-life caught her eye, by Jan van Huysen.
Schumacher didn't seem to care for the moderns, or even the
impressionists, which seemed a pity.

She came to a Madonna and Child, by Pierino de Vainci.
Something about this painting particularly intrigued her;
the artist's name meant nothing to her, but the painting itself seemed very familiar. It was annoying, but that had
happened before with paintings, and she knew it would
come back to her.

It was an amazing private collection, the kind that Lydia
had occasionally heard about, but never seen. She was totally
absorbed, and time flew by unnoticed. As she came to the end
of a row she noticed an antique clock on the wall. The time!
She glanced at her watch—incredibly, about two hours had
passed. The housekeeper would already be back, and even
Schumacher as well if he had finished early. My God, suppose he caught her down here? It came as a shock when she
realized that she was far too frightened to him to broach the
subject of his secret gallery.

She closed the door behind her and walked softly up the

staircase. She turned the lights off, then eased open the steel door very slowly. No crack of light came through the concealed door in the bookcase. She pushed it open cautiously until she could peek into the study. No one to be seen. She pushed it further and slipped into the study as the steel door clicked shut behind her. The door in the bookcase was taking its own time in closing, and nothing she could do would hurry it up. With maddening slowness it swung back into position, then with a quiet thump, shut tight.

Lydia hurried out of the study and almost ran up the main staircase to her room, slamming the door shut behind her. It was dark now, but the rain was still pattering on her window. She could see her own reflection on the pane. . . . Then she remembered the Madonna and Child.

Abruptly, she sat down on her bed. It was one of her professors in college. He had been thumbing through a book that dealt with the art treasures looted by the Nazis during World War II, and she remembered him pointing to a photograph of the Madonna and Child, one of the many missing paintings that had never been recovered.

Then what was it doing downstairs, in Schumacher's private gallery? Maybe she was wrong, but it wouldn't be difficult to check.

Schumacher was in his cabin, with charts spread out on the table in front of him, making certain of his course, when Hendrick knocked on the door.

"You asked me to hold all phone calls before putting them through?"

Schumacher didn't look up. "Yes?"

"There is an art dealer on the line. He says he knows you and that it's urgent."

Schumacher did glance up this time. "His name?"

"Gerrie Meijer, Captain."

Schumacher always insisted on the title when on board *Pandora*, even though they had not left port.

"Put him through."

When the ship-to-shore extension rang, he picked it up immediately.

"Yes?"

"Ah, Mister Schumacher, I am very sorry to trouble you when you are preparing to go to sea. . . ." Meijer sounded anxious, eager to please—as well he might.

"How did you know I was here?"

The art dealer became even more obsequious. "I, er, called your house first, of course, and the housekeeper informed me of your whereabouts. Naturally, I would not have called you on board *Pandora* if it was not important . . ." He paused, then added delicately, "I know how you value your privacy."

"Go on," Schumacher said, trying to control his impatience.

"Well, er, the young lady . . . Lydia Bowen, I believe." He coughed to cover his embarrassment. "I don't know her personally, of course, but you once mentioned her to me because of her interest in art, and so I came to know of your, er"—he hesitated again, searching for the right word—"friendship," he finished lamely.

"Yes, Meijer, I remember. Now what is it you want to tell me that is so urgent?" The edge on his voice cut through Meijer's waffling.

"Yes, of course, sir, forgive me. She, er . . . came to see me this morning on what she described as a confidential errand." He paused, then blurted out suddenly, "It was about the de Vainci Madonna."

Schumacher's tone altered at once. He spoke quietly, almost casually.

"What about the Madonna, Meijer? Did she seem interested in it?"

"Oh, yes, indeed she was, sir, most interested, although she didn't actually say that she had seen it—which was what worried me, of course. No, what she wanted to know was whether it was one of the paintings that had disappeared during the war, and if so, whether it was still missing."

"And how did you answer, Meijer?" Schumacher said gently.

"Well, it occurred to me that I could pretend that it had in fact been recovered. But then I thought, if she knows this much already, she may become suspicious and check this information somewhere else. May I assume that I acted correctly?" It was more of a plea than a question.

Schumacher stared out through a porthole at the busy quayside, where Hendrick and Albert were loading supplies that *Pandora* would need for the voyage.

"I don't know yet, Meijer," he said patiently, as though to a child. "You haven't told me how you answered Lydia's question."

The art dealer was frightened; he detected the iciness beneath the apparently simple questioning.

"I . . . I told her the truth." He hesitated, and there was a dreadful silence. Meijer gushed with fear. "I thought it was the best thing to do—now you can deal with her before your position is compromised. If she had gone to someone else, you might have lost everything." He waited in an agony of fear, sweating profusely.

Several seconds went by before Schumacher replied.

"You did absolutely the right thing, Meijer. Believe me, you have nothing to reproach yourself for. Many would have lied and endangered us *all*." He emphasized the collective. "But you can leave it safely with me now. I shall deal with it immediately . . . and I shall not forget you for this, Meijer."

Schumacher hung up the receiver. For a long time he stared blankly at the maps on his desk, then he picked up the dividers and continued to check his course meticulously. Nothing had changed, only now there would be an extra passenger. Lydia was attractive, but perhaps a luxury he could no longer afford, and he would have to do something about Meijer as well.

NEAR HEILBRONN
November 1963

FRANZ stood by the door for a long time, and he was about to knock again when he heard someone slowly making his way down the hall. Schlenke was much older, frailer, and his back a little more bent with the years of poring over exam papers. But his eyes were the same, sharp and intelligent.

"Yes?"

"Herr Schlenke?"

"That's right. I'm sorry I took so long coming to the door, but my housekeeper sometimes goes out in the afternoon, and I don't usually have visitors."

He gazed up at him curiously. Franz smiled a little hesitantly. It was odd how he suddenly felt exactly like a schoolboy again.

"I was passing through this part of the country and I wanted to come and see if you were still. . . ." His voice trailed off and he felt awkward. He tried again. "It's Franz, Herr Schlenke."

The old man blinked, leaned forward, and stared at him incredulously.

"Franz . . ." he said, almost to himself, then louder, "Franz!" and his face lit up. "Franz Hagen!" The name that had been imprinted on the headmaster's mind for more than nine years sprang from his lips. The old man was unaware of the irony.

Franz nodded dumbly. Herr Schlenke grabbed his hand and pumped it vigorously. "Franz, my dear boy!" He was delighted, and Franz could see he was close to tears.

He put one hand on Schlenke's thin shoulder and tried to think of something that might take the emotional strain out of their meeting.

"Headmaster," he began, then continued feebly, "you haven't changed at all, you know."

"Haven't I?" The old man sniffed and pulled a handkerchief from his pocket. "A bit older, I suppose, but no wiser." He blew his nose thunderously, then looked at him quietly for a moment. "But *you* have, Franz." He shook his head. "I'm sorry, I didn't recognize you." Franz said nothing. So much had changed, more than the old man would ever know. The headmaster scrutinized him closely, as if reading his unspoken thoughts; then he waved an arm impatiently. "But what are we doing standing here? Come inside."

He turned and led the way, calling out over his shoulder. "Shut the door, and come in here."

Franz followed him into the familiar room—the old leather chair, the battered desk, and the musty smell of books and tobacco smoke.

"Sit down." He flapped an arm, indicating the chair that Franz had always sat in. "Would you like some coffee? I think we've got some biscuits in there somewhere."

Franz shook his head. He knew it would take ages for Schlenke to find anything. The kitchen was the domain of his housekeeper, Erika, and the headmaster only set foot in it cautiously and at his own peril, rather like a soldier negotiating a minefield.

"In that case, we will have a glass of port together." He busied himself around the liquor cabinet. "I think the occasion warrants it." He handed Franz a glass and sat down in his leather armchair across from him.

"To you, Franz." He raised his glass and added quietly, "I hope we are treating you better now." He took a sip, then sat back, almost engulfed by the chair.

Franz swallowed some of the excellent port and glanced at him over the rim of his glass. "I was surprised to find you still here, headmaster."

The old man chuckled. "Probably thought I was dead, eh?" He silenced Franz's protests. "No, it's all right, young man, and you needn't call me headmaster anymore. Alfred is my name. You're old enough to use that now." He paused for a moment, then took another sip and smacked his lips. "Lovely port." He waved his arm in the general direction of the school. "They've got themselves a new man now, excellent chap in many ways. I don't agree with all his ideas, of course, but that's only natural, and they've been kind enough to let me stay on here. Not that Erika would ever leave." He laughed again. "They'd never get rid of her."

A pleasant silence fell between them. Then came the inevitable questions.

"And you, Franz. How are you? Have you done the things you wanted to do?"

Franz glanced at him sharply, wondering what the old man meant by his question exactly, but Schlenke was gazing down at his glass, turning it slowly in his fingers.

"I've been busy—working abroad most of the time, which

is why I haven't been to see you before. I'm sorry, I know it's been a long time, but here I am nevertheless."

"Don't apologize, Franz. Few of my students visit me, but I'm glad that you have. I've often wondered what had become of you. I would not have blamed you if you had never wanted to set foot in this place again." He held up one hand. "It's all right. You don't have to spare my feelings. I know about the terrible things that happened to you while you were here. The 'race-science' classes, the Jew-baiting that you had to take part in. I understand the strain you must have been under, the effect it must have had on a sensitive, intelligent young boy. So"—he shrugged his shoulders—"I was not surprised when we didn't see you again." There was a tremor in his voice now. "I could understand it if you felt nothing but hatred for all of us." He slumped back in the armchair and seemed to be exhausted.

Franz spoke quietly. "I do not hate you, Alfred." The words seemed to hang in the air.

The headmaster replied without looking at him. "But there are those that you do?" He lifted his head and their eyes met, Schlenke's old and sad.

"Yes, there are some that I hate—some still to be found."

The old man turned away. "And that is what you do—you find them."

The silence deepened, and Franz could hear the clock ticking in the hall. He was stunned.

"How did you know?"

Schlenke inclined his head. He spoke slowly.

"It wasn't difficult, and I have had a long time to think about it. You must remember that it is, or was, a part of my job to know what boys are thinking. That way I could stay one jump ahead of them." He was staring into the empty fireplace, and for a moment Franz thought that he was not going to go on, but he was just trying to remember. "It wasn't difficult to know what you were thinking sometimes. I'd watch you playing with the other boys from my window, and occasionally, when you thought no one was looking, I could see the desire for revenge on your face." He turned and looked at him helplessly. "It was awful, Franz. You were just a boy, but there was nothing I could do to help you in those moments."

Franz didn't know what to say. He felt compassion for the old man, an emotion that was almost alien to him, and he was confused. He wanted to reach out and touch him, try to give him some comfort, but he just sat there silently and the moment passed. He heard Alfred talking, and saw him stand up and walk toward the kitchen, but he didn't move. His thoughts were chaotic. So many preconceptions shattered. He needed time to think, to reassess, be sure of himself.

The headmaster was in the kitchen trying, unavailingly, to find the kettle. Franz found it and filled it for him. Schlenke was sitting down by the kitchen table, still watching him intently.

"What will you do, Franz?"

"I have to go now. I have a long journey in front of me." He spoke matter-of-factly and busied himself with lighting the ancient gas stove. The old man looked distressed.

"Won't you stay and have some coffee?"

"No, I'm sorry, Alfred, I must be on my way." He paused. "I wish I could have seen Erika. Perhaps you will give her my regrets and explain for me."

"Yes, of course." He smiled and rested his hand lightly on his arm. "I will see you to the door."

He led the way slowly out of the kitchen and through the hall. Franz glanced into the study, remembering the first time he had come into this house so many years before. He paused by the open door and looked back at Schlenke. The old man offered his hand and Franz grasped it—once again what he wanted to say refused to come.

"I'm glad I came to see you, Alfred." His voice was tight. Schlenke held his hand in both of his.

"You're a good boy, Franz. You always were, and I'm so glad that I had this chance to see you again. I hope you will forgive an old man for being so sentimental." He cleared his throat. "I . . . I only wish I could have done better for you."

Franz squeezed his hand tightly.

"You saved my life, Alfred."

Then he turned, walked back to his car, and drove away without looking back.

OFF THE
HOOK OF HOLLAND
November 1963

THEY HAD ridden out the worst of the storm, and Wally spotted the lighthouse at Ijmuiden as the gray watery light spread slowly from the east. Manderson was exhausted after battling most of the night with the sea and the storm, but Wally seemed to have been unaffected by it. The irony of this did not escape Manderson, particularly after his fears about Wally's ability to survive.

Once they passed the point at Den Helder and were into the bay of Amsteldiep, the sea became comparatively calm. He radioed his position and destination to the harbormaster at Den Helder and got clearance into Den Oever. They made good time and entered the sluice system in the Great Barrier Dam at around eight A.M. Manderson had never seen the Barrier Dam before, and though he was so tired he could hardly keep his eyes open, he still marveled at the incredible skill and industry that must have gone into its construction.

It stretched away into the far distance, a thin strip of land and concrete right across the mouth of the Ijsselmeer, separating it from the sea and transforming it into a freshwater lake.

He remembered that the Germans at the end of the war had tried to delay the Allied advance by breaching the dam with explosives, and flooding land reclaimed from the sea. It hadn't worked. The Dutch, who had lived with the sea over their heads for centuries, quickly filled the gaps, and there had been no loss of life.

Once inside the Zuyder Zee (Manderson persisted in thinking of it as that, although it had officially been known and mapped as the Ijsselmeer for forty years now), the wind abated considerably, and Wally dozed off in the corner, oblivious of the dam stretching away behind them. Danger past, he slept like a baby. Manderson took the opportunity of having another look at the documents Pennyman had given him. Their thoroughness was impressive.

The first postwar draining started in Eastern Flevoland in 1950. The Zuyder Zee had been used extensively by both British and American air forces as a safe corridor of entry to, and exit from, occupied Europe—at least until the Germans surrounded the inland coastline with heavy concentrations of antiaircraft batteries and a number of Luftwaffe fighter stations. This led to many bitter aerial clashes over the Zuyder Zee and heavy casualties on both sides, and returning bomber formations had to run the gauntlet of the heavy flak, which accounted for a lot of tired crews. Estimates varied that there were between six and twelve hundred Germans and Allied airplanes lying beneath the Zuyder Zee.

In 1960 the Royal Netherlands Air Force set up a recovery unit, "Operation Harvest," to trace and identify these aircraft as the reclamation of the Ijsselmeer progressed. The missing columns steadily got shorter as planes were recovered, and the crews identified and given decent burial. Soon South Flevoland would be drained and the opportunity of recovering the plane would be lost.

Manderson put the documents back into the envelope and tucked them in an inside pocket of his reefer jacket. He glanced at Wally, who was still asleep, and checked his position. The East Flevoland polder was off his port bow, and he looked curiously at the new township of Lilystad, already springing up on the drained lands. He followed the coastline around the island until they reached the Harderwijk bar, then cruised quictly up the channel, past the heavy asbestos plant on the left, and docked her gently in Harderwijk yacht basin without ever waking Wally.

LONDON
November 1963

HE SAT in the high-ceilinged elegant first-floor room of the embassy, alone apart from the heavy oil paintings of Bismarck and Helmholtz staring stonily at him from the walls. Miss Flohe, his secretary, came through on the telephone.

Always somewhat excitable, she seemed particularly overwrought on Mondays, and it usually took her most of the day to recover. He didn't know what she did on Saturdays and Sundays that caused this rush of blood to her head, and he thought it wiser not to inquire.

"There's a Mr. Roland Schumacher on the line, Mr. Ambassador, and he insists on speaking with you immediately," she announced, a little huffily. "He says it concerns land reclamation in the Netherlands."

He sat absolutely still as the sentence reverberated in his brain. Such a banal phrase—"land reclamation in the Netherlands." His mouth felt dry, and a shudder of unreasoning fear went through him like a hot knife.

He could hear a voice calling to him, from far away. He stared stupidly at the receiver. Slowly, he put it up to his ear and cleared his throat.

"Yes?" His voice sounded strangely calm.

"Is everything all right, sir?" she asked anxiously.

"Yes, perfectly all right. I was just looking for my notes."

"Of course, sir." She added a little distractedly, "And shall I put the call through, sir?"

"Put him through, Miss Flohe. Er, you said his name was . . . ?"

"Schumacher, Roland Schumacher."

"All right, put him on please." The phone clicked as she connected him, and there was a silence.

"What can I do for you, Mr. Schumacher?" he asked, as matter-of-factly as he could.

"Hello, is that Herr Koessler?"

The voice was precise, almost affected, with just the slightest trace of an accent.

"Yes, that's right."

"Werner Koessler?"

"Of course."

"Thank you for speaking to me," the voice said politely. "You see, I have a problem, and I think you could be of some help."

Koessler continued to make the correct diplomatic noises. "Perhaps you could be more explicit, Mr. Schumacher."

"*Herr* Schumacher, please. No, I don't think so." He paused. "You see, it is a matter of some delicacy, concerning certain salvage operations, that I need your advice on."

Koessler felt a cold trickle of fear slide slowly down his back. "In what possible way could I advise you?"

"You will know the location." There was a long silence. Then the voice in his ear, gentle, almost chiding. "Koessler?"

"Yes?" His voice was strained, unnatural.

"Did you hear what I said?"

"Yes."

"Well, I think we should meet somewhere. Don't you?"

"Yes, all right. Where?"

"There is a nice restaurant in Richmond, on the Kew Road. They serve traditional English food, which might be appropriate under the circumstances." He chuckled. "Besides, I have a particular weakness for steak and kidney pie."

"What's the name of the restaurant?"

Schumacher told him, then added, "Shall we say at eight this evening?"

"Yes, at eight o'clock."

"Good." Schumacher sounded pleased. "The table will be booked in my name." He paused, then chuckled again. "Schumacher," he said pointedly, "Roland Schumacher. Just ask for me. I'll be waiting, Koessler—don't be late."

The line went dead. Koessler sat there for a long time, his thoughts chaotic. Someone knew, but how?

It was raining when he parked the Mercedes in one of the side streets off the Kew Road. A few drops went down his neck as he got out of the car, and he quickly turned up the collar of his raincoat as the moisture trickled uncomfortably down inside his shirt. The restaurant was set back a little from the main road, and he glanced right and left before crossing.

There were two sets of doors, one outer and one inner, to prevent draughts. The restaurant was warm and welcoming after the rain. A waiter quickly relieved him of the dripping raincoat.

He stood inside looking around uncertainly, but the restaurant was just a crowded sea of faces. Then he heard the waiter asking him if he had made a reservation.

"No, I am joining Mr. Schumacher. Is he here?"

The waiter nodded and said something that was lost in the babble of conversation, then led him into an adjoining room. A man of medium height stood up as they approached his table. He was stocky but with no excess weight. He smiled, extending his hand. The grip was firm, the hand rough.

"Hello, Koessler, nice to see you again after all these years. I often wondered what you looked like," he added ambiguously. "Do sit down. I'm glad you could make it."

Was he mocking him? Koessler tried to study him unobtrusively as he sat down. He looked about fifty, but his hair was almost completely gray, which probably made him look older than he was. His eyes were blue, the accent German or Dutch. But where had he met this man before? Plainly Schumacher felt they had met, and there was something vaguely familiar about him that troubled Koessler.

Schumacher sat for a moment eyeing him quizzically, then leaned forward to reach for the menu. As he did so, the dim ceiling light fell across the top half of his face, illuminating it for the first time—and Koessler saw the scar on his forehead.

Suddenly he felt physically sick; the blue eyes seemed to be boring into his head, reading his thoughts. Schumacher leaned toward him.

"I think perhaps you ought to have a drink, Koessler." He beckoned to the waiter. "What would you like?"

"A whiskey," he murmured hoarsely.

Schumacher ordered two whiskeys, then sat back in his chair, gazing at him ironically.

"No doubt my presence has shocked you, but you must try to pull yourself together, Koessler, and think constructively."

It was the old voice of authority that Koessler remembered most of all. It droned on and on, reveling in his discomfort. Schumacher explained, almost gloatingly, how he had regained consciousness as the Liberator was sinking to the sea bed, how he was still strong enough to make it to the surface, lucky enough to find the dinghy had floated free, and luckier still to crawl into it before he passed out again. Koessler was only half listening, his thoughts rattling around in his head like a pea in a can, but always they came back to the same question. If this man was his passenger, and Koessler didn't doubt it—how could he be Bormann?

If Bormann was still alive he would be much older, and he certainly could not afford to walk openly through the streets of London. Besides Koessler had seen one or two pictures of Bormann since the war, had tried to match them with the shadowy figure in the Liberator, and this Schumacher looked nothing like him. The voice had stopped, and he was studying the menu now. Koessler's thoughts were chaotic—here he was sitting opposite the man he had transported out of Germany eighteen years before, in pleasant, normal surroundings. But, there was still something about him, even in this warm, very English restaurant. Something alien, nightmarish.

"I thought you were still down there," Koessler said quietly. "I thought you were Bormann."

"I'm sure you did. You were meant to." He smiled indulgently, but the smile did not reach his eyes.

The waiter returned, and Schumacher ordered his promised steak and kidney pie; Koessler, fish soup and a steak. After the waiter walked away, Schumacher buttered a piece of bread and picked up the conversation.

"You have done well, Koessler. Remarkably well for an ex-Luftwaffe pilot. What led you to politics?"

Koessler ignored the question. "How did you know my name? where to find me?"

Schumacher leaned forward with his elbows resting on the table.

"You have a good friend in Munich. Remember Lange, at Rechlin?"

Koessler nodded.

"He told me all about you. He was a little difficult at first" —he smiled expansively—"but once he realized who I was, he was most forthcoming."

The fish soup arrived in a huge tureen, and Koessler helped himself. Schumacher sniffed at the soup.

"Mmmm, that smells delicious. Do you mind if I have some? I didn't order a first course." He didn't wait for Koessler to reply, but picked up a spare plate and delicately ladled out two huge spoonfuls.

Koessler asked, as casually as he could, "How is Lange? I haven't seen him for ages."

Schumacher spoke through a mouthful of soup. "Oh, he's fine, very cooperative, as I told you. That is, he was fine. He, er, has since had an accident."

Koessler looked surprised. "Accident?"

"Yes, with his pillow. He fell asleep with it over his face." He sucked up another mouthful of soup. "Suffocated, poor chap." His eyes were cold and hard as he spit the words out with bits of fish. "I don't like loose ends, Koessler." Then he smiled again. "Lovely soup."

Koessler was shocked. The war had been a long time ago, and he realized he had gone soft. Death frightened him.

"What do you want of me?" It was almost a whisper.

"We are going on a trip, Koessler. There is something in that Liberator that I need now, and you will show me where it is. Just think, Koessler—another journey for us together. We've almost come full circle—this time we'll be *starting* from England. It is appropriate, don't you think?" He raised his glass mockingly and swallowed the whiskey neat. "*Prosit!*"

HARDERWIJK
November 1963

IT WAS Wally's snoring that woke him. He was sprawled across his bed, the covers mostly on the floor. Manderson pulled the sheet back and swung his feet onto the linoleum. He had not slept well. The central heating had been impossible to turn down; nor could the windows be opened. He had complained to reception, but they evidently thought he was mad to want to have the bedroom cold at night.

He glanced at his watch—ten past five. Good! That gave him plenty of time to get out to the location before many people were about. He washed and shaved, then woke Wally up.

"What time is it? It's not light yet."

Wally rolled over and tried to go back to sleep. Manderson looked at the recumbent figure, exasperated; then he went into the bathroom, filled a glass with cold water, and slowly tipped its contents over Wally's head. Wally sat up in bed, coughing and sputtering.

"What the bleeding hell did you wanna do that for?"

Manderson sat down on the other bed, facing him.

"Listen, Wally, let's get one thing straight. I didn't ask you to come on this trip."

"I know that, Tom, but—"

Manderson cut him short. "Wait a minute. Now understand me, Wally. There's a lot at stake here."

The old rummy looked at him gravely.

"You guessed right when you decided to follow me—there may be a lot in this. More than you think."

Wally licked his lips, and his interest quickened visibly. Manderson held up his hand.

"Now don't get excited. I don't know yet. We have to locate a crashed bomber from the last war out in the bay there. I've been given a map, so it shouldn't be too difficult. The difficult bit comes later, getting up whatever is inside it."

Wally stood up and gave him a triumphant look. "That's why you bought the air compressor."

Manderson shook his head in disbelief.

"You old bastard! You followed me there as well."

Wally grinned abashedly—obviously pleased with himself. "You didn't see me then?"

Manderson stood up and thrust his finger under Wally's nose. "Now . . . you get one thing wrong, if one drop passes your lips before we get up whatever's down there, you get nothing."

Wally grasped the finger, tugging it gently.

"You don't have to worry about me, Tom. I won't let you down." Then he grinned absurdly at a sudden thought. "Besides, you're gonna need me. Who'd cook your breakfast for you?"

They cleared the harbor at Harderwijk by six o'clock and headed south down the coast toward Spakenburg, keeping about a mile offshore. Manderson let Wally take the wheel while he scanned the coastline with the glasses, looking for the road indicated on the map that led down to the coast from Ermelo. Wally kept up a running commentary on the hotel breakfast.

"Two bloody rolls and some jam. Not even a cup of tea, just stupid coffee—and why didn't they have some bacon and eggs? Who ever heard of a hotel without bacon and eggs for breakfast?"

Manderson tried to shut him up.

"They don't normally have bacon and eggs over here. It's called a Continental breakfast. Now, for Christ's sake, stop moaning. I'm trying to find something."

Wally continued to mutter under his breath. "Continental breakfast—bloody incontinent, if you ask me."

Manderson spotted the road and told Wally to cut the engines. The light was not good yet, but he could see it clearly enough as the early morning mist rolled slowly back from the shoreline. The location was supposed to be directly in line with the road from Ermelo and about half a mile offshore. He told Wally to bring *Lucky Lady* around until her bow was pointing directly toward the road, then he eased up gently on the throttle, and Wally brought her in slowly until they were about half a mile from the coastline. Manderson gave Willy the signal to cut the engines, the sea anchor rattled noisily through the blocks, and *Lucky Lady* was resting quietly on the flat oily swell—they'd arrived.

HARDERWIJK
November 1963

FROM the maps that he'd bought in Munich Franz learned that the Ijsselmeer had already been drained in Eastern Flevoland, creating an island of approximately thirty kilometers by twenty, which stretched from almost opposite Harderwijk up the coast as far as Kampen to the north.

It seemed possible that the Liberator might have been re-covered already from this polder, and its significance over-looked; in any case it would have to be checked out.

The records of the Dutch Recovery Unit were housed at Spui 32 in The Hague, and they proved to be very useful. Every plane that had been recovered was listed, type of air-craft, date of excavation, country of origin, parts found, and bodies recovered.

None, however, was a B-24, which meant that it was still beneath the Ijsselmeer somewhere south of Harderwijk. He drove slowly from The Hague, through Gouda, Utrecht, and

Amersfoort, past the road that led down to the sea at Ermelo, reaching the outskirts of Harderwijk around four in the afternoon. The light was already beginning to draw in as he paused at an intersection. Just ahead of him, he could see the medieval wall that still surrounded most of the old town, and as soon as he passed beneath it the road narrowed, and the tires began to beat a tattoo on the cobblestones.

He slowed right down and switched on his headlights, wondering if this was a one-way street. Almost at once the question was resolved as a local motorist came racing toward him from the opposite direction, just as if he were on the autobahn. Franz gripped the wheel tightly, swung it hard over, and brought his car screeching to a halt, nearly running up on the sidewalk. He caught a glimpse of the driver staring at him curiously as he went tearing by, and one or two pedestrians gave him a cursory glance before continuing on their way. Franz started forward cautiously, hugging the curb, and finally parked with some relief next to several other cars in front of a church.

The Hotel Baars was just a few paces away, next to the church, and he had no difficulty getting a room. The place was nearly empty in the off-season. He unpacked, washed, and changed, then went downstairs to the dining room, which was long and low; the tables along the righthand side faced out on the street. To Franz, the dining room seemed dangerously close to the traffic, separated as it was by only a thin strip of sidewalk. He decided to sit on the opposite side, away from the window. He didn't feel like sharing his dinner with a passing motorist.

He ordered steak and fried potatoes. While he was eating, a party of about a dozen men and women came in and occupied a long table at the far end of the room. They all seemed to be in an expansive, jocular mood, and were obviously on some kind of annual outing, which made it all the more surprising when, at a signal from the man at the head of the table, they bowed their heads and said grace.

Franz suddenly felt like an intruder in the dining room, though it was empty except for him and the celebrants at the long table. He quickly finished his meal, collected his overcoat, and walked out into the cold, brightly lit street.

At first Franz thought that there must be some kind of local celebration or pageant taking place. He hadn't noticed in daylight that the street was festooned with emblems of huge fish, cut out of what looked like silver cardboard, outlined by tiny white electric lightbulbs. They stood out now, slung high across the street from one side to the other. All the shops were open, although it was nearly nine o'clock, and crowded with excited flocks of children shepherded by their parents. Then he remembered. It was late November, and the Dutch celebrated Christmas on December 5, Saint Nicholas's Day.

The shops were well-stocked, and nobody seemed to be short of money. It was a happy, bustling scene, but it meant little or nothing to Franz—mothers with children, sometimes fathers dragged from the warmth of the fireside to help with the annual ritual. Occasionally some would glance curiously at the solitary figure gazing through the shop windows. There was something about him that attracted their attention. An ambivalence, vaguely menacing. Like the antelope, uneasy under the gaze of the carnivore even when they know the lion is far enough away not to be a danger; nevertheless they feel threatened.

Franz was aware of this reaction, but he ignored it. It was something he had learned to live with these past fifteen-odd years. Curiously, he did not feel alone, not even at Christmas. He did not share their feelings for family, the ordinary desires of men and women—or if he did, the feelings were so securely locked away he was not conscious of their presence.

Even now as he walked through these streets teeming with people, eager children tugging at their arms, he was a haunted, strange figure. Guarding his flanks, automatically flicking his eyes over any man that might resemble his quarry.

He knew he was getting closer; he sensed that his quarry had passed by here, and his reactions sharpened as he walked along the narrow sidewalk, past windows with curtains thrown wide open. Sometimes only the thickness of a pane of glass separated him from someone watching television or reading a book.

Evidently the Dutch did not feel their privacy had been invaded if strangers stared curiously into their homes, though more than one householder shifted uneasily as Franz walked by. The rooms were clean, polished, like showplaces. Perhaps that was what they were, he thought contemptuously. He turned up his collar against the cold. His breath hung in the frosty night air, and he was suddenly aware that everyone on the street was puffing out steam as he was, like ridiculous trains passing in the night.

He walked past the town hall, asked a passerby for directions, and was pointed down a side street that led into a square fringed with bare trees. One side of the square was bounded by the wall of the old town, and Franz made his way through an archway in the wall. He could feel the breeze coming off the water and he noticed the shadowy outline on top of the wall of what must have been at one time a lighthouse or warning beacon. He walked through the archway, and found himself facing the inland sea; the water, glittered slightly, reflecting the bright lights of the town behind him. He turned right, toward the quay. Some fishing boats were still unloading their catches, but he didn't see a boat that might be suitable for diving purposes.

He didn't have much to go on, but a B-24 was not a small

object, and he was hoping that he could hire a boat with some echo-sounding equipment and sweep up and down the coastline as far as Spakenburg until he came up with something. If he failed here, then would come the laborious task of tracing Werner Koessler. But he was sure the key was the Liberator, somewhere under this stretch of water. . . . Now all he had to do was find it.

ZUYDER ZEE
November 1963

MANDERSON was exhausted. He flopped down in the stern and didn't move for about three or four minutes, just getting his breath back. Wally came and sat beside him, handing him a mug of sweet, hot tea. Manderson gulped most of it down gratefully and began to feel a bit better.

"It's as black as pitch down there. If I so much as brush the bottom with a flipper, the lamp is practically useless."

Wally looked at his watch. "It's nearly four o'clock, skipper"—a title he only gave Manderson when they were working— "light's beginning to draw in. I think maybe we ought to call it a day. Have another go tomorrow."

Manderson hauled himself up on one elbow.

"No, think I'll have one more circuit. We've checked the map reference and the area on either side. I'm going to move in a little closer to the shore, Wally. If that's no good, we'll move out again first thing in the morning. Besides, the light doesn't make much difference down there."

Wally made some last-minute adjustments to the regulator, and helped him pull the headpiece back on; then Manderson inserted his mouthpiece, climbed down over the stern onto the diving platform, and eased himself into the water. Wally handed down the sealamp, and he gripped the metal stake tightly in his other hand, then disappeared below the surface.

He was using precisely the same method of finding the Liberator that Koessler had before him. This was not surprising, since it was fairly commonplace. The stake was rather like a long metal needle with a tough nylon line threaded through the eye at the top of the stake. Here the analogy ended, because the eye of the metal stake could rotate freely, which prevented the line from becoming tangled. By playing out the line gradually and slowly circling the stance until the line was taut, Manderson could avoid going over the same area endlessly, in spite of being practically blind. When the line was all played out, he would simply jerk the stake loose, haul it toward him, and thrust the stake down from his new position. It did mean partly covering some old ground, but it also halved the risk of missing something.

He swam to the marker buoy he had left after his last fruitless dive and hauled it about seventy-five yards closer to the shoreline. With a hundred yards of line he would not overlook anything. He could see Wally standing on the high prow of *Lucky Lady* watching him, so he waved, then swam slowly down to the seabed.

Almost immediately, the water turned from milky gray to black, and he could see nothing outside the narrow beam of his sealamp. His instructions had given the correct depth, but he still found the shallowness of the water surprising.

He carefully pushed the metal stake into the mud but he brought up a flurry of sediment. When it had settled again, he began playing out the line and started circling the stake, moving the beam of the sealamp from side to side.

He reset the stake three times. The cold was getting to him, and he knew he was reaching the limits of his endurance. Then the beam of the sealamp passed over something. It was the nose section of the bomber, which had broken off on impact, and he knew now that the rest of the Liberator would not be far away.

He jerked the stake loose and reset it again, close to the nose section, then started to circle once more. He'd almost pulled the line taut when he saw the twin tailfins of the bomber sticking up from the mud, about fifteen yards to his right. There was no mistaking it. He swam the length of the fuselage, over the flat, narrow wings, then he saw the broken windscreen of the flight deck, just as it had been described in his instructions. He pushed the sealamp through the aperture and saw that the mud had almost completely filled the cockpit.

Wally was having a quiet pull on the flask he always kept in his hip pocket when he heard Manderson's shout. One swallow nearly went down the wrong way, but years of experience averted the waste of the precious fluid. He quickly stowed the flask away and peered guiltily over the gunwale. Manderson was about two hundred yards away, off the port bow. He waved an arm in triumph and yelled something that didn't quite seep into Wally's befuddled brain, but he knew what it meant.

He quickly raised the sea anchor, coasted over to the spot where Manderson was still treading water, picking up the marker buoy on the way. He dropped the buoy down beside him, then hauled Manderson back on board. Manderson pulled off his dripping headpiece, then looked up and grinned at him.

"It's there, Wally, just like the man said. But the mud is gonna take some shifting."

Wally threw his cap in the air and did a little jig of joy. When he stopped his face was flushed and he was breathing heavily. He rested a hand on Manderson's shoulder.

"Skipper, do you think I'm gonna have enough to be rich?"

"I don't know about that"—he leaned forward confidentially—"but I'll tell you what I'm gonna have."

"What?" Wally asked cautiously.

"I'm gonna have a drop of that whiskey you've got in your pocket."

Wally let out a wild whoop of delight, ceremoniously cleaned the top of the flask with the palm of his grubby hand, and gave it to Manderson. Manderson took it, inclined his head deferentially, and lifted the flask.

"Here's to us, you old bastard."

HARDERWIJK
November 1963

IT HAD been a fruitless day for Franz. By the time he had breakfasted and walked down to the dock area, most of the working boats had already put to sea, and those that remained were mostly pleasure craft like the open-topped *Kasteel Staverden*, docked opposite the asbestos plant, the date she was built, 1932, marked on her stern. She was probably used by daytrippers for runs up the coastline as far as the Barrier Dam.

He had made some other inquiries about sonar equipment that had raised a few more eyebrows, and he finally resolved that he would have to hire a boat in Amsterdam the next morning, where it would cause fewer ripples.

There was a small café bar facing the yacht basin where he could observe all the vessels coming in to anchor off the Harderwijk bar. Outside were some fuel pumps placed right on the dockside to service the motor cruisers. He had been sitting there for almost an hour sipping a cup of strong black coffee when *Lucky Lady* came in to berth. It was already dark, but the harbor lights clearly picked out the diving platform on the stern of the converted trawler and the English name above it.

Franz paid his bill and strolled back along the dockside. He watched curiously as the old man at the wheel brought her expertly into the quay. Then a younger man, about thirty years old, around six feet tall and strongly built, emerged from the cabin. He waited until she was almost alongside, then leaped ashore and tied her up. It struck Franz as unusual for a British vessel to be in these waters at this time of year. He hadn't noticed any others in the harbor, and closer inspection revealed the diver's suit and equipment lying on the deck.

He watched from behind a store shed about twenty yards away as the two men got *Lucky Lady* bedded down for the night. They were apparently in an ebullient mood, but he heard the younger man remonstrate with the other, then give him some money, together with a warning of some sort, and a lot of finger-wagging.

When they came ashore, Franz followed them as far as the archway in the wall. There they split up and Franz decided to stay with the old man, who continued through the archway, across the square, and into the town—oblivious of Franz's presence and apparently searching for something. Even Franz, twenty-five yards behind, could sense his relief when he sighted the bar and entered it with an elaborate show of anticipation.

It was a typical Continental bar restaurant, with stools along the counter for snacks and drinks, and a few tables in an alcove for meals. There was a group of men, apparently seamen, playing cards at a center table. One had his shoes off for comfort, which added to the atmosphere of the place. There was a pool table in the corner, and photographs stuck

up behind the bar displayed the winners of various competi-
tions, clutching their trophies and grinning triumphantly.

The old man was perched on one of the stools, waiting for
his drink to appear. When it did, he downed it in one gulp
and immediately ordered another. Franz sat down on a
nearby stool and in a mixture of English and halting Dutch
ordered himself a whiskey. He caught the old man's eye and
shrugged his shoulders.

"I don't speak Dutch," he explained.

Wally tapped the side of his nose knowingly. "No need,
just say whiskey—they understand that in any part of the
world."

Franz smiled. "You're English?"

"That's right—all the way from bloody Chatham."

"Me too"—Franz extended his hand—"from bloody London. My name's Ronald. Ronald Harris."

The old man seized Franz's hand in his horny palm, and
Franz felt his bones crunch.

"Wally Bannen," he announced, then swallowed his second whiskey.

"What're you doing down here?"

Franz reached into his pocket. "I'm on holiday. Came over
from Amsterdam on the train just to take a look at the
polders and see the Barrier Dam." He signaled the barman.
"Can I get you another?"

Wally licked his lips. "I don't see why not. Same again,
please."

When the drinks arrived, Wally said, "Cheers!" and
downed half of his in one gulp, while Franz surreptitiously
poured his into an empty coffee cup on the bar.

"Have y'seen that Barrier Dam yet?" Wally asked, scratch-
ing an unshaven cheek.

"No, I haven't been out there. What's it like?"

"Well, I came through it the other day, but I didn't see
it."

Franz stared at him curiously.

"I was fast asleep." Wally grinned. "Skipper brought us through."

He tossed the rest of his whiskey down his throat and beckoned to the barman.

"Two more of the same." As an afterthought, he added, "Better still, bring us a bottle." He grinned at Franz, exposing a row of discolored teeth. "That okay with you?"

Franz nodded. There was going to be no problem getting Wally to drink—how long he could keep up with him was another matter.

"Do you fish around here then?"

Wally shook his head emphatically.

"Me—fish? No, not me, sonny boy. Used to years ago, but not anymore. Too much like hard work." He drained his glass, then picked up the bottle and pointed it at him. "But I can sail any tub anywhere, and keep her in one piece." He refilled his glass and looked balefully at the full one in front of Franz.

"Come on, drink up! Mustn't let this lovely stuff go to waste." He patted the bottle affectionately. Franz had no choice this time. He swallowed it quickly, giving a passable imitation of Wally's technique.

The old man laughed and thumped him on the back. "Good boy, keep it up. You may pass me one day."

Franz smiled, splashing his whiskey into the coffee cup as soon as Wally tilted his head back.

Wally refilled his glass and swirled the golden liquid around, squinting at it with one eye. "This is the best drink in the world—and I should know, I've tasted the booze from Shanghai to San Francisco. Must've got drunk in more places than me wife's cooked me dinners."

He was starting to get maudlin, and Franz encouraged him.

"You've been married a long time, Wally?"

"Me?" Wally turned, eycing him curiously, as though he had forgotten he was there. "No, not long, just about a year, then she packed it in. Don't think she liked me much after that." He paused ruminatively. "Loved her though." He glanced down at the glass in his hand. "It's the smell of the drink, y'see. Women don't like that." He turned and looked sternly at Franz. "Blast 'em!" He lifted his glass and tipped back his head.

Franz knew the moment was ripe. "What sort of boat have you got, Wally?"

"Converted trawler. Not mine though, belongs to the skipper."

"Converted?"

"Yeah, been turned into a diving rig." He grinned wickedly. "And if we find what we're lookin' for, I may be able to buy me own boat."

Franz filled Wally's glass. "Well, let's hope you're lucky—is it valuable cargo?"

Wally thrust his face close to Franz's. His breath reeked, and although Franz did not draw back, he understood why Wally's wife had fled.

"Listen, you keep your mouth shut, right?"

Franz nodded and sucked his breath in sharply as Wally leaned closer.

"There's a load of German booty out there," he whispered hoarsely. "Stuffed in some bloody aeroplane, and we're gonna get our hands on it tomorrow." He tapped the side of his nose. "And only we know where it is."

Then he climbed back up on his stool, and Franz took his first deep breath in nearly two minutes. Wally grinned and picked up the bottle. "Let's have a drink to celebrate." He filled both their glasses and they clicked them together.

"Here's to your new boat, Wally."

"Yeah, me new boat." He frowned thoughtfully. "As long as I don't sink it."

It was late by the time they emerged from the bar, singing a bowdlerized version of "When You Walk in the Garden, the Garden of Eden," Franz allowed Wally to steady him along as far as his hotel, where they indulged in a lengthy and maudlin farewell, vowing eternal friendship and promising to do the same again soon.

As soon as Wally had set off, the inebriated pose slipped from Franz like a cloak, and he watched coldly as Wally made his drunken way down the street and out of sight.

Although he had drunk an enormous amount of alcohol, which he knew he would pay dearly for in the morning, his concentration and alertness were unaffected. Franz ignored the displeasure of his solitary lady receptionist, who sniffed conspicuously when she smelled his breath. Gravely, he bade her good night and made his way quietly to his room. He carefully set the alarm on his watch; he could not afford to miss the early morning departure. Then he got into bed and fell asleep almost at once.

RICHMOND ENGLAND
November 1963

"WHY ARE you taking me to school today, Daddy?"

Koessler looked at his son anxiously; he had never really noticed he spoke English without a trace of accent.

"I thought it might make a change. Give Mummy a rest."

Perhaps it wasn't as surprising as it seemed. Uli was six now, and they had been in England for two years. He had been so preoccupied with his own affairs that he had paid almost no attention whatsoever to his son these past eighteen months. When was the last time he had taken Uli to school? It must have been the day he started, over a year ago. He remembered how upset Greta had been on her way back in the car, but she had kept her chin up when Uli's teacher had taken him into the classroom, though the sight of his brave little face had almost caused Koessler to lose his composure.

He braked the heavy Mercedes as it crested Star and Garter Hill. Thankfully, the rush-hour traffic was all going the other way, into town, though the narrow, twisting road still made driving difficult. He half turned in his seat and called out over his shoulder, "I'm going away for a few days."

Uli didn't answer. Perhaps he wasn't curious, or had just come to accept his father's frequent absences as a matter of course.

"When I come back, I'm going to have a bit more time to spare. Is there anything special you'd like to do?"

There was a long, puzzled silence, then: "What do you mean, Daddy?"

Koessler swore silently to himself. *Poor little sod, he didn't even understand the question.* Had it been so long since he and his son had gone somewhere together?

"Look, Uli, on Saturdays when you're not at school, maybe you and I could go to the zoo or see a film. Would you like that?"

He turned right off the main road in Petersham, then right again almost at once.

"I'd like to go to the fair, Daddy. Martin went to the one on the common last week and they've got a Ferris wheel."

Koessler guided the Mercedes into a parking space, then switched the engine off.

"All right. You stay here a minute while I open the door."

He waited until another car, laden with children, drove slowly by, then he got out and walked around to open the door for his son. Uli bounded out of the car as though released by a spring, and Koessler grabbed his hand, thinking he might make a dash across the road.

The playground was already full of screaming children, and a number of young mothers standing in little groups waiting for their children to be called in were taking the opportunity to catch up on the local gossip. They mostly wore jeans and wooly cardigans to keep out the early winter chill. One or two of them glanced curiously at him as he passed, and he became very aware of his rather formal suit and tie. He had hoped there might be one or two other fathers around, but he couldn't see any. They were nearly at the gate now, so he stopped, knelt down in front of his son, and attempted to straighten his tie, but it was useless. Somehow it had already got itself so tightly knotted up that he couldn't do anything with it. He pushed his hand through his son's forelock, trying to get it out of his eyes, but it just flopped back again.

"You are going to have a haircut, young man."

Uli looked pained but still stood dutifully in front of him. He seemed embarrassed, and Koessler realized he wasn't very good at this sort of thing. He tried again.

"Uli, about the fair on the common. If I get back by Saturday, would you like to go?"

There was a brief glow of interest.

"Oh, yes. Can I go on the Ferris wheel?"

Koessler nodded and reached out to straighten Uli's jacket, but he had already spotted some of his friends and was trying to pull away.

Koessler stood up and tousled the boy's hair. "All right, off you go. Mummy will pick you up this afternoon."

The boy darted off at once, and Koessler called after him, "See you on Saturday." But already he was lost in a swirling mob of short pants and gray jackets.

The Mercedes was crawling up Star and Garter Hill behind an electric milk float that must have been doing all of five miles per hour. It was impossible for him to pass it on the steep hill, and by the time they reached the crest there were about twenty cars lined up bumper-to-bumper.

Koessler turned right, through the tall ornamental gate into Richmond Park, stunningly beautiful at this time of year, especially so on a morning like this. The autumn reds and golds were splashed against a clear blue sky, and there was just enough nip in the air so the deer's breath came out in little clouds. He saw a small herd grazing by the side of the road and he slowed down, then stopped as first one, then the others, began to walk unconcernedly across. The park often reminded him of South Africa, where he had spent some time in the fifties. There was a lot of scrubland, coarse grass, and small twisted trees, not much different from the countryside around Johannesburg.

A stag, who had waited until all of his does had gotten safely across, ambled slowly and majestically in front of the car. It turned and eyed him contemptuously as it passed, fully aware of its right of way in a Royal Park, its superiority once again confirmed. Koessler smiled to himself—the stag, with its head upraised, gazing down its nose, was quite like some of the haughty dignitaries he had to entertain from time to time.

He slipped the Mercedes back into gear and left the park by Sheen Gate, turning sharp left into a leafy, secluded road. Greta had fallen in love with the house the moment they had seen it. They had spent a lot of time trying to find something suitable. The apartment in the embassy was luxurious, but no place to bring up a lively six year old. The house they had found was beautiful—a long, low, two-story building, white fronted, with a reddish gabled roof and two garages, one on each side of the house.

There was a circular driveway leading to the front door, and a garden enclosed by a yew hedge and rose trellis. In spite of its size, it had a charming country-cottage air about it. Greta had not had any doubts, and Koessler felt much the same way. There was more than enough room for his family, the housekeeper, and his secretary, and the large back garden gave him all the seclusion he needed. They had lived here comfortably for over a year.

Greta was still asleep when he returned to pick up his suitcase. He stood at the foot of the big bed looking at her; she was lying on her back, her fair hair falling over her face. She still looked just the way she had that first day on one of the practice slopes at Gstaad.

He had been gazing out over the impossible Christmas-card view, when she had quite literally swept him off his feet. Both of them ended up in a confused white heap ten or twenty yards farther down the slope, her hair tumbling over her face, just as it was now.

He knelt down by the side of the bed and removed a strand that had fallen across her mouth. She brushed her cheek with her hand; her eyes opened and gazed directly into his. He smiled.

"Morning, sleepyhead."

"Hello," she said, and stretched luxuriously. "What time is it?"

He glanced at his watch. "Twenty-five past nine."

She sat up, startled. "Oh, my God! I've got to take Uli to school."

"It's all right," he said, pushing her gently back against the pillows. "I've taken him."

She stared up at him, puzzled. "You don't usually."

"I know. That's the trouble—I don't do anything with him. So I took him in today. I don't have to be at the station until noon."

"Oh, really?" She smiled, putting her hands behind her head. "Then perhaps you'd like to spend a little time with me this morning."

He leaned down and cupped her cheek in his hand, kissing her lightly on the lips. "Greta," he said regretfully, "I wish I had woken you before." He smiled ruefully. "There just isn't enough time. I haven't finished packing yet, and I have to leave in an hour."

"Of course," she said, turning her head away.

He knew he had upset her, and he longed to slip naked into the warm bed beside her, but he couldn't. Schumacher was waiting for him, and somehow that had to be dealt with. If only he could tell her. He wanted her to put her arms around him, tell him it would be all right. For a moment he was on the verge of confiding in her, telling her the whole story. But whatever it would cost him now, it was better to say nothing. He could not place her and Uli in the same danger he faced. He turned her head around tenderly, so that she was looking at him.

"I'm truly sorry." He grinned at her. "Come on, help me pack. You know I always forget something."

"All right, cheat." She kissed him on the nose and pushed him away, throwing back the covers. "Let me get dressed first, but then you sit there and let me do it, otherwise we'll just get in each other's way."

"Fine by me." He swung his legs up and slid into the warm space on her side of the bed. Greta pretended to ignore him; she knew he liked to watch her dress and undress, and without making it obvious, she did it as provocatively as she could—slipping the long silvery nightdress up over her head and brushing each breast lightly once with her hand, then pulling her silk underwear on before splashing her face over the sink in the corner of the bedroom.

She leaned over the sink, her breasts still uncovered, the silk underwear pulled tight over her buttocks. Although it seemed ridiculous, he always found that far more seductive than if she had been completely unclothed.

He slid off the bed quietly and crossed the room until he was standing immediately behind her. Greta reached blindly for the towel, but he was already holding it.

"Let me," he said. He turned her around and she held up her face as he dabbed away the water with the towel. She opened her eyes, looking up at him, as he concentrated on drying her face. For a moment, at least, he seemed free of the worries that had haunted him for weeks now. He reminded her of a little boy she had adored when she was a child. She reached up and touched him.

"I love you, Werner. So much."

He wrapped the towel around her neck and kissed her passionately, as though somehow he could communicate all the unspoken things he longed to tell her. It seemed to matter, this special private moment together.

Koessler had given himself plenty of time for the journey from Richmond to Paddington Station. It was mid-morning now, and the traffic wasn't heavy. The car radio was playing, for the umpteenth time, the current rage of the pop world— "She Loves You, Yeah, Yeah, Yeah." He had tried to resist the Beatles for a while, but the insistent tunefulness of their music stuck in his mind and wouldn't go away. He started to hum the song quietly to himself, but was interrupted when Greta abruptly leaned over and switched off the radio. Koessler suddenly realized that she hadn't spoken since they'd left the house. He glanced at her anxiously.

"Anything wrong, darling?"

She turned and smiled quickly.

"No, no, of course not." She knew she was lying. Well, it wasn't a lie really—she just didn't want him to go, not this time. She couldn't explain it, and she knew it was unreasonable. Werner often had to go away like this unexpectedly, and it had never really worried her before. But he had been strange lately, withdrawn, quiet. She had mentioned something about it to him, but he had laughed and assured her it was just something to do with his work. For a time she had been reassured.

She clung to him at the station and he held her tight,

oblivious of the crowd. She leaned back in his arms and looked up into his face, touching him lightly on the cheek with her hand.

"I need you so much, Werner." Her eyes were filling up with tears, and he pulled her toward him, holding her, his mouth close to her ear.

"Come, Greta, this is not like you," he whispered. Then he stepped back a pace, his hands on her shoulders. "I shall be home soon. I've promised Uli a ride on the Ferris wheel." He brushed aside the persistent strand of hair from her face. "I'll miss you." They kissed and he got into the carriage and leaned out the window, making small talk until the train began to pull out of the station. He waved. "Good-bye, darling."

She raised her hand and mouthed a good-bye. She remained there unmoving until the train had left the station and she could see him no more. Then she turned and slowly walked back toward the ticket barrier.

He made his way to an empty first-class compartment; he was grateful for the privacy. The parting from Greta had disturbed him. He knew that she felt something of his private turmoil, but there was nothing he could tell her now. He vowed to himself that when this was over, somehow he would make it up to her and Uli. He had notified the British Foreign Secretary that he would be absent, due to illness, for a few days, and that the Minister Plenipotentiary would be representing him. His secretary had a number, provided by Schumacher, where he could be reached, and his only fear was that Greta might ring the embassy for some reason and discover that he was supposed to be home in bed.

He sat back in the well-upholstered seat and gazed at a long narrow photograph above the opposite seat that bore the yellowing label *St. Ives*. Strange how the British always filled their trains with pictures of the seashore.

The filthy black interior of the Liberator flashed across his mind, and his hands clenched the armrests. He remembered how close he'd come to being entombed in that muddy grave. He pushed the fear to the back of his mind and thought about the journey ahead. One way or another he intended it to be conclusive, and now that he had made his decision he felt a lot better.

The English diver would recover the map-case, he would dispose of Schumacher, and that would be the end of the whole affair. Koessler had decided that he would have to kill Schumacher. It was clear and simple. There was simply no alternative if he was to continue in politics.

He was met at Weymouth by two men. The older one introduced himself as Hendrik von Hoff. He was tall and lean, well wrapped-up in a duffel coat and wearing a battered sailor's cap. The other, Albert, was younger, with a blond straggly beard and Wellingtons; he merely nodded and said nothing, his hands stuck firmly in his pockets. Hendrik hunched his shoulders against the cold wind blowing in off the sea, picked up Koessler's suitcase, and led him down to the dockside, where Schumacher's small motor cruiser was tied up.

Albert preceded him down the stone steps in the seawall, jumped on board, ignoring the gangplank, and disappeared around the stern. Koessler made his way more carefully down the slippery steps and across the gangplank. He had already noted that the boat was called *Pandora*, registered in Amsterdam. Hendrik was Dutch, and he suspected Albert was as well, and he wondered what significance that might have. Schumacher emerged from the aft section of the boat; he was plainly delighted to see him and took great pride in showing him around the beautifully appointed bridge and lower deck.

He referred to him openly in front of his crew as the German ambassador, which surprised and disturbed Koessler. Plainly Schumacher had no fear of detection. Hendrik and Albert did not strike him as typical seamen—they too were wary. Wherever Schumacher had established his new identity, he had done it carefully and well—he seemed to think that there was no need to take the more ordinary precautions. Koessler still puzzled over Schumacher's true identity. That he was a highly placed ex-Nazi and well connected was self-evident; how else could he have been in a position to take Bormann's place and assume his identity? And yet, he deliberately flaunted himself and his money in such an obvious way. Perhaps that only served to deflect suspicion, and thus had enabled him to remain undetected all these years.

If Schumacher had any weakness at all then, it must be his vanity. Koessler was going to have to make him believe that he would cooperate in every way possible. Perhaps a few references to the good old days, a hint here and there that if only things had gone differently—that might cause him to lower his guard.

There were more surprises for Koessler after the *Pandora* put to sea that evening. The first emerged from her cabin to join them for dinner—a tall, leggy, dark-haired girl in her early twenties. Her name was Lydia, and she was an American. She gave Koessler an unfathomable look, inclining her head as he scrambled belatedly to his feet, and sat next to Schumacher, who introduced her to Koessler as he sat down again.

"Lydia, I'd like you to meet Werner Koessler, or to give him his full title, the Ambassador of the Federal Republic to the Court of St. James. Isn't that right, Koessler?"

"Not entirely, Herr Schumacher"—he smiled—"but it will suffice."

"Lydia is my secretary." He paused to give ironic emphasis to the word *secretary*, and added, "She does things for me; she does them very well."

If the American girl was embarrassed by the crudity, she gave no sign of it.

"And why not?" Lydia sipped some wine. "Since you can afford the best, you should have it."

She glanced at Koessler over the top of her glass, her eyes amused, and he began to wonder how much she knew. Was she aware of the purpose of this voyage? The dinner continued, along with the somewhat barbed conversation between Lydia and Schumacher. There seemed to be a strange, dreamlike quality about it, as though there were a subtext to the dialogue that he was not privy to. Koessler felt as if one half of him were present, and the other half suspended somewhere, waiting, listening.

The second surprise came after the brandy, when Hendrik entered soundlessly and whispered something into Schumacher's ear. The mood of after-dinner conviviality dropped from him like a cloak. He nodded curtly to the Dutchman, who left the cabin as quietly as he had come. Both Koessler and Lydia were watching him closely, and Schumacher was aware of their gaze. He spoke to Koessler.

"Your embassy have been trying to get you." He paused, and added quietly, "Kennedy has been assassinated."

Koessler stared at him, trying hard to make some sense of what he'd just heard.

"Kennedy?" Lydia said unbelievingly.

Schumacher nodded, his face grave. Then Koessler knew it was true.

"How?" Koessler asked. "Where?"

"I don't know how. It was in Dallas."

Koessler half rose from his seat.

"I must call them. They'll need me."

Schumacher leaned forward, his eyes unblinking. "Sit down!"

Koessler found himself back in his chair.

Schumacher went on, "They may need you, but they'll

have to do without you, I'm afraid. They may assume, since they can't reach you, that you are already on your way back. But that does not concern us now. We are going to Holland; we have a job to do, you and I. Now, I suggest we finish our drinks. If there is any further word, Hendrik will bring it."

Koessler had felt nothing yet. The thoughts were racing through his head so fast that each moment seemed to hang slowly and heavily like a slow-motion film. He looked at the girl. Her eyes were no longer enigmatic or amused—they were shocked, frightened. It was November 22, 1963.

HARDERWIJK
November 1963

THE ALARM went off at six o'clock, galvanizing him into wakefulness. He fumbled desperately for the clock, then remembered it was only the alarm on his watch that was reverberating in his head like the great bell of Notre Dame. He lay back on the pillow, his head pounding. Oh, God, his head hurt, and his teeth felt like they were wearing fur coats. Beware of old men who drink, he thought sadly. Wally must be a walking sponge to absorb so much with so little effect. Franz groped his way to the bathroom, the linoleum freezing cold under his feet, and stuck his head under the tap. The shock to his system was considerable, but afterwards he felt better, though not much.

He dressed quickly; the cold was beginning to get to him. After he had put on his sheepskin coat and fur hat, he carefully checked the safety catch on his pistol before slipping it into his pocket.

The small hotel was deathly quiet, and no one would be up for at least a couple of hours. He crept down the wooden stairs, which creaked abominably, echoing in his hungover head like a belltower. He winced and silently cursed the old man. The lights had been turned off in the reception area, and it took a lot of groping around in the dark before he found the switch. He blinked in the harsh light and wished he could crawl away and hide somewhere until the pain in his head stopped. His mouth was dry, and the thought of food made his stomach turn, but he had no intention of facing the day without something inside him—God only knew when he would get his next meal. He made his way through the dining room to the kitchen. Everything was neatly tidied away, but he found some orange juice in the fridge, and forced down some dry bread, which sat solidly in his stomach like a lump of concrete.

The narrow streets were still dark and the cobblestones slippery with frost. He made his way gingerly through the town to the quayside. By the time he reached it, the light was just beginning to show in the sky behind the old town.

The yacht basin was deserted and silent, just the slapping of the water against the hulls. Manderson's converted fishing boat stuck out like a sore thumb among the smart yachts and motor cruisers. He climbed on board and went aft. The door to the wheelhouse was unlocked; he went inside and closed it behind him, then climbed down the narrow steps into the cabin below, settling himself down on a bunk and pulling the blanket over his head. No harm in a snooze. It might be the last he'd get for a while, and it was going to be a long wait.

PANDORA

SLEEP was impossible. Koessler lay in his luxurious bunk and tried to evaluate the likely possibilities. His absence at the embassy would be impossible to account for now, and Greta . . . she would call and start to worry when he couldn't be found. There was only one explanation left to cover it— an accident. He smiled grimly to himself. That might not be necessary to invent. . . .

He was finally beginning to drift off into a troubled sleep when he heard something. He sat up wide awake. There it was again—two almost inaudible knocks on his door. He slipped out of his bunk, walked swiftly across the cabin, and flattened himself against the bulkhead beside the door.

"Who is it?"

"Lydia," she whispered. "Let me in."

He closed the door softly behind her as she crossed the cabin and stood looking out of the porthole; he caught the scent of her perfume as she passed. He waited for her to say something. Finally, she turned around and looked at him, her dark hair hanging down around her shoulders, the satin nightgown clinging to her flat stomach and prominent breasts.

"I had to come and see you. I couldn't sleep. The news has upset"—she stopped—"has frightened me. You're a diplomat. What will happen now? Do you know?"

Koessler indicated the chair. "Sit down please."

As she leaned forward to sit down, the loose folds of her nightgown parted, and he was suddenly aware that he was only wearing his pajamas, and that Lydia's eyes were on his rising awareness of her sexuality. She looked up, totally unembarrassed, and smiled.

He hastily took his dressing gown from the hook on the door and put it on, tying the belt around his waist. He faced her, trying hard to maintain his composure, his mind on her question.

"It's difficult to say," he began, "without knowing the full circumstances, but American presidents have been assassinated before with no great international repercussions. There are provisions in the American Constitution for dealing with this—provided it was an internal matter," he added. He had intended to say something reassuring but had succeeded only in sounding portentous.

She looked up at him. "You mean, if he was killed by someone from Russia or Cuba, then it would be different? This could be it—World War Three." It was a statement, matter-of-fact and to the point. He was surprised by her change of attitude. Before, she had been apprehensive, vulnerable; now she was hardnosed and fatalistic.

"Yes, if you want to put it in a nutshell—this could be it."

She sighed. Was it with relief? Then she spread her legs out in front of her and relaxed in the chair.

"That being the case, Mr. Ambassador, I think I might as well enjoy myself while I can. You wouldn't have a drink on you, by any chance?"

Koessler was disconcerted. "No. I mean, yes. Well, only a flask, I'm afraid." He opened his suitcase, took out a silver flask, and handed it to her.

"What? No glasses?" she cried in mock-horror as she stood up to take the flask, then unscrewed the cap and took a long pull.

"Are you really the West German ambassador?"

"Of course. Why do you ask?"

She took another drink, rubbed the mouth of the flask with her hand, and proffered it to him. He didn't want any, but he decided to accept. It might make her feel more secure, more talkative.

"Thanks."

She turned and glanced out of the porthole again. "I know you and Schumacher plan to do something together, but I don't like those men he keeps on this boat. I never have— they scare me."

Koessler needed to know more. "I'm sure they are perfectly all right—" he began reassuringly.

"They are *not* all right," she interrupted. "There's something very odd about them, and they wouldn't let me go ashore at Weymouth."

"Why not?"

"I don't know." She looked down at the carpet. Koessler guessed she was lying.

"Are you sure you don't know?"

She walked over to him. "Give me another drink." She took the flask from him, but didn't take a drink. She looked him over appraisingly. "How much can I trust you?"

"Is there anyone else you can trust?"

"Sit down."

Obediently, Koessler sat down. Lydia began to pace the cabin again. She started talking, slowly at first, and then with increasing momentum as she continued.

"I met him two years ago in Paris. I was working as an interpreter for NATO. A friend of mine, a model, had gone there ahead of me from New York, and she said I ought to come over, that I'd have a good time.

"Well, I guess we did, but I was getting pretty bored with the men I was meeting. Her friends—mostly advertising guys on one-night stopovers and Frenchmen who thought I made an interesting change—for about a week. Mackie—I call Schumacher that, he doesn't like it, which is a good enough reason for me to do it—well, he seemed different then.

"He'd come to Paris with a Dutch politician who I had to interpret for. We met through him. He was charming, in an old-fashioned sort of way, and he asked me to come back to Amsterdam, to live with him. He said I could have anything I wanted. Well, I was tempted. He was obviously incredibly wealthy, and to cut a long story short, I said I'd come just for a vacation. As you see, I'm still here."

Koessler was intrigued. The connection with the Dutch politician was interesting. It might explain a lot.

"What's the problem then? Why do you feel threatened?"

This time she did take a swig from the flask, and started pacing some more, the nightgown parting enticingly at the thigh. Koessler took his eyes away from her legs and concentrated on what she was saying.

"I lived in his house in Amsterdam. It's a huge place, very beautiful. Downstairs, in the cellar, he has a private art collection. Very few people had ever seen it, least of all me. I didn't even know of its existence until two weeks ago when I got suspicious of these little gatherings in his study—"

"Gatherings?"

"Yes, he'd have people over to the house, mostly businessmen, colleagues, and so on. The point was that I wasn't invited, *verboten*. He'd use any excuse to get me out of the
house, but he wasn't very good at it, and naturally I was
curious."

She related to Koessler how she discovered the gallery and
her suspicions about the Madonna and Child.

"It was by Pierino de Vainci. . . . Finally I remembered
where I'd heard of it before. One of my professors in college
mentioned it once." She looked directly at Koessler, emphasizing every word. "It had disappeared during the war, in
Italy. I think from the Uffizi around 1944."

Koessler nodded. "Go on."

"Anyway, I decided to check it out with an art dealer in
Amsterdam, which turned out to be a really bright move—"

"He contacted Schumacher?"

"Right the first time. Mackie came home that night and
confronted me. We had a terrible fight and I told him I was
leaving. But since that night I haven't been allowed out of
the house, until now. I didn't want to come, but he insisted.
Then yesterday they wouldn't let me ashore."

She had stopped pacing now. "To tell you the truth, Mr.
Ambassador, I'm just a little bit scared."

And with good reason, Koessler thought. This explained
why she was on board, and she had as much to fear from
Schumacher as he did. Perhaps this made her the perfect
ally. He would not have to incriminate himself to get her
help. On the other hand, it might be some kind of trap set by
Schumacher, possibly a test to see which way he would jump.
He took the flask from Lydia and swallowed some himself,
wiping his mouth with the back of his hand.

"Well, this looks like it will be an exciting voyage, one
way or another. But you're welcome to come ashore with me
whenever you like, either in Amsterdam or when we return

to England. I shall be delighted to have your company, and I promise you will be in no danger, at least not from the crew." He held out the flask. "Would you like some more?"

A smile tugged at the corners of her mouth. The implication was obvious; her eyes were questioning. She reached for the flask, but he took hold of her wrist with his other hand and pulled her toward him. She had not taken her eyes from his face.

"The flask," she prompted.

He tipped it up—it was empty. He threw it on the bed and slipped his arm around her waist. She did not resist—she had invited it, and the satin nightgown was not unintentional. Her mouth found his hungrily, her hand slipping inside his dressing gown and down his back, pulling him hard against her. He was sweating slightly, but she liked his smell and the lean muscularity of his buttocks.

She pushed the dressing gown from his shoulders and felt inside his pajamas, holding and caressing him lightly. The carpet was thick and soft—they had Schumacher to thank for that. Perhaps the evening would not be without its compensations, unlike the non-events she had performed with Schumacher. Koessler was on top of her, between her legs— he thrust hard. She gasped and started to enjoy it. He's good, she thought. If this is going to be the last one before the balloon goes up then it might as well be memorable. She arched her back, and responded. . . . Lydia was nothing if not practical.

LUCKY LADY

THE NOISE woke him instantly. He pulled back the blanket, swung his legs over the side of the bunk, and dropped silently to the floor of the cabin, moving quickly into the dark corner at the foot of the stairs. He listened as the boots clumped aft to the wheelhouse above him. Then he heard somebody else climb aboard, but he stayed forward, evidently checking the diving equipment. The man in the wheelhouse coughed, and the faintest suspicion of whiskey wafted down the companionway. It turned Franz's stomach—the old man must have the constitution of an ox. He heard Manderson call out, and after three unsuccessful tries, the diesel engine turned over, and he heard Wally start to sing tunelessly.

Wally took another swig at the bottle and watched Manderson cast off forward, then head aft to the other mooring. He slid the flat bottle into his pocket, but Manderson caught the smell of the whiskey and glanced curiously at Wally. He showed no sign of ill effects; Manderson would have been surprised if he had. His seamanship had never been affected by drink, only his tongue.

He undid the aft mooring, pulled it through the ring on the quayside, and told Wally to take her out. Wally eased *Lucky Lady* slowly out of the yacht basin and into the main channel, picking up speed and holding her at a steady eight knots. They passed the long bar and headed toward the southeast and the sunken Liberator.

The weather was cold, bright, and calm, a pale wintry sun just beginning to appear behind Harderwijk. Manderson busied himself with the equipment, checking that the compressor for the airlift pipe was working smoothly. He was elated and trying hard not to show it. He knew exactly what they had to do, and although it was not going to be easy, today was going to answer some of the questions.

Wally felt blissful, not a thought in his head, the wheel in his hands, and the engine chugging rhythmically beneath his feet. The smell of whiskey pervaded his nostrils delightfully, and he was happy in the element that he understood and could deal with. Then he felt the gun in his back and heard a familiar voice.

"Hello, Wally. No need to get excited. Just your drinking companion from last night, along for the ride."

Wally half twisted round and saw Franz standing behind him. He was startled and confused, and he momentarily released his hold on the wheel.

"What the hell!" he exclaimed, and quickly grabbed the wheel again. Manderson felt *Lucky Lady* start to yaw, and he glanced quickly back to the wheelhouse. Wally was beckoning to him. He dropped the rubber suit he'd been about to put on and made his way aft. The moment he entered the wheelhouse he knew something was wrong. Wally was gazing stolidly forward, his position at the wheel tense and unnatural. He paused in the doorway.

"What is it?"

Wally jerked his thumb over his shoulder without looking around. "We've got company."

Manderson turned and saw Franz smiling at him, the gun in his right hand steady, pointing directly at his belly.

"Stand by the wheel, please, next to Wally."

Manderson didn't move. He stared coldly at the intruder, wondering if he could jump him. Franz stopped smiling.

"Do as I tell you, Manderson. It would be a pity to impair your diving abilities at this early date."

Manderson took two paces into the wheelhouse, keeping his back to the cabin wall. He would have to wait, bide his time.

"That's better. I'm sorry to intrude on your little expedition, but you see, I, too, am interested in the contents of the B-24 that you've found. Perhaps you would be kind enough to tell me what you know about it."

Manderson tugged at the peak of his cap.

"I've no intention of being kind, particularly to you. Furthermore, I don't know what the hell you're talking about."

"Shall I tell him, Wally, or will you?"

Wally shook his head; he couldn't bear to look at Manderson.

"I'm sorry, skipper. It's all my fault." He paused, confused. Manderson remained silent. "I met him in a bar last night. We had a few drinks. I suppose I must have said something. . . ." His voice trailed off.

Manderson looked at Franz contemptuously. "That's how you make your living, is it—filling an old rummy full of booze?"

"I assure you, Mr. Manderson, I felt a lot worse than he did this morning."

Wally grinned. "Can't hold your liquor, eh?" He suddenly felt a lot better.

"No. I envy you your capacity, and to be fair I already knew something of this Liberator before I saw you and your boat come in yesterday."

Wally grunted and added disgustedly, "Ah, shit! Just my soddin' luck."

Manderson shifted his ground and sat down behind the chart table. He turned to look at Franz. "What do you mean? You knew something about it?"

Franz pondered the question for a moment—he didn't really have to tell them anything, and he could get all the information he needed with methods that had long since ceased to affect him. But he did not wish to subject these palpably innocent Englishmen—innocent, at any rate, of being involved in Bormann's escape—to such extreme measures unless he had to. Furthermore he needed Manderson's cooperation; perhaps he might get it if he doled out a little information.

"That Liberator, as you know, crashed during the war." He waited. Neither of them spoke. "What you probably don't know is that when it crashed it was carrying an important Nazi official out of Berlin."

Wally started to say something, but Manderson cut him off. "Wait a minute—what would an important Nazi official be doing on an American bomber?"

Franz looked from one to the other. "The Germans had a squadron of captured Allied planes. The Liberator was one of them, and it was the only chance he had of getting out of Europe at the end of the war." He stopped, then pointed at Wally. "Now, perhaps you will tell us how you came to know of this plane."

Wally laughed derisively and kept his back to him. When the gun went off, the report was shattering in the small cabin. The bullet splintered the top spindle of the wheel, next to Wally's hand. Manderson leaped up, then froze as the pistol swung toward him.

"That was deliberate, Manderson," Franz said softly. "I could just as easily have taken off his finger, and unless you tell me what you know, I assure you the next one will."

Manderson didn't doubt it. He knew now that there was an implacable streak, a steely resolve behind the civilized exterior of this man; and what he'd said about the Nazi in the bomber only made Manderson more eager to get down to the wreck. He sat down again at the chart table.

"All right, I'll tell you."

"Don't say anything, skipper." Wally looked at him pleadingly. "It's my fault anyway."

Manderson shook his head. "Forget it, Wally. I've got to tell him." He turned to Franz. "I was approached by a solicitor in London. His name is Pennyman. He told me that a Dutch businessman had found the wreck—he didn't say how. He had recovered something valuable already, but he couldn't do the job by himself. He didn't want to report the find to the Dutch authorities, for obvious reasons—that's why he hired me. Besides, they're gonna drain this area soon." He smiled. "Now you know everything I know. So where does that leave us?"

It made sense. Franz knew that, and he could easily check out the story about Pennyman later.

"It leaves us in a position to cooperate. I want to know as much as you do—for different reasons, perhaps—what is inside the Liberator. I have no interest in the cargo as such. I just want the Nazi, and if he's not down there, I intend to find him, possibly through your Dutch 'businessman.' "

Manderson nodded. "Okay. That suits us fine. If he's in the wreck, I'll tell you. Now I'd better get the suit on." He made a move toward the door, then paused as Franz raised the gun to his head.

"Look," he said scornfully, "if you're going to fire that gun, you'd better do it now, because I've got work to do." Then he pushed past him and went forward. Franz watched him pulling on the diver's suit and slowly lowered the weapon, but he didn't put it away—not yet.

PANDORA

THE SWEEPING arc of the lighthouse at Ijmuiden periodically lit up Koessler's cabin, then gradually began to fade against the morning light. He opened his eyes and gazed blankly at the roof overhead, wondering if last night had been real or imagined. He'd half expected her to question him, but if she was curious about his reasons for being on board, she had kept it to herself. Perhaps she had foreseen that this might make him wonder about her motives, and deliberately avoided questions.

She had stayed with him until the early hours, loving him, plainly disturbed by Kennedy's death, and reminiscing about her own childhood in Texas. She was from a small town called Raymond, which, aptly enough, was only thirty-odd miles east of Chandler. She had lived there with her father and two elder brothers, acting as a sort of miniature mother for the boys. She talked lovingly of her father; her mother had died when she was born. Now her brothers were married, and her father lived alone. This worried her, and from what she had said, Koessler got the impression that she preferred the company of older men. This was a common syndrome—Koessler himself was twenty years her senior.

Texas reminded him of Dallas, and he got up from his bunk abruptly—he needed to know what had happened. Strange, he reflected, how most of the traumatic events of his life had been associated with the sea, and now here he was again, approaching the low, characterless coastline of Holland.

The Englishman that Pennyman had hired should have reached the area by now, and if Koessler was lucky, he may have already recovered the map-case and whatever else was inside the sunken bomber. He wouldn't want Manderson involved in this situation. If Schumacher was to be eliminated, he would have to do it alone, and he had not brought a weapon on board. That would have been folly, since, undoubtedly, his bags had already been searched.

Somehow he had to get hold of a gun, though how he was going to carry out the rest of his plan with those two cold, taciturn Dutchmen protecting Schumacher was something he preferred not to dwell on. Perhaps Lydia. . . .

As soon as he had washed and dressed, he joined Schumacher on the bridge. They were entering the North Sea Canal at Ijmuiden, and Koessler held out his passport.

"Do you want this?"

Schumacher shook his head. "There is no need. This vessel is registered in Holland."

The remark seemed to hang there for a moment, and Koessler gazed out of the windows of the bridge trying not to show his interest.

"I thought you might need it for customs, that's all."

The derricks and heavy industrial plants began to slide by,

and the traffic in the canal was quite busy, but Albert, at the wheel, seemed unperturbed. Koessler finally broke the silence.

"Have you had any further news of Kennedy?"

Schumacher continued to gaze out over the busy waterway.

"They are charging someone with the murder today—I believe his name is Oswald." He smiled to himself. "An American. Strange!" He went on, half to himself, "They inflict more damage on themselves than we ever could have. Perhaps we should have left them to their own devices."

He looked at Koessler from beneath his heavy eyebrows, his eyes squinting from the reflected light off the water. Koessler waited. He knew there was more to come.

"I have lived here in Holland since the end of the war."

Koessler did not look around.

"I tell you this for a good reason." He stepped closer and lowered his voice so that only Koessler could hear. "When I swam ashore eighteen years ago I had nothing—nothing, that is, except a little knowledge." His voice was gloating, and Koessler was repelled yet eager to hear Schumacher's story.

"I had already made the acquaintance of several prominent persons who had all been very cooperative during the war in ways that were not . . ." he paused, choosing his words carefully, "generally known." "The Dutch, as you know, Koessler, have always excelled in the service industries to Europe, especially in the area of transport. They had done so much for us, in fact, that it was not difficult to persuade them to do another small favor for me." He waited for the implications to sink in, then he leaned back and laughed.

Koessler looked at him curiously.

"Why are you telling me this?"

"Why?" Schumacher said softly. "I told you I had a good

reason, Koessler. I want you to know everything." He smiled coldly. "Well, almost everything. Thus, your secret will be safe with me as long as mine is safe with you." He waited for Koessler's reply.

"I think I can guarantee that, Herr Schumacher," he said dispassionately.

"Good!" he exclaimed. "Good! Let us go and have some breakfast." He waved his arm. "I find this coastline boring."

Over breakfast Koessler fawned a little more, feeding Schumacher's vanity and listening attentively to his reminiscences. It was a strange, eerie conversation, as though they had both slipped back twenty years in time. Koessler had to remind himself of where he was, and was shocked to discover how easy it was for him to assume all the old attitudes. The air thickened with excuses and justifications, and now Koessler felt the moment had come.

"Herr Schumacher, bearing in mind what you have told me of your life here in Holland"—he scooped another spoonful of the delicious lime marmalade onto his toast—"I find it difficult to believe that whatever lies beneath the water inside the Liberator. . . ." he paused, indicating his puzzlement.

Schumacher leaned back in his chair. "Go on, Koessler."

"I find it difficult to believe that you find it necessary from a financial point of view."

Schumacher said nothing, but Koessler knew there was no going back now.

"Whatever is in those packing cases—much of it will be worthless; it has lain beneath the sea for eighteen years!"

Schumacher stared at him expressionlessly. The silence grew longer, then slowly he began to smile, and a chuckle started deep in his throat, turning to laughter.

"Ah, my dear Koessler, I can see why you survived the

Luftwaffe to become our ambassador in London." The smile faded. "You are quite right, the packing cases do not interest me, but there is something else down there that I want—in my coat."

Koessler suddenly had a vivid mental picture of the slimy interior of the Liberator and his gloved hand finding the sleeve beneath the mud.

"In your overcoat?"

"Well, not really *my* overcoat, Koessler."

Schumacher spoke slowly, carefully. "Someone else was wearing it when we left the Fuehrerbunker." Koessler sat very still, realizing the significance of this remark, but unsure where it was leading.

"Seven of us broke out between eleven and midnight on May 1. There was no point in staying—there seemed little point in anything anymore. The Fuehrer and Eva Braun had already killed themselves the day before, and Goebbels, who had poisoned his six children, had himself and his wife shot by an SS orderly shortly before we left. Before he died, Hitler gave Bormann a copy of his testament. I knew Bormann had an escape route planned—he would never have stayed that long beneath the Chancellery without one." There was no sound in the smoke-filled cabin, just the soft chug of the motors as *Pandora* made her way through the North Sea Canal toward Amsterdam.

Schumacher pulled on his cigar, which glowed red for a moment. He seemed lost in thought, and Koessler was about to make some comment when he spoke again.

"Bormann was carrying something else, something much more valuable. He held a power of attorney, appointed himself sole trustee of the fund for the organization of SS veterans—ODESSA—and Die Spinne, which you may not know of, Koessler, but it is—how shall I say?—another aspect of the same organization, but much more interesting.

However, access to the fund is only possible by means of the five code-numbers that are on that document." He smiled. "The Swiss are very punctilious about such details."

Koessler was beginning to see daylight. "The document that you refer to—it still exists?"

"Sealed in oilskin in the leather coat that I was wearing when I boarded your Liberator."

Koessler stared, unbelieving.

"That's right, Koessler"—his teeth were bared in a smile —"I killed Bormann and Stumpfegger, his companion, after the escape party had split up. I took his coat and the documents, and by using the route he intended to follow, I got to Lake Havel and took his place in the Ju-52, then flew to Rechlin, where I joined you. I gambled that in the confusion no one at Rechlin would know exactly who might try to escape, and I was right. Your Hauptmann Lange did not question me—he was more than satisfied when he saw that I was the bearer of Hitler's testament."

Koessler could only sit and nod dumbly. It all fitted together, and poor Lange, who had survived the Russians, had fallen victim to this monster once he had given him the information he required. Only one question remained unanswered.

"The ODESSA Fund . . ."

"Yes, Koessler?"

"If the code on the manuscript is still intact in the Liberator, why have you waited till now to look for it?"

"I did not need it. My position in Holland was secure— but more important, there was no way I could make proper use of it. I had to wait until the moment was ripe. Until the war was far enough in the past to enable us to start afresh and use the fund to rebuild National Socialism. We are getting near that point now. Soon, the lack of an outlet for man's natural aggressions here in Europe will lead to the formation of extremist groups, and mass outbreaks of violence will threaten to destroy society. Already we have had the assassination of an American president. When this frustration, this dissatisfaction, is felt most keenly, then—that is the time for us, Koessler. And you are in the perfect position to help."

He drew again on the cigar and regarded Koessler coldly from behind a veil of smoke.

"You cannot condemn me, Koessler, without condemning yourself—so why not choose to help instead? You are German, you come from a good German family, and your help could be invaluable. I think it would be a pity to see your political career end, before it had really started. Besides, I, too, think you would make an excellent leader in the Bundestag."

Koessler's mind reeled. My God, he had even heard about all that. He felt boxed in. The air in the cabin was stifling. He stood up and made his way to the deck, leaving Schumacher to puff meditatively on the cigar. They were now in the main harbor of Amsterdam, the tall derricks and cargo ships towering above them. It would have been easy to leap overboard and swim for the quayside, thirty yards away, but that would have accomplished nothing. Then, as though he had read Koessler's mind, Hendrik swung down from the flying bridge and leaned against the wheelhouse, watching him carefully.

Koessler took a deep breath and stretched his arms, making it clear he had come up on deck for a breath of fresh air. He leaned on the guardrail. Deliberately, he pushed everything he had heard to the back of his mind. He needed time to digest it.

Koessler watched the office workers pouring over the bridges on their way to work, and the convoys of cyclists weaving expertly in and out of the traffic. He remembered the cobblestones and tramlines and wondered why they never broke their necks.

He had been to Amsterdam once during the war, in May

1943. Goering had chosen to inspect the Atlantic Wall in Holland and Koessler, along with eighty-nine other Luftwaffe pilots, had been ordered into the area to provide protection.

It had been a running joke among his colleagues that the ratio had worked out to about one kilogram of Goering per Messerschmidt 109. A squadron of New Zealanders in Lockheed Venturas flew into this unexpectedly high concentration of fighters and suffered heavy losses. They had known nothing of Goering's visit—it had been a tragic coincidence.

Koessler and his comrades had celebrated long into the night. In fact, Koessler remembered nothing until he woke up in the old seaplane base, Schellingwoude, which was somewhere down there in the harbor. He could vaguely remember the seaplanes moored offshore, but the rest of that morning was a haze of throbbing pain behind his eyes and an agonizing ride back to Schipol.

The low-pitched sound of a tugboat's siren brought him back to the present, and he watched it cheerfully pulling a long line of heavily-laden barges toward the docks. He made his way back to his cabin, watched all the time by Hendrik.

LUCKY LADY

MANDERSON and Wally anchored *Lucky Lady* securely fore and aft, so that the air compressor on the deck behind the wheelhouse would have a firm platform. Wally laid a tarpaulin out nearby that he could fling over it should any-one get too nosy. Manderson buried himself in his prepara-tions, blocking out all thoughts of the gunman and con-centrating his efforts on the job at hand. It was going to be difficult, possibly dangerous, and experience had taught him that he could easily come unstuck if he started to worry about events unconnected with the diving operation. The gunman was no immediate danger, and until he found out exactly what was down there, he didn't know how far he'd have to go to carry out the terms of his contract with Penny-man. He planned to carry a wire-reinforced flexible pipe about four inches in diameter, an airlift pipe, down to the wreck to suck up the mud inside the fuselage. They had secured the other end of the pipe to a small buoy far enough away from the bomber, so that the sediment would not impair his vision when it poured out of the pipe and filtered back down. The airlift pipe was suspended from the buoy and was invisible from the surface.

A narrow rubber tube ran down from the air compressor and was attached to the side of the airlift pipe when the diver reached the bottom. Then, the compressed air was injected through the tube and into the airlift pipe, which created a suction at the mouth of the airlift pipe and carried away the mud. The flow of air could be regulated by a valve on the tube, and Manderson had taken the precaution of fixing some coarse wire mesh across the mouth of the airlift pipe to prevent any documents or clothing or other small articles from being drawn into it.

He had already donned his rubber suit; Wally checked the cylinder on his back and gave it a few tugs.

"What about him?" He jerked his thumb at Franz, who was watching from inside the wheelhouse.

"Ignore him and concentrate on me. Okay, Wally?"

Wally looked down and shifted his feet uneasily. "All right, skipper, no more mistakes. You can count on me."

Manderson grinned. "Sure I can." He sat on the gunwale and put on the flippers as Wally unwound the loops in the airpipe, then gently lowered it into the water. He positioned the temporary ladder over the stern on the diving platform that Manderson would use. It was important to disturb the shallow water as little as possible.

In addition to the battery-operated sealamp, Wally had strapped a smaller light around his headpiece, which would free his hands for working below. Wally had already got the line from the derrick over the side, which he could attach to anything he found in the wrecked bomber. Manderson climbed down the ladder onto the diving platform and immersed his facemask in seawater before slipping it on. Wally handed him the end of the airlift pipe, and Manderson held it below the surface and gave Wally a signal. Wally started the compressor and Manderson twisted the valve, testing it— the suction was strong. Franz had joined Wally at the rail.

"Good luck, Manderson. If I can help in any way, I will." Manderson felt a surge of anger.

"Just stay clear of it and don't interfere. Leave everything to Wally." He looked at the old man. "Is that clear? He touches nothing!"

"Sure, skipper, I'll see to it."

"I don't expect the mud down there to be packed hard, but have the water jet standing by, just in case."

"Right."

Manderson gave the line from the derrick a tug. "All right, one last time. One tug is to lower a little, two to raise, and three to bring it up, okay?"

Wally nodded his head vehemently. "Understood."

Manderson pulled the facemask down over his eyes, took one last look around, then lowered himself and the sealamp into the water and slid beneath the surface.

He pushed the sealamp ahead of him and swam slowly down to the bomber. The light was better today, the sunshine filtering down a little way below the surface, and he could see the Liberator with its long, slender wings stretching out from the fuselage, looking not unlike a giant starfish. Manderson proposed to make his way into the fuselage at the point where the tail assembly had broken off, just behind the waist guns; the bulkhead behind the cockpit would effectively block movement of any large objects. First he did a quick check on the broken nose section, which had been wrenched off some distance away. It was full of mud and he could see nothing, but he didn't expect to find anything there. The most likely place would be in the fuselage, particularly the bomb-bays.

He swam around the tail section and fastened the clamps

of the sealamp to it. The metal was in remarkably good condition and showed no sign of corrosion; perhaps it was the low salt content of the water. In any case, it supported the lamp perfectly and he adjusted the beam so that maximum light was falling on the rear of the broken fuselage. Then he pulled down the airlift pipe slowly until he'd got it into the right position.

All he could see above the mud were the loop and whip antennas on the top of the fuselage, and the upper edge of the sidegunner's windows.

He released the valve on the air-compressor tube, gradually building up the pressure. At once the mud began to stir, clouding his vision, but he kept the nozzle pointed in the right direction and increased the suction. The mud that had been collecting inside the bomber for the past eighteen years slowly began to disintegrate.

PANDORA

IT WAS about ten A.M. when Hendrik came to fetch him. He had heard him coming along the companionway, and he kicked the cabin door right back before entering, to be sure Koessler wasn't hiding behind it, then came in when he saw him lying on the bunk.

He was carrying an automatic rifle, which he leveled at Koessler, and he spoke quietly, without emotion. "Get up. The captain wants you."

Koessler rose from the bunk and started to walk to the door.

"Wait, you'll need a coat. It's cold on deck."

Albert was still at the wheel, and Schumacher was studying the coastline through a pair of binoculars, but it was the girl, Lydia, who attracted his attention. She had on a fur coat with a white mink collar, and a woolen sailor's hat perched incongruously on her head. She smiled as he came onto the bridge.

"It seems the world did not come to an end last night, after all." Schumacher broke in before he could reply. "Koessler, time to make use of your services. We are clear of Amsterdam now and into the Ijsselmeer. Kindly give Albert the course, please."

"May I have the glasses?"

Schumacher glanced at him briefly and handed them over. They were heading almost due east, into the wider reaches of the Zuyder Zee. A decision had to be made now. His failure to extract the information he needed from Schumacher meant that he could not risk misdirecting him to some other part of the inland sea, since if Schumacher had the slightest inkling of the correct position, then any trust he might have built up over the last forty-eight hours would be destroyed.

"Bring her around," he said, "to a heading for Harderwijk. Do you know it?"

Albert stared at him impassively.

"Keep the coastline about a mile to starboard, and I'll tell you when we are almost there." He glanced at Schumacher, who was staring out over the water, apparently immersed in his own thoughts.

When he spoke it was so softly that Koessler could hardly hear him. "How did you get ashore?"

Koessler considered the surprising question for a moment. "I'm not sure. After the impact the nose section was torn off. I managed to get up on top of the fuselage and tried to release the liferaft cradle, but the hatch seemed to be jammed. I managed to open it a little, but then it stuck fast and I had to swim for it."

Schumacher was still staring out to sea. "Could you see the coastline?"

"Yes, it wasn't far away."

"And you know where that was?"

"I've got a pretty good idea."

There was a long silence, broken only by the sound of the engine as the motor cruiser sped over the calm, dappled water.

"The weather is good this time," Schumacher remarked. "Better than that day." He paused, then added quietly, "I must have been unconscious. It was the water that brought me round. That's what I remember most, the cold. I don't know how I got out, but the plane was just sinking as I did—and that liferaft you spoke of?"

Koessler nodded.

"Well, it had floated to the surface. Perhaps if you had been more persistent. . . . However, that's all I remember until I woke up on the beach."

Koessler didn't comment on this. There was nothing to say. He realized with a sickening feeling of disgust that he'd been outwitted—Schumacher had had absolutely no idea of the Liberator's location but he had covered himself so well that Koessler had been afraid to feed him false information —the risk was too great. Schumacher must have been aware of his maneuverings from the start. God, how he'd underestimated this man. The self-satisfaction and delusions of grandeur—it was all a front, or at least most of it. Behind all that was a sharp, cruel, analytical mind, carefully weighing the odds. He should have known that no one like Schumacher could have survived for so long, in such style, on luck alone. Of course it was all very obvious—in retrospect; then he realized that Schumacher had said something and was staring at him.

"I beg your pardon?"

"The glasses." He pointed. "May I have the glasses?"

Koessler lifted the strap from around his neck and handed them over.

"You seem preoccupied, Koessler. I trust there is nothing wrong with your directions. Remember, I am relying on you."

"No, no, of course not. I was just remembering a few things, that's all."

Schumacher scanned the coastline. "Let's hope your memory is good, and that politics haven't blunted your reactions."

It was as if Schumacher had read his mind, and he was right. He had treated it as a political situation—trying to make use of diplomacy, talk, to outwit this monster—and it had all been so useless. There was still only one way out.

Schumacher was peering intently through the glasses, and suddenly Koessler was very aware of everything around him —from the fresh smell of the breeze and the cold metal of the rail his hands rested on, down to the specks of dandruff on Schumacher's dark coat. All his senses seemed to have quickened. Schumacher lowered the glasses.

"Unusual!"

Koessler followed his line of vision and felt his stomach turn over. He tried to speak calmly.

"What is?"

"That fishing boat." He pointed. "I know these waters; the boats from Harderwijk don't normally fish in this area."

Koessler shrugged his shoulders. "Perhaps he has broken down. Some of these boats are very old."

Schumacher nodded. "Yes, he does seem to be having difficulties. Perhaps we can help." He turned to Albert. "Bring us alongside that boat nice and gently, Albert. We do not want to disturb whatever it is they are fishing for." Then, to Hendrik: "Find yourself a good position, but don't let them see that automatic"—he smiled—"unless, of course, you have to." Then he glanced at Lydia. "But first, take her below and lock her in her cabin."

"Aw, c'mon, Mackie, what the hell difference does it make?"

The nickname seemed to make no impression on Schumacher. "Take her below," he repeated. "Now."

The Dutchman nodded curtly and gestured with the automatic toward the door. Lydia shook her head in disbelief.

"You want to know something? You guys are a real load of laughs. I knew from the start I was going to enjoy this trip." She gave Hendrik an icy look. "C'mon, cowboy, take me to my cabin. I'll switch on my sunlamp and start working on my tan."

Koessler admired her spirit, but he knew she was better off in her cabin. Clearly, she did not understand the risks she was running. A minute or two later Hendrik came back on deck, but he kept well back of the bridge, as Schumacher had instructed him to.

As they drew closer Schumacher indicated the steps that led down onto the deck. "After you, Koessler. Let us see how the Dutchmen are doing."

Koessler led the way. The low November sun reflecting off the water was dazzlingly bright, and he put up one hand to shield his eyes from the glare. He had seen Manderson once in the hotel bar at Chatham, and the old man standing near the rail amidships was certainly not him. At first he couldn't see anyone else, but then as the motor cruiser drew up alongside he saw someone in the wheelhouse, who then came out on deck. His hair was blond, almost white, his eyes blue, and he was staring at Koessler intently. He reminded Koessler of someone. At first he couldn't place him; then he remembered—he looked incredibly like himself, twenty years ago.

He was standing in the doorway of the wheelhouse; his gaze went past Koessler to Schumacher, who was standing just behind him, to his right. Koessler saw recognition dawning in his eyes and with awful clarity he knew what the man on the trawler was going to do. He saw his hand go into his pocket, and then Schumacher screamed. Koessler saw Hendrik sliding quietly around the corner of the cabin leveling the automatic at the young man on the trawler, whose eyes hadn't left Schumacher for a moment.

Koessler jerked into action, throwing himself desperately at Hendrik. "No!" he screamed. "No!" Franz saw Koessler leaping sideways and fired at him instinctively. The bullet hit Koessler with stunning force, smashing him back against the side of the cabin.

Hendrik let off a round in the same instant, but Koessler's scream had been enough to affect his aim; the bullet hit Franz in the upper part of his chest and shattered his collarbone. A moment later the Dutchman was dead as Franz's second shot hit him in the face just below his nose and took the back of his head off.

As though in a dream, Koessler watched the young man slide slowly down the side of the wheelhouse, until he collapsed onto the deck. He was looking up at him, his face wracked with pain. Koessler opened his mouth to speak, but nothing came out. He looked down at his legs, willing them to move; they seemed to mock him, to grow longer and heavier. He wasn't going to ride the Ferris wheel on Saturday— no more Saturdays. Koessler was dying, and he knew it. He made a supreme effort and staggered forward, trying to focus his eyes on the figure slumped on the deck of the trawler, but he was distorted and in shadow. Koessler looked up at the sky for the light and the sun, but it was black. Then his body lurched against the guardrail, toppled over, and disappeared beneath the water.

Manderson turned off the water jet and waited for some of the mud to settle. It had packed hard inside the fuselage, and he'd had to loosen it from time to time with the water jet before continuing with the suction pipe. He'd already made considerable progress that morning, clearing enough mud to remove one packing case. The metal strips that had originally secured it were still in place; nevertheless, he had very carefully wrapped the line from the derrick around it before Wally hauled it to the surface with the light diesel engine, and swung it aboard.

To Wally's disgust Manderson hadn't come up to examine the packing case; he didn't know how long this weather was going to last. Now he had cleared the fuselage as far as the rear gun-platform, and he could just discern what looked like the top of another case in front of the ball turret shaft. He looked for the line from the derrick and thought he saw something moving in the muddy water. At first he dismissed it as a trick of the light and the eddying currents, but then he saw it again as it dropped toward him through the cloud of mud. It turned over, and Koessler's lifeless eyes stared down at him. His hand appeared to reach out, and frozen with fear, Manderson could only watch as it touched him lightly on the shoulder.

He jerked up the water jet and released a blast that hit Koessler's dead body in the chest and sent it twisting and turning grotesquely toward the nose of the plane, like a straw man flailing in the wind. The corpse sank to the bottom, coming to rest near the shattered remains of the pilot's compartment that Koessler had occupied eighteen years before.

Franz couldn't move his right arm. He cradled it against his chest with his other arm, trying to lessen the pain. The bullet had splintered his collarbone and passed right through his shoulder; he could feel the blood trickling down his back.

He felt Wally groping for the gun and he realized that he was still clutching it in his useless right hand. Then came an excruciating pain in his shoulder as the broken ends of the bone ground together. He cried out, and Wally drew back at once. Franz screamed at him, "Take it! Take it! Kill him!" Wally hesitated. He didn't know if he could make it, and his own reactions were slowed down by the numbing shock of the last sixty seconds. He reached for the gun again, then heard a voice cut through the silence. "Don't touch it, old man." He froze.

Franz stared at Wally, his pupils dilated with pain—and something else, a madness, an icy hatred. "Kill him," he said quietly. "Take the gun and kill him."

Wally was no coward, but he'd lived a long time and been in enough brawls to know that this was not the time to make any sudden moves. He stretched out his empty hands, then turned and faced them.

The man with the gray hair was standing by the guardrail, holding what he thought must be a Luger. The younger man stood on the roof of the bridge, with an automatic rifle that was trained on Wally's chest.

Schumacher waved the gun at him. "That was very sensible of you. Now take the gun from him, please, barrel first, and if he tries to use it—that will be the end of both of you."

The voice was quiet, almost pleasant, but Wally could feel the hairs prickling on the back of his neck as he turned and faced Franz again.

His face was gray and contorted with pain; he tried stubbornly to pry his fingers from the grip of the pistol. Wally leaned down and put his hand on the barrel.

"Give it to me. There's no chance. They'll kill us both."

"Leave it." Now Franz spoke slowly, emphasizing every word. "Get . . . out . . . of . . . the . . . way, I want him."

Wally had no alternative. He gripped hard on the barrel and ripped it out of Franz's hand. Franz screamed with pain, and Wally waited for the bullets to smash into his unprotected back. Nothing happened, and slowly he held out the gun by the barrel so that they could see it.

Schumacher's voice was still calm and pleasant. "You did well. Now turn and throw the gun over the side."

Wally did as he was told, the gun flashing in the morning sun as it fell into the water.

"I'm going to ask both of you to come on board, please."

Wally glanced down at Franz. His eyes were closed, and the blood had soaked through his clothing. "I can't move him. He's unconscious. I think he's lost a lot of blood."

Schumacher looked at Albert and nodded. "Throw him a line, then search the vessel, and bring them on board. I will keep you covered." He reached out and took the rifle.

The search revealed nothing, and it took some time for Wally and Albert to get Franz's unconscious body over the high gunwale of *Lucky Lady* and onto the deck of the motor cruiser; Schumacher kept the rifle trained on Wally.

Following Schumacher's instructions, they carried him below and into the galley, leaving a trail of bloodstains behind them. After they had propped him up in a chair, Wally called for the first-aid kit and did his best to staunch the flow of blood and get the arm in a sling. The broken collarbone protruded horribly, and it was just as well for Franz that he did not regain consciousness.

"We've got to get him to a hospital so the bone can be set," Wally said. "He could get gangrene."

Schumacher busied himself about the galley. He removed a foil-wrapped frozen-food container from the fridge, then put it in the microwave oven, and took it out a few moments later.

"I don't care if he dies—as long as someone gives me the answers I want."

He sat down at the table and started to eat his meal; Albert stood by the door, cradling the rifle.

Schumacher put a forkful of what looked like shepherd's pie into his mouth and wiped it with the back of his hand. "Who told you about this place?"

As Manderson swam upward through the murky water, he saw the hull of the motor cruiser along *Lucky Lady*'s portside; then something glinted and splashed in the water. It was a pistol, plummeting straight toward the bottom. He swam toward it, tried to catch it before it reached the bottom, but he was too late. His clawing hand missed it by inches and it sank into the thick sediment, threw up a little cloud of mud, and disappeared.

Manderson started to swim back up to the surface; when he had almost reached the starboard side of *Lucky Lady*, well away from the motor cruiser, he pulled off his headpiece and poked his head above water, ready to slip back below should anyone spot him. He heard a voice ordering someone else to bring the body on board the motor cruiser, and he was relieved when he heard Wally reply. Manderson continued to tread water, waiting for the opportunity to pull himself up over the rail and see what was happening on board.

The man's voice that had spoken to Wally sounded Dutch, maybe German, but that did not concern Manderson at the moment. Somehow he had to get Wally out of their hands.

Gradually the noises faded, as Franz was carried below. There was just the gentle slap of the water against the two hulls and the occasional squawk of a seabird. Manderson swam around to the stern and pulled himself quietly onto the diving platform, then slowly raised himself up until he could peer over the railing.

The decks of both boats, as far as he could see, were deserted. He pulled the flippers off his feet and swung his legs over the rail, easing himself down onto the deck. He padded quickly across to the wheelhouse, keeping it between him and the cruiser. He could see no one on the bridge, and then, half-hidden behind the superstructure, he saw Hendrik's body. That meant that, including the corpse on the sea bed, the gunman had killed at least two of them before he was hit, but Manderson had no way of knowing whether he was still alive, or how many of the others were left.

He found a large oily wrench down by the side of the engine housing, and silently cursed himself for not having a real weapon on board, apart from the knife in his belt. Then he saw the bloodstains that trailed across the deck. He followed them to the gunwale and as silently as he could he lowered himself over the rail and onto the deck of the cruiser.

Schumacher pushed another huge forkful of meat and mashed potatoes into his mouth, and without looking up, repeated the question.

"Who told you about this place?"

Wally didn't know the answer. Manderson had been secretive about his trip to London, and that had annoyed him. He was naturally curious, and had an almost proprietary interest in the old fishing boat, but the one thing he couldn't do was to let these bastards know that Manderson even existed.

"I don't know much about it, sir. This man here"—he indicated the unconscious figure—"asked me if I could get hold of an old fishing boat and bring him out here."

Schumacher continued to eat. "And that packing case on your deck?"

Wally's mouth was dry. He needed a drink badly. His eyes flicked around the galley until he saw the whiskey bottle on top of the cupboard. He licked his lips and stared at it thirstily.

"We, er, we brought that up this morning. He seemed to know where it was, and I just helped."

He couldn't take his eyes off the whiskey bottle; Schumacher got up from the table, went over to the cupboard, and reached for the bottle.

"Perhaps you'd like a drink."

He took two glasses from the cupboard and poured a generous amount into each. "It might help you think of something else to tell me."

Wally nodded vigorously. "Yeah, well, maybe I could think of a few more details that you might like to know."

"Of course." Schumacher took a sip from one of the glasses, then started to walk toward Wally. He offered the glass to Wally, and his hand was nearly on the glass when Schumacher flicked the whiskey into his face.

Wally winced, then swore as the alcohol stung his eyes and trickled down the stubble on his cheeks. He closed his eyes tightly, grimaced, and stumbled over to the sink. He put his head under the tap and let the cold water pour over his head, splashing it in his face until the burning sensation began to subside.

He faced them, his vision blurred, and then he heard that toneless, polite voice again.

"Now. Perhaps the alcohol has helped you remember. Who told you about this place?"

Wally could almost taste the hatred burning inside him, but he checked the dockside language he would have liked to use. "I only know what I've told you," he said sullenly, refusing to look directly at Schumacher.

Manderson climbed the steps to the bridge. It was empty, as was the main cabin aft. Now came the tricky bit. He had to go below, and he wouldn't stand much chance against the automatics if he let himself get trapped down there.

He went down the companionway and heard the mumble of voices coming from the galley. He followed the blood-spattered carpet along the passageway, past the doors of several cabins. He came to the end, the voices much louder now. He risked a quick glance around the corner, then ducked back again. He'd caught a glimpse of one of them getting up from behind a table, but he could see only one tenth of the galley and he had to know who else was in that cabin.

He heard Wally cursing and obviously in pain. The temptation to go rushing in was too much for him. He took three steps toward the door of the galley, then stopped as he heard the click of a safety catch being slipped. Wally was blundering around the cabin and Albert was taking no chances.

Manderson backed away from the door and stood by the corner, listening. He jumped as someone in the cabin next to him started to pound on the door.

It was a woman. "C'mon, you creeps! Let me out! What the hell's going on out there?"

Manderson flattened himself against the corner of the bulkhead so that he could not be seen immediately should anyone emerge from the galley.

He heard Schumacher order Albert to ignore the woman in the cabin. God, if only he had a weapon! Then Wally started splashing his head under the tap and he remembered the water jet.

Franz dragged himself wearily back to consciousness. He could feel his face stinging as someone slapped it viciously, then the sudden shock as cold water was thrown over him, bringing him gasping back to reality and the indescribable pain in his shoulder.

The face that he had seen from the fishing boat was swimming in front of him, the mouth opening and closing. He heard a voice echoing back from the boarding school at Heilbronn, taunting him.

"Why do you wait, Franz? Why do you hide behind the others? Are you afraid of the little Jewboys?"

Gradually the voice penetrated. It was coming from that mouth in front of him.

"How do you know of this place? What brought you here?"

It repeated the same question patiently, but with infinite menace, again and again.

"How do you know of this place? What brought you here?"

"You did," Franz answered. "You brought me here."

The voice spoke again; the eyes looked slightly puzzled.

"Say that again please—repeat that in English."

Only then did Franz realize that he had spoken in Hebrew. He looked around the room. Wally was standing by the sink, staring at him anxiously. Another man stood with his back against a bulkhead, holding a rifle. The face loomed up in front of him again. There was no sign of Manderson, so perhaps there was a chance. It seemed that Lutz Beyer hadn't recognized him yet.

Beyer repeated the question once more. Franz started to shake the water out of his eyes, and instantly, the pain in his shoulder almost made him pass out. He bit into his lip and felt the salty taste of blood in his mouth.

"I wanted what was down there," he whispered haltingly. Beyer had to lean closer to hear. "Is that why you shot at me?"

He remembered not to nod. "Yes."

"How did you know something was down there?"

The face did not change expression; only the eyes told him what to expect. He didn't answer. There was no point. He resigned himself to whatever would come next.

Beyer stood up, his face seeming to swim up and bob somewhere above him. He gazed down at Franz contemptuously.

"Jews! Always the same, always ready to die, to martyr

yourselves." He swung round toward Wally. "Well, old man, your noble friend will say nothing—I speak from experience. Now, perhaps you know nothing, but I will have the truth. Put the handcuffs on his wrists, Albert. In front of him."

Albert took the handcuffs from his belt and clicked them in place, then pushed him toward the galley.

"These microwave ovens are very useful. You saw how quickly it heated up my meal. They cook anything in seconds, from the inside out—by boiling off the water molecules contained in any organic material." Schumacher sounded almost like a salesman. "The makers tell me that they are absolutely safe and cannot go on unless the door is closed, but look."

He put a piece of raw fish in the oven, left the door open, and turned on a red switch at the side. Almost immediately, the odor of cooking fish pervaded the galley. Schumacher watched until all that remained was a dessicated, blackened slab, then switched it off.

He turned to Franz. "I have had it adapted to my own uses. It's an old principle, but much more up to date now, don't you think? I promise you, the old man will suffer."

He nodded briefly to Albert, who started to push Wally toward the oven. Wally struggled, but Albert merely smashed the butt of his rifle across the back of his head.

Wally slumped toward the floor; Albert picked him up under the arms, then thrust his hands into the oven. As Schumacher's finger went toward the switch Franz struggled up from the chair.

"No! Don't touch it, Beyer. There is no need."

Schumacher's finger was poised over the switch; he stopped and looked at him intently.

"Beyer?" he asked softly.

"Yes. Beyer. . . . Lutz Beyer. That is your name."

"Is it?" His hand had come away from the switch. "And what do you know of Lutz Beyer?"

Franz managed a smile in spite of the pain. "I know you were never very good with the girls, Beyer, in spite of your prowess on the track and the uniform you were so proud of." He stopped for a moment to look at him. "You preferred me, didn't you, Beyer . . . you preferred little boys. Did you ever realize, Beyer, that you had made love to a Jew?" Franz laughed, a strange sobbing sound. "I wonder what you would have done if you'd known—cut it off, perhaps?" He grinned at Schumacher, gloating.

Schumacher screamed at him. "Shut up!" His hand shot out, catching him squarely in the chest. He tottered back into the chair. A burning shaft of pain went through him, and he started to slump forward.

"Franz Hagen?" Schumacher stared down at him, his eyes wide, shocked. "So you are little Franz." Schumacher spat out the words. It was naked now—the raw stinking hate exposed. "You were the one who didn't want to hurt the Jews." He spoke slowly, quietly. "But you did, didn't you, Franz, eh?" His teeth were bared in a snarl of triumph.

Franz rocked slowly back and forth, cradling his arm, his eyes shut tightly, trying to block out the taunting voice, the insidious memory.

"Oh, but you did, Franz, you hurt them. Remember the jeweler's wife, Frau Dreifuss? You hurt her, Franz." Schumacher grabbed him by the hair, jerking back his head. "You crushed her skull with that stone jug, didn't you? And it wasn't difficult, was it? Killing a Jew."

Franz said nothing, his eyes were dark empty pits, fathomless. No hate, no fear—nothing.

Schumacher let go of his hair, and Franz's head fell forward lifelessly. Schumacher turned away.

"That's right, Franz. You killed her, and she wasn't the

only one you helped us deal with. That's right, you had to, of course. In fact, afterwards you were a shining example to us all, Franz. A perfect little Nazi. You led the way, otherwise we might have guessed, mightn't we? And poor little Franz wouldn't have liked that. You might have been sent away to that filthy camp, with all your other friends."

It was true. Franz knew it; he had always known it—feared it for years. The shame of wearing the uniform of the Hitler Youth. Surviving by brutalizing his own people. He had tried to blot that out, hide it from himself. But here it was erupting from inside, where it had been rotting, eating him alive, like a cancer. As always, Beyer had pierced to the heart of it, to his most vulnerable point, and torn him apart.

The hate he felt for Beyer was exceeded only by the disgust he felt for himself. He looked up at his tormentor, the agony in his shoulder forgotten for the moment.

"You forget that I *know* you, Beyer. We went to assembly one morning, long after you had left school. The headmaster told us you had won a medal in the war, and we cheered. We cheered for you, Beyer. I don't think I've ever hated anyone the way I hated you that morning." The galley was silent; there was just the sound of the water slapping against the hull.

"And now, do you know what you are? You are an anachronism, a poisonous remnant. You pollute those around you, the minds of all you contact with your sickness." His voice had dropped to a whisper. "Oh yes, I know you, Beyer, better than I know myself. And I know that you were at Babi Yar—you stood and watched while thousands were slaughtered. When I found that out, I wished I could have brought that stone jug down on your head, splattered your brains all over the street in Heilbronn. I always knew I would find you one day, Beyer."

Schumacher took the Luger from his belt. "So, you have

found me, but nothing has changed, Franz. You are sitting there, helpless as usual, and I have this." He brandished the pistol. "Killing is not difficult, you should know that. And in this case I shall really enjoy it."

He pulled back the catch and walked around behind him. Franz felt the cold barrel on the back of his neck. He closed his eyes, wondering if he would feel anything.

The steel drum crashed down onto the deck, and for an instant Franz thought it was the sound of the gun. Momentarily he wondered how he could hear it, but then the drum rolled across the deck and splashed into the sea. Schumacher and Albert stood motionless, staring up at the roof of the galley, listening.

There was nothing, and the silence hung heavily. Schumacher exchanged a look with Albert and signaled him to go up on deck.

The Dutchman nodded, and left the galley quietly. Schumacher stationed himself near the door and put his finger to his lips. Franz sat absolutely still; the barrel of the Luger was pointing directly at his stomach.

Albert didn't make a sound as he crept along the passage, ready at any moment to slip into one of the cabins. When he reached the companionway, he waited a full minute. There was nothing—just an empty patch of blue sky and the gentle *putt-putt* of the pump on the fishing boat.

He flattened himself against the bulkhead and climbed one step at a time until he was near the top. He inched up slowly until he could peer over the edge of the housing. The afterdeck was empty, but *Lucky Lady* rode much higher in the water and he couldn't see over the rail. He slipped around the corner of the housing, keeping to the port side, away from the trawler. When he reached the front of the bridge superstructure, he carefully scanned *Pandora*'s entire deck, gazing steadily at any possible hiding place until he was sure it concealed no one.

Slinging the rifle over his shoulder, he climbed up a ladder. From the flying bridge, he could see onto the deck of the fishing boat. The wheelhouse was empty and the deck clear, apart from a hose about four inches in diameter snaking up out of the water on the far side of the trawler and across the deck to the port gunwale. He didn't know why it continued to attract his attention—then he noticed it was glistening, wet, as though it had just been pulled out of the water. In the instant that he raised the automatic, Manderson stood up from behind the gunnel. Albert didn't have time to get off a round; the water jet struck him with incredible force, and he crashed to the deck.

Manderson trained the jet on the canvas around the flying bridge and tore it to shreds. Albert's body was pressed against the far side of the bridge until that too was torn apart. He clung desperately to the rails, but Manderson brought the jet closer until his fingers slipped from the rail. He fell backward; his head caught the side of the deck, splitting like a melon, with an obscene, squashy sound. Then he disappeared over the side and into the sea, a small patch of blood and bubbles marking the place where he had fallen.

"How many are up there?"

Franz stared at him impassively. "I don't know."

Schumacher stood behind him and repeated the question softly. "How many?"

Franz sensed the danger. He could feel the cold sweat running down inside his damp shirt. He wanted to leap up from the chair and make a run for it, but he forced himself to sit still. "I don't know."

Schumacher wasted no more time. He brought the barrel

of the Luger down across the back of his head, and Franz crumpled to the floor of the galley.

As soon as Wally heard the water crash onto the deck of the cruiser he realized that Manderson was using the jet as a weapon, but now that the advantage of surprise was gone, he knew that Manderson had little chance against the Luger. Somehow he was going to have to help, but so far there had never been a moment when Schumacher could not have killed him the instant he made a move.

Schumacher threw him the keys to the handcuffs. "Undo them."

It was difficult to manage the handcuffs, and all the time the Luger was trained on him. Schumacher waved him through the door of the galley, then grabbed his arm and pinned it behind his back. The gun was thrust under his jaw, and Schumacher forced him slowly down the passage, stopping every few yards to listen.

It was eerie; silent, apart from the creaking of the boat as she rocked slightly in the swell, and the occasional bump as the cruiser rubbed against the hull of *Lucky Lady*.

They could hear the soft sound of the diesel pump when they reached the companionway. Schumacher pushed Wally up the steps and kept Wally ahead of him as they stood in the entryway. He scanned the flooded deck; the scuppers were overflowing, and water dripped steadily from the cabin and bridge above them. Schumacher called out, his voice echoing back from the hull of *Lucky Lady*.

"I've got the old man. He's here." He jerked Wally's arm upward sharply, and Wally cried out, cursing him. "I want you to come out here onto the deck, otherwise he will suffer for it."

He paused; there was still only the panting of the engine. "There is no need for this; whatever you have found down there, we can share. This is stupid and unnecessary. There is only me left, so you and the old man will get most of it anyway."

The *Lucky Lady* was lowest at its center, where the gunwale was just about level with the deck of the cruiser. Wally could see the hose looped over the rail. He knew roughly how long it was, and he estimated that Manderson must be somewhere near the stern, probably by the wheelhouse, but Manderson was powerless as long as Schumacher was shielded by his body.

Schumacher was getting impatient. "All right. If you are not going to be sensible, I shall have to report this to the authorities. I am going to take the old man with me to the bridge, and I warn you not to interfere, or I shall be forced to kill him."

He pushed Wally ahead of him onto the deck and started to edge slowly toward the steps leading up to the bridge. Wally knew this was the last chance he would have.

He kicked back hard, his heavy boots crunching into Schumacher's leg, and in the same moment he dropped to his knees, throwing his weight backward, pushing Schumacher up against the cabin. His arm was yanked up into the small of his back, and he felt a searing pain as he heard his elbow crack, but he had broken Schumacher's grip. Wally stumbled to his feet, running as fast as he could toward *Lucky Lady*.

"Tom!" he yelled hoarsely. "Hit him now!"

Schumacher gasped with pain. He thought his leg was broken, but he wasn't going to let the old man get away. He raised the Luger and took aim. Manderson leaped up, turned on the jet, and directed the nozzle at Schumacher, who was only about twenty feet away. Nothing happened. The hose was looped over the gunwale and tangled up behind him, and there was a momentary pause before the water came bursting out.

Wally had reached the rail of *Lucky Lady* and was trying to scramble over, his broken arm hanging uselessly at his side. Schumacher got off one round before the jet struck him and flung him back down the companionway. The bullet hit Wally squarely in the back, tearing his heart open and emerging just under the ribcage, before burying itself in the wooden side of the boat.

He died instantly, his body draped over the rail. Manderson automatically switched off the jet and dropped the hose. He didn't know what had happened to Schumacher. He didn't care. He walked slowly over to Wally's body. He stooped, and tenderly lifted the old man up, and carried him through the wheelhouse and down the steps to the cabin. He laid Wally down on the bunk and slid a pillow under his head. He pushed the thinning gray hair back from his face and pulled the eyelids down with the side of his hand to cover the empty stare of his eyes.

Manderson covered the old man's body with a blanket and methodically began to prepare himself and his boat for the final assault.

Schumacher's fall down the companionway had crushed one of his small vertebrae; his legs were totally paralyzed. He dragged himself painfully over to the spot where the Luger had fallen and propped himself against a bulkhead in the passage, holding the pistol in both hands to steady it, but no one appeared in the entrance.

Suddenly the diesel pump stopped and all he could hear was the wind whipping up off the sea, then the splatter of rain on the deck. Somehow he had to find out what was happening, and he remembered the porthole in the galley. Clutching the pistol in his right hand, he dragged himself forward on his elbows, the veins in his neck bulging with the effort.

Lydia was frightened but trying hard not to let it get to her. She had not been able to identify the sound of the water jet, but there was no mistaking the shot that had killed Wally. She was not afraid of going into the water, and she had searched the cabin and found the lifejacket under her bunk. It would at least keep her afloat if she had to slip over the side, though how long she would last in these wintry seas was another matter, and she decided to keep on her coat and boots.

She heard something outside the door. Once again she pounded on it, pleading to be let out. Schumacher reached up and turned the key in the lock, then pushed himself back until he was sitting against the bulkhead, facing the door.

"It's open," he called weakly. "Come out, but make no noise."

He saw the doorknob turn. She came out into the passage; her eyes wide when she saw the Luger.

"What's wrong? Are you hurt?"

"Don't waste time, woman! Help me up."

She put her arm around his shoulders and tried to get him to his feet. Schumacher almost screamed with the pain, and she drew back. He wedged himself against the bulkhead, yelling at her not to let him slip back down. Somehow they reached the galley.

Franz was still lying unconscious on the floor, but Schumacher was only concerned with the porthole. By gripping the sides of the sink, he was able to support his weight on his elbows and look out. He could only see the trawler's port bow section—it was impossible to see the deck. Then the cruiser began to shudder as the anchor chain of the trawler was hauled up, scraping between the sides of the two vessels, the noise echoing through the galley like a huge mallet pounding against the hull.

Schumacher realized he might have a chance now that

Manderson was not manning the water jet. He turned to the girl, who was staring at the unconscious figure of Franz.

"I have to get back up onto the deck. Help me."

She slipped an arm around his waist. With Lydia half dragging, half carrying him, they made their way down the passage. Schumacher was sweating profusely from the pain and the exertion.

Once the forward sea anchor was up, *Lucky Lady* began to crash against the side of the cruiser with ever increasing force. The wind was beginning to gust severely, flinging sheets of rain into Manderson's face as he struggled to raise the temporary sea anchor at the stern.

Finally it was up, and he made his way along the pitching deck to the wheelhouse, slamming the door behind him as the rain lashed furiously at the windows. The motor cruiser shuddered every time the old fishing boat crashed into her.

Twice Schumacher slipped from Lydia's grasp and fell helplessly onto the deck before they reached the foot of the companionway. He pushed her away and began to drag himself up the steps.

The rain was bouncing high off the deck of the motor cruiser as he started to pull himself across, flat on his stomach. He was soaked to the skin almost immediately, and the chill of winter turned the sweat cold on his back. He remained totally unaware of this, every ounce of his attention concentrated on getting in a shot with the Luger before *Lucky Lady* was out of range.

Schumacher reached the rail of the cruiser and hauled himself up until he could see the shadowy form in the wheelhouse, half obscured by the rain pouring down the windows. He braced himself by looping one of his legs through the lower rail, held the gun in both hands, and fired twice.

The first shot missed the wheelhouse altogether, the rise and fall of the cruiser making accuracy impossible, but the

second smashed into the top corner of the window, shower-
ing Manderson with broken glass. He ducked down beneath
the sill, hardly noticing the gash in his head. The engine
caught on the second turn of the starter, and *Lucky Lady*
gradually began to pull away, stern first, from the cruiser.
Twice more Schumacher fired, but the bullets smacked
harmlessly into the heavy woodwork.

The muffled sound of the shots was the first thing Franz
heard through the fog of returning consciousness. A hazy
pattern of lines danced in front of his half-closed eyes, then a
hideous gargoyle grinned at him, moving in and out of focus.
He tried to escape from its mocking smile and rolled his
head sideways. Immediately the pain in his shoulder shocked
him back to full consciousness and the gargoyle faded into
the electric-blue pattern of the linoleum.

He heard a woman shouting, then felt her arms around his
waist, trying to lift him up, and he found himself sitting
upright on the floor of the galley. She whisked off the table
cloth and ripped it in half, then knotted it behind his neck as
a makeshift sling for his injured arm. He thanked her. She
seemed concerned but unafraid.

A saucepan fell from the edge of the sink and careened
across the floor until it struck the far bulkhead; then it
started to slide back as the deck tilted the other way. Franz
realized that the boat was pitching badly.

Now that the cruiser was no longer in the lee of *Lucky
Lady* she was taking the full force of the wind, and Schumacher's hold on the rail was precarious. He decided he
would have to get to the bridge, but found it almost impossible to haul himself up the steps.

He had to bear all of his weight on his arms, but the will to
survive was as strong as ever, and by looping each arm in

turn through the rungs of the ladder he was able to drag himself up toward the bridge.

Manderson kept "Lucky Lady" in reverse until he was far enough from the cruiser to get maximum way on the old boat.

He slammed the throttle forward, and she began to pick up speed, crashing her way through the heavy swell toward the cruiser. Manderson braced his feet wide apart on the pitching, rolling deck, gripping the wheel tightly in both hands, and kept the bow pointed directly at the bridge of the cruiser.

Schumacher hauled himself up the last few steps onto the bridge and lay there for a few seconds, exhausted, unable to move, the blood pounding in his ears. Then he became aware of a different sound. Above the gusting of the wind he could hear the old trawler's engines screaming at full throttle, as though they were about to tear themselves from their mountings.

He turned, propping himself against the side of the bridge, and stared out toward the sound. *Lucky Lady* was almost obscured by the rain and the plumes of spray tossed up by the blunt prow boring through the heavy seas, but there was no mistaking her skipper's intentions. Manderson was going to sink the cruiser with the only weapon he had left. The wind kept trying to swing *Lucky Lady* around to starboard, but he kept the prow aimed squarely amidships, and the distance between the two vessels was closing rapidly as the trawler picked up speed.

Schumacher fired off the rest of the Luger's magazine, the sound of the shots lost in the wind, but still she came surging toward him. For the first time in his life Schumacher was frightened. There was a numbing invulnerability about that half-seen ghostly fishing boat smashing its way through the water. He dragged himself over to the control panel; he knew that if he could escape Manderson's first onslaught, he could easily outrun him. He tugged frantically at the starter, but the engine didn't engage. He pulled the choke full out and tried again.

He was whimpering and cursing with fear—a filthy stream of invective and abuse directed at everything he hated most, interspersed with pleas addressed to his God, to Jesus—then back to cursing the Jews again.

Franz and the girl had reached the companionway, and now they were only able to climb the steps by clinging tightly to each other and hanging on to the rail. The wind was whipping the rain through the open doors of the housing, drenching them at once, but above the noise of the gale Franz could hear something else. At first he couldn't identify the sound, but as they neared the top of the steps it grew in intensity and an instant before he saw the misty outline of *Lucky Lady* plowing through the last twenty yards of water toward them, he knew what it was. He dragged the girl the last fifteen feet to the stern, furthest from the onrushing trawler, and threw her, then himself, headfirst into the numbing cold water of the Ijsselmeer.

Schumacher actually got the engine started twice, but he was so terrified and so nearly deafened by the squall that he failed to hear it turn over, and continued to fumble with the starter switch. Finally, as the boat was almost upon him he turned and flung the Luger in a last gesture of defiance at the gray shape towering above him. At that moment *Lucky Lady* struck the cruiser just forward of the bridge.

Schumacher was first thrown against the binnacle by the impact, then through the disintegrating window of the bridge. There was a terrible grinding of metal and wood as

Lucky Lady rammed into the side of the cruiser, then started to ride up over her as she heeled completely over on her port side. *Pandora* sank beneath the weight of the trawler, her fabric being torn and opened to the sea as she was crushed beneath the heavy keel of *Lucky Lady*.

Schumacher's body came up among the debris of *Pandora*'s bridge as it rolled free of the stern. The vortex of water sucked him toward the thrashing screw, and a red, billowing cloud stained the turbulent water behind *Lucky Lady*. The cruiser drifted down toward the seabed, landing stern first on top of the Liberator. Gradually, inexorably, the whole weight of the sinking vessel began to crush the Liberator downward into the mud until nothing more could be seen.

Manderson stared briefly at the widening stain on the surface of the water. He automatically checked that his steerage and engine were not damaged before switching off. He had seen the gunman and a girl dive off the stern of the cruiser moments before the impact, and now he could just see their heads bobbing above the surface some twenty feet off the port beam.

He grabbed the lifebelt and threw it out to them; it landed close enough for the girl to take hold of it on the first cast. Franz would have died but for her; with the lifejacket she was able to keep both arms around him, even when the cold had so numbed him that his one good hand was unable to hold on. The fur coat had kept the cold from Lydia long enough for Manderson to get a line out to them.

He walked the line around to the diving platform aft and slowly pulled them in. The waves were slapping over the platform, soaking him, but it was still more effective than trying to haul them up over the high gunwales of *Lucky Lady*.

Franz was only half conscious; the girl was able to walk. Manderson carried Franz below, and after gently removing his wet and bloodstained clothing, he wrapped him in a blanket and forced some whiskey between his lips. He heard the girl scream behind him. Lydia had stripped off her wet clothing and pulled the biggest blanket she could find off the other bunk, uncovering Wally's body. She dropped the blanket and stood there shivering and naked. Manderson picked it up and wrapped it around her, then handed her the whiskey.

"Thanks," she said laconically. "I was starting to wonder if you knew I was there."

Manderson did not reply and the cold eyes repelled any further attempts to communicate. He covered Wally's body with another blanket, then left the cabin and made his way forward and down into the bilge.

The sea was spraying in through a number of open seams where the timbers were damaged, but he got the pump rigged and started. It seemed to be holding its own against the inrush of water, and Manderson figured they were safe— provided the leaks didn't get any worse.

He climbed wearily up from the bilge and staggered along the rain-washed deck to the bows. They were scraped and splintered in a number of places, but the old boat had been built to last and she would see him safely home.

The rotting packing case lay on the foredeck, and he gazed at it without curiosity. He felt empty, drained, and his muscles ached, but there was no time for sleep. He manhandled the packing case across the deck until he got it alongside the cabin. There he slung a line around it, opened up the skylight, and lowered it down onto the deck below and out of sight. After refastening the skylight he cleared the broken glass from the frame of the window in the wheelhouse, swept the decks clean, and stowed the water jet away, making sure that the air compressor was well secured and covered by the tarpaulin.

There remained the bullets embedded in the woodwork, but perhaps the risk of them being seen at night was negligible. Manderson switched the engine back on, and pointed the battered old boat toward the lock gates at Den Oever and the North Sea. He was going to make a run for home. There would be too many tricky questions if he risked putting in at Harderwijk, and he still had a final responsibility to Wally.

Manderson had two alternatives. He could choose the canal through Amsterdam to the North Sea, but he imagined there would be more risks, more prying eyes to wonder how he had damaged his bows or lost a window in the wheelhouse. Furthermore, he had arrived through the lock system of the Great Barrier Dam, and he would be less likely to attract attention if he returned the same way.

He knew the chance he was taking. If Wally's body was found, it would mean arrest and imprisonment, possibly for a number of years. He could put Wally over the side here in the Zuyder Zee, but he had no intention of doing so. Wally didn't belong here. Manderson dawdled his way up through the inland sea, wasting as much of the afternoon as he could, and as the light started to fade from the leaden gray skies, the rain eased off, and the wind was dying down.

The girl—her name was Lydia—had brought him some hot soup, but he was hardly aware of her presence; his thoughts were elsewhere. He had given them an outline of his plan; they hadn't raised any objections—perhaps they realized they had no choice.

Manderson prepared himself as best he could, putting on a couple of old sweaters, a reefer jacket, and a cap. By the time he'd shared some sweet, hot tea with them and the sandwiches Wally had prepared that morning, the light had drawn right in and the Barrier Dam was looming up on the starboard bow.

He warned Franz and the girl not to show themselves, and took the added precaution of locking the cabin door. He was lucky at Den Oever. The fishing fleets from Harderwijk and Lemmer were coming in through the locks and no one paid much attention to him. By six that evening he was clear of the Zuyder Zee and heading for the Marsdiep Gap, between the promontory at Den Helder and the island of Texel.

Manderson had been at the helm for a long time; the trawler was well out to sea, and keeping her on course was now merely reflex. He had passed the need for sleep and his thoughts kept returning to the cabin below. He looped the line over the wheel and lashed it down securely. *Lucky Lady* would stay on course and there was little risk of collision. Conditions had improved, the wind had died completely, and a fitful moon was trying to break through the low cloud formations.

He picked up a crowbar that he'd fished out of the bilge and made his way down to the cabin door. He unlocked it and pushed it open. The girl was in the bunk with Franz, trying to keep warm. She turned over, ignoring him. Franz sat up, his face pale, with dark rings under his eyes; his gaze flickered down to the crowbar in Manderson's hand.

"You don't need that. I don't think I could get myself off the bunk—let alone take you on."

Manderson glanced at him briefly. "It's not for you."

He walked past them and stood looking down at the packing case. "It's for this." He stared at it uncertainly for a few moments, then looked over at the body on the other bunk.

"Well, you old bastard, I expect you're more curious than I am."

He took the crowbar and tried to snap the metal bands around the case. They proved tougher than he expected, but eventually he managed to force them clear of the top. The wood was sodden and beginning to rot. The mud stank horribly. He broke through the top and saw something glittering through the remains of what must have been the packing material.

He reached in a little gingerly and fished around until his hand touched something hard and metallic. He pulled it out and rubbed the slime and muck off it with his sleeve. It was a beautifully embossed gold plate. He heard Lydia's sharp intake of breath behind him.

Manderson didn't have to look at the hallmark; he could tell by the feel and weight of the metal that it was solid gold. There were several more plates, both gold and silver, and some magnificent pieces of ornamental jade, at least one of which had been smashed. Manderson cleared away as much as he could from the packing case, poking through the residue, then throwing the remains over the side.

He returned to the cabin and stood, a little bewildered, among the litter of treasure he'd taken from the wrecked bomber. Franz was lying on his bunk, staring at the roof of the cabin. Lydia had gotten up, and was putting on the clothes that had dried over the galley stove. The light from the single bulb reflected off a dozen pieces of precious metal, casting strange shapes and patterns on the interior of the cabin as *Lucky Lady* rolled slightly in the swell.

Manderson bent down and opened a drawer below the bunk that Franz was lying in. He took out a roll of canvas and put it down on the foot of the other bunk. Then he started to wrap the blanket tightly around the old man with infinite care and tenderness.

Franz stared at Manderson's back and felt curiously uncomfortable, like an intruder. He got up to leave.

"I, er, I think I'll get a breath of fresh air. Feel a bit queasy." He nodded to Lydia. "Come on." She followed, glancing back once. Manderson didn't answer him, and they climbed the steps to the wheelhouse, leaving him standing alone in the middle of the cabin.

When Manderson had gotten the blanket wrapped around the body to his satisfaction, he went back to the drawer and found his sewing kit. He took out the largest needle, some strong thread, and a thimble. Then he began to sew up the edges of the blanket.

Perhaps Manderson was feeling a little lightheaded, perhaps weariness had blunted his mental reactions, perhaps being alone with Wally for the first time played some part. Whatever the reason, he felt strangely close to the old man. He could feel his presence in the cabin, curious, birdlike, interested. He whispered, half to himself.

"What do you think, Wally? Should be enough money from that to give the old girl a refit and buy some new equipment." He glanced down. Was it imagination, or did there seem to be the faintest of smiles on that lined and battered face? "I'm gonna miss you, you old sod."

He went on with the sewing, talking to the old man. "I know why you did it—as if it mattered. Now look where it's got you." He could have sworn that Wally grinned at him. Then he had a thought and an irrepressible desire to laugh. He chuckled quietly to himself, then reached down for one of the heavy gold plates, slipped it between Wally's legs inside the blanket, and laughed out loud.

"There you are, Wally—that's your share. Hope it keeps you down." He laughed again, tears of mirth and grief intermingled, running down his face. He heard a sound behind him, and saw Franz staring at him, shocked.

"What's the matter?" he said anxiously.

Manderson burst into another paroxysm of laughter. "It's

all right," he said, wiping away the tears. "I'm not going mad. I just hope the fishes don't take a bite at that." He pointed between Wally's legs. "They might get gold poisoning."

Manderson waved him away, and Franz walked back up on deck, puzzled by Manderson's macabre humor, even if he understood what lay behind it.

Manderson had sewn the blanket up as far as the neck. "Good-bye, old man, sleep well."

He covered Wally's face and started to wrap the canvas sheet around him.

Lydia and Franz sat by the helm, not daring to unlash it, and stared out at the water glinting coldly under the moon. Occasionally they heard Manderson laugh or talk to the old man, or curse as the needle snapped on the thick canvas.

Lydia stirred and shivered. "Do you think he's all right down there?"

Franz shifted his position awkwardly, favoring his arm, and gave her a bit more of the blanket they were wrapped in.

"Yes, he's all right. It's probably the best way."

She looked at him curiously.

"They were very close, I think, closer than he realized. He is preparing the old man for burial at sea and this—" They heard Manderson laugh again. "This is maybe the only way he can get through tonight without cracking."

Lydia did not reply. It was easy enough to understand. The events of the last twenty-four hours had made *her* crazy enough. God knows what they had done to that poor man sewing his friend up for the sea to take. A comfortable silence fell between them.

Franz lost track of time. The engine continued to pound

soothingly, pushing them through the North Sea to England. His thoughts drifted back over what had happened since the night in Munich with Lange. His head sank slowly down onto his chest, and Lydia cradled him gently.

He was almost asleep when he realized that he too had found a release—there was no one left to look for. A great sense of calm came over him. He felt light, empty, as though he could float away on the merest puff of wind. Everything was clear, like sunlight on a cold bright day. He felt removed, apart. He could see himself asleep on the boat, Lydia's arms around him, warm, and he was content.

Lydia heard Manderson coming up the steps. He was carrying the body tightly sewn up in the canvas. She whispered to Franz, "He's coming." He was awake instantly. Manderson put the body down in the stern, then leaned past Franz and switched off the engine. Franz could see his fingers were bleeding from his struggle with the tough canvas, then he glanced up at his face. The eyes were red-rimmed with fatigue.

"Are you going to bury Wally now?"

Manderson nodded.

"Do you mind if we come with you?" He glanced at Lydia inquiringly. She nodded.

Manderson looked down at them coldly for a moment, and Franz thought he would refuse, then he shook his head.

"No, that's all right. Just don't start saying any prayers. I think Wally might get embarrassed."

Franz nodded. "I promise."

Manderson carried Wally down to the diving platform, then helped Franz and Lydia down the steps. The water was lapping almost at their feet, and Manderson knelt down beside the body for a moment, his head bowed.

Then he pushed Wally gently over the side, and he slid silently into the water. Franz, who was standing by the ladder, heard Manderson whisper, "So long." Nothing more.

Manderson trudged slowly up the hill around the point to the hotel. It was late afternoon, and a huge red sun, magnified by the early winter mist, was setting behind the hills across the harbor.

Was it only five and a half days since he'd sailed *Lucky Lady* out of that bay, with Wally tagging curiously along behind?

No doubt there would be questions that he would have to answer, but the gale on the outward trip had been severe, and perhaps wreckage from the boat Wally had taken would eventually be washed up, and it would be assumed that Wally had drowned. Manderson did not intend to enlighten them.

He hitched the kitbag higher up on his shoulder. It was heavy, but Maggie would be pleasantly surprised. Manderson wondered about Franz and Lydia. Franz had been as good as his word, shown no desire whatsoever to take a share of the contents of the packing case. But Lydia had been shrewder; she had three of the heavy gold plates wrapped up in brown paper.

Manderson had given Franz some dry clothes and a hundred pounds—which was most of what remained of Pennyman's expense money. They hadn't said much. Manderson told him where he could find a good doctor and had walked with them both as far as the dock gate, where they had paused awkwardly for a moment, each of them conscious that this was probably the last time all three of them would be together. Then Franz held out his left hand, and Manderson shook it gently. Lydia put her arms around him and kissed his unshaven cheek. Manderson smiled, said good-bye, and watched her help Franz down the cobbled street until they disappeared from sight.

He arrived at the hotel and peered through the heavy glass door. Maggie, her head down, was reading a paperback. As he got closer he could see the title—*The Lady in the Lake.* Still on Chandler.

He dumped the kitbag heavily on the floor in front of her desk. She looked up, saw him, and smiled.

"I'm back," he said.

AUTHOR'S NOTE

ONE OF the most interesting areas of research into KG 200 for me was the subject of the draining of what was formerly the Zuyder Zee and the recovery of over a hundred World War II aircraft from its shallow, muddy waters. In fact one of the planes recovered led me directly to the existence of KG 200 itself, and the continuing operation forms part of the authentic background of *The Last Liberator*.

The truth behind the fiction is so dramatic and interesting that it certainly bears recounting here. As the war ended the Dutch resumed their struggle to wrest the land from the sea, and small areas called polders were slowly drained from within the Zuyder Zee, now a huge freshwater lake called the Ijsselmeer.

As they did so, the wrecked aircraft emerged one by one, together with their potentially dangerous high-explosive bomb loads and ammunition. In 1960 the Dutch authorities set up the Royal Netherlands Air Force Recovery Unit, consisting of fifteen men under the command of Major Arie de Jong, to recover and remove these wrecks and their cargoes.

The work was hard, filthy, and potentially dangerous, and few of them regarded it with much enthusiasm. But this attitude altered as time passed and the emphasis, if not the objectives of the operation, changed.

It became their task to track down the identities of the drowned fliers whose bodies were recovered in the Ijsselmeer —to put together the tragic jigsaw puzzle from the pieces of wreckage and human remains, until they knew who these men were, where they came from, and finally, to inform their relatives that these airmen had not just disappeared off the face of the earth, but had been found and given a decent burial.

The Ijsselmeer is in fact a graveyard of sunken planes. Pilots had tried to use the fifty miles that were free of flak, only to fall victim to the fighter or the air gunner. The estimates vary, but between five hundred and seven hundred wrecks may still be lying beneath the water, and the men from the recovery unit regard it as a moral responsibility to see that all the airmen whose bodies are recovered, whether they were British, American, or German, are given some final dignity.

In September 1963 a British Mosquito that had crashed in 1944 was discovered. The wooden wing was still in good condition, but no markings could be found, and, strangely enough, the paint had a white-gray finish that was unfamiliar to all of the investigators. But the most curious fact to emerge was that the weapons system held German ammunition.

This was the plane that led me to Holland when I learned of its existence in 1968, and it was there that I learned for the first time, from Major Arie de Jong, of the existence of KG 200.

Another plane recovered in December 1975 was, unsurprisingly, a Liberator—a B-24 out of Shipdam, Norfolk, carrying ten crewmen—that crashed into the Zuyder Zee on December 22, 1943, after being hit by German flak over Holland. It was returning from raids on targets in Muenster and Osnabrueck. Records disclosed that four of the crew were washed ashore and had been buried in Holland, so it appeared that there might still be human remains within the sunken bomber.

The only survivor of the crew, Lt. Charles Taylor from Scotch Plains, New Jersey, was invited by NCRV, the Dutch television network, to come to Holland; he arrived in the autumn of 1976. His story is interesting and probably typical; I quote from an interview.

"After being hit by German flak over eastern Holland, gradually three of the four engines gave up, and seeing we were unable to fly the aircraft back to England, the pilot gave a bail-out order, assuming that we were still flying over land in the overcast. I believe that four of us did bail out before we spotted water below through the bomb-bay doors. It was at this time we all decided we would be better off sticking together and ditching the plane. I thought at the time I had floated through the open escape hatch, but found out during this return visit that it was the side of the cockpit, for the nose had broken away from the fuselage."

Eventually he managed to free the dinghy, but was too weak to crawl into it. His Mae West kept him afloat and he was picked up later unconscious by a German antiaircraft boat and taken to Amsterdam. Lt. Charles Taylor's war ended in Stalag 1, near Rostock on the Baltic coast.

For compassionate reasons the men of the recovery unit had avoided telling Lt. Taylor of the possibility that some of his crewmates might still be inside the Liberator. A few days after he returned to the U.S., five of them were found, braced behind the armor plate for protection. It had buckled on impact and blocked the escape hatch—their only way out.

The Dutch Recovery Unit paid its usual homage to these no-longer-missing men of World War II—each of the coffins was draped with the Dutch flag—and their humane work continues.